CU00540398

A CIP catalogue record for this title is available from the
British Library.
Cover photo by Darren Wilkins of The Tudor Roses
Edited by Cas Peace

About the Author

Judith Arnopp lives on a smallholding in rural Wales. She graduated from University in 2009 with a Bachelor's degree in English Literature and a Master's in Medieval Studies. She now combines those skills to create masterful historical novels. She also blogs and lectures on her favourite subjects.

Intractable Heart is Judith Arnopp's sixth novel and her third set in the court of Henry VIII.

Her other books include:
> The Kiss of the Concubine: a story of Anne Boleyn
> The Winchester Goose: at the court of Henry VIII
> The Song of Heledd
> The Forest Dwellers
> Peaceweaver

All are available in paperback and are also on Kindle.

Intractable Heart:
A story of Katheryn Parr

Judith Arnopp

For Laura, with love

Best wishes
Judith x

England, 1536

As the year to end all years rolls to a close the Holy Roman Church reels beneath the onslaught of the reformation. And, as quickly as the vast abbeys crumble, so do the royal coffers begin to fill.

The people of the north, torn between their loyalty to God and their allegiance to their anointed king, embark upon a pilgrimage to guide their errant monarch back to grace.

But Henry is unyielding and sends an army north to quell the uprising. In Yorkshire, when unrest breaks out again, Katheryn, Lady Latimer and her stepchildren, Margaret and John, are held under siege by the rebels at Snape Castle.

Part One
Margaret Neville

January 1537 - Snape Castle

"There she goes, grab 'er!"

As they lunge for me, I dive into the bushes and scramble up the incline toward the house. The ground is damp. Wet, slippery leaves hinder my progress but I struggle onward, desperate to reach home. Katheryn, my stepmother, told me not to come. I should have listened but, resentful of her taking my own mother's place, I ignored her and came outside to spite her.

I hate it in the castle; the heat of the fire, the chattering of the women, the never ending unpicking and re-stitching of the tapestry I am working. Usually I like it in the woods; I feel free. I can breathe and run, and love the sensation of the wind on my face, but now I am sorry I disobeyed. The stifling women's quarters are suddenly a haven. I wish I'd never left it. I should have remained at the fireside and attended to my detested needlework as I'd been told.

"Oh dear God," I gasp. "I promise, if you just help me get safely home, I will never be bad again."

At last, the angry voices behind me begin to dwindle, and the pain in my side forces me to stop, just for a moment. I am not far from the hall now. Through the branches I can just glimpse the red brick walls of Snape Castle. Hiccupping in fear, I crawl on until I am close to the drive where, gathering all my courage, I throw myself from the safety of the covert and dash beneath the gateway into the barton.

There are men massing before the house. Not soldiers, not gentlemen, but peasantry. Ordinary men who, on a normal day, would pull their caps and treat us with respect. But yesterday I saw their leaders bear my father away, leaving us defenceless and the castle to be ruled by rough-clad farmers, millers, dispossessed monks and the like.

They are angry, shouting, waving their arms at the blank castle windows. Keeping my head down, I sneak along the wall, sidle up the steps to the hall where the bailiff, Layton, is bravely trying to contain their anger. I duck behind him and almost fall over the threshold. The warmth of the hall engulfs me.

"Miss Margaret, where have you been? You were told not to leave the house."

"I'm sorry," I wail. Relieved beyond words to have escaped, the terror turns to tears on my cheek. I cling to Dorothy. "I really am so very sorry. I will never disobey again."

I am trembling, overwhelmed to be safe, and yet perhaps not as safe as I would have it.

"Look at your gown, look at your shoes." Dorothy slaps at the filth on my skirts as she scolds me, and for once I do not resent it. I am glad of her rough nurturing, glad that there is someone bigger and wiser than myself. Dorothy's reproaches are cut short by a footstep behind us, and I hear my stepmother's voice.

"Oh, Margaret, thank God you are safe." She swoops toward me, sinks to her knees and holds out her arms. For the first time I fall into them, lose myself in the comfort of her bosom. Katheryn smells of rose water and camomile.

Scents of summer.

"I am sorry, Mother. I will never disobey you again." My nose is running all over her fine brocade gown but she doesn't appear to notice. She cradles my head beneath her chin, her hand on my hair, and makes the soft motherly noises that I have missed so much. My brother John is scowling at us from the stairway; he will punish me later for this show of affection.

"Did they hurt you?" Her voice seems to come from far away. I shake my head.

"No, but I am sure they would have had they caught me. I had to escape through the shrubbery. I am sorry, Mother, but I lost my hood."

She holds me a little away, plucks a few twigs from my hair and looks at me, her heart-shaped face warm with affection. "What does a lost hood matter when it might have been you, Sweet-one? Come, let me take you to your chamber. Dorothy, see that warm water is brought up, Margaret will want a bath and an early night."

An hour later, although it is just a few hours past noon, I am tucked up in bed while Mother spoons broth into my mouth and Dorothy tut-tuts over my ruined clothes. The servants come one by one to take away the dirty bath water. They tread softly, their eyes averted, while Mother holds the spoon beneath my nose, tempting me to eat.

Although I am not hungry, I open my mouth obediently. I have so many questions, so many doubts. I swallow the broth, lick my lips.

"Who are those bad men, Mother? What do they want?"

"They are not 'bad men' my sweet-one. They are frightened, angry men who urge the king to change his mind."

"Change his mind about what? And why are they here bothering us? What have we to do with the king?"

She replaces the spoon in the half empty bowl and hands it to Dorothy, tucks the sheet higher about my chest.

"So many questions."

She smiles and bids me sleep but, forgetting my recent declaration of obedience, I sit up again.

"How can I sleep if no one will tell me what is happening? I am afraid."

She leans forward, kisses my hair. "Very well. In that case I shall do my best to answer." She clasps her hands and I wait while she considers how best to begin. "They want the king to change his mind about many things. They did not like his treatment of the late queen and the Lady Mary, or his marriage to Anne Boleyn..."

"But she is dead now, isn't she? I heard the maids gossiping about it. Didn't the king cut off her head?"

"Yes, Margaret, but you really shouldn't listen to gossip. The king has a new wife now and Queen Jane will lose no time in bearing him a son ... God willing. It is the changes to the church that these men are protesting about. They don't like the religious reforms or the closure of the monasteries. They cling to the old ways."

"Why has Father gone with them? Does he cling to the old ways too?"

She straightens up, her gaze straying to the window as she considers my question.

"Your father will do as the king wishes, to ensure your safety and mine, regardless of what he really thinks."

"But what about the monks? Who will speak out for them? And what about God, what will He think about church reform? Do you think the king has consulted Him about it all?"

"I am sure the king has searched his soul, which is much the same as consulting God. Now, be a good girl and lie down, get some sleep."

I slide down my pillows, keeping hold of her slim white fingers.

"Everything is changing. Why can't things always stay the same?" My mind drifts back to my mother and how it was before she died. Her memory drifts across me in a wave of scent – a sense of happiness, security and love. Even after all these years my heart is sore for need of her. Katheryn, my stepmother, although only just past twenty, has been married before. When she came here, John and I made up our minds not to like her. We hoped she'd go away, back to her old family, but she stayed, and disliking her has not been easy.

"Nobody likes change," she whispers as she gives my hand a squeeze. I increase my grip so she cannot pull away.

"No. But sometimes change isn't as bad as we imagine it will be."

She looks up quickly, understanding flickering in her eyes. Her face softens. "I am lucky to have such a wise daughter. Now, go to sleep. You are exhausted after your adventure. I can see it in your face. Tomorrow you can help me begin work on a new set of chair covers for the hall."

"When will Father be back?"

"Soon, my darling. He will come back to us soon."

I snuggle into my pillow, listen to the hush of her skirt as she crosses the room and softly closes the door.

The shutters are closed, the fire glowing red in the hearth, all but three of the candles snuffed. Cocooned in my bed, I am safe at last, the terror of the day receding. Today, amid the upheaval of rebellion a new alliance has been forged. The king and the northern rebels may well be enemies, but my stepmother and I are now friends.

***

A noise disturbs me. My eyes snap open, my heart begins to thump. I pull myself up on my pillows and peer into the darkness, listening. Footsteps hurrying along the corridor, a door slamming, and an angry voice cut off mid-sentence. I throw back the cover and slide from the bed.

The floor is cold underfoot as I creep to the door, open it just a crack. I sneak across the upper landing. The carved oak bannister is cool beneath my hands as I look over the balustrade to the hall below.

A huddle of servants, and Mother in her nightgown, her hair coiled into a serpentine braid, her face white and tight. My brother John hovers behind her, as if uncertain, as acting baron, he should intervene.

Raised voices, crude words and a glare of torchlight accompany the gang of rebels as they intrude into the hall. The household, with Mother at its head, retreats backward. One of the rebels is clutching a flagon, his lips loose and wet, his eyes unfocussed.

"It's bitter cold in the stables, we're coming in 'ere, whether you like it or not."

"Your leaders have forbidden that. I was promised you would stay outside the house. I have the servants to think of ... my children ..."

Only a slight quiver in her voice betrays her lack of certainty, her fear, but it is enough to strike terror into my very soul. I sink to my knees and press close to the newel post as the rebel spokesman steps forward, his face thrust menacingly toward mother. John moves backward, treads on our dog Homer's paw, who yelps loudly.

"Well, our leaders ain't 'ere, are they?"

As the rebel shoves her aside, Mother falls back against the wall. My brother darts out of the way. The servants fall like wheat as the mob passes through them, their snivelling protests robbing me of the last of my courage. The dogs will stop them, I tell myself; they will come no farther. I dig my fingers into my face, praying I am right.

Behind the doors to the great hall the castle hounds are slavering and growling loud enough to deter even the most foolhardy. But when the doors are forced open, the dogs betray us, and the great fickle beasts leap up to lick the rebels' faces in greeting.

From my hiding place I hear the scrape of wooden chairs on the stone flagged floor as the rebels make themselves comfortable, calling for victuals, for more wine.

From my place on the upper floor it is as if the scene below is frozen. The servants are all looking to Mother for direction but she remains where she is, hovering undecidedly. Then, suddenly making a decision, she turns on her heel, her braided hair whipping in her wake.

"Come," she orders. "We must barricade ourselves into my apartments. Layton, be quick, see that food is brought up from the kitchens, enough to last a few days." She ushers the snivelling women up the stairs. I feel the waft of their skirts as they pass me by, snatches of their terrified conversation instilling me with further dread.

I see Mother reach out and grasp the knob of my chamber door. I want to call out to her but she hurries in before I can speak, cries out in fear when she sees my bed is empty. The flurry of her skirts raises dust from the corners as she rushes out again, belatedly spying me cowering in the shadows.

"Margaret!" She grabs my wrist in relief and drags me in her wake to her apartments that stretch the length of the house. I drop my nightcap in our haste and my hair falls on to my shoulders. Once inside, she clasps me briefly to her chest. I close my eyes, hear her heart hammering, the energy pulsing in her throat. Then she wraps me in a fur, sits me beside the hearth, and her voice when she speaks is high and wavering. "We will be safe here once the door is locked and barred. Don't worry."

I turn my face toward the huddle of female servants who have taken refuge by the shuttered window, blubbering and weeping and seeking comfort in numbers. Mother does her best to soothe them, promising that my father will soon be returning.

"We must pray," she says. "And take comfort that God is watching over us, for we know he must have some influence over these ungodly pilgrims."

Obediently they fall to their knees.

Bread, cheese and wine is brought up from the kitchens, my mother's ante-chamber is stacked high with casks and pots. At least we will not starve, not for a while.

Layton and the male servants tug their forelocks and shuffle away to resume their duties, leaving John the only male in a roomful of women. I can see from his face that he resents it.

8

"Will our men be safe?" I blurt out. "Won't the rebels hurt them too?"

Dorothy perches on the arm of my chair. "No child. They may be rough-handled a little but it is always womenfolk who are most in danger when men run wild."

She picks up her comb and begins to tease the tangles from my hair, throwing small knots on to the fire where they shrivel and burn – like the heretics I have heard them gossip of in the kitchens.

I know what she means. I know the dangers women face. When I was eight years old I was betrothed to the son of my father's friend, Sir Francis Bigod. I met Ralph Bigod only once; a skinny little boy who would not look me in the eye.

Thankfully, our marriage will not take place until I am older and, as far as I am concerned, they can postpone it for as long as they please. I learned a few weeks ago that Ralph's father is leading the band of rebels. I heard father whispering of it to Katheryn, but they have said nothing to me. I am too young to be involved in their discussions. Instead, I pick up servants' tittle tattle, and it seems that Sir Francis is an angry, foolhardy man. Instead of letting the unrest die down, he is stirring up hatred and will surely bring down the wrath of the king upon us all. Father has ridden away but I don't know whether it is to intervene with the king or to ride against him. My mind doesn't linger on it for long.

I wonder what it is like to be married and what sort of husband Ralph will make. I know that some men make harsh partners, demanding much and providing little, and I do not relish the thought of lying with any man skin to skin.

I am not as ignorant as they suppose about the things that go on between men and women. I have seen

9

the servants sporting in the stables, misbehaving in the wine cellar. It is my virtue and reputation that Mother is keen to protect for, once taken, a woman's chastity can never be redeemed.

***

My belly growls loudly and Mother looks up from her needlework. "It's not long until dinner now," she smiles. I try to look enthusiastic but the meagre fare we have been living on for the last few weeks is anything but appetising. Cold cuts of meat and cheese, hard bread with no broth to soften it, is far from the delights we are used to but Mother won't surrender. A few weeks ago I left the crumbled remains of a deep meat pie on the edge of my plate, too full to finish it. I dream of that pie now, mourn the unappreciated thick glazed crust, the rich dark gravy.

Dinner is a meagre affair. The bread I am chewing is dry, it refuses to soften, resists when I attempt to swallow it. I turn my watery eyes to Mother and try to smile. "I wish we could go outside," I complain for the hundredth time. "I miss the fresh air."

Mother refuses to allow any of us to leave the chamber, and is determined not to weaken in the face of our gaolers. She doesn't even allow us to open the windows wide for fear that they might scale the walls.

Each night the rebels carouse in the hall, the sounds of destruction, splintering wood, and drunken song used to keep me awake. I would stay alert, ready for the sounds of immediate attack, but now they scarcely disturb me.

At first I asked every day, every hour, why Father isn't doing anything to help us, but now I have come to realise that either there is nothing he can do, or he doesn't want to help us. All we can do is wait and see, and the tension is killing me.

It doesn't help that John is in my company far more often. Usually he is off with his hawk, or riding the estate with Father and the bailiff, learning his trade. Now, cooped up with us all day, he is bored and the darker side to his nature is getting the better of him. I have become his target. He vents his spleen on me, imbibing me with his own fears, his own uncertainty.

"Maybe they've killed him," he whispers when the adults are not close by. "Maybe he has sickened on the road and can't come back to us. Maybe the king has taken him up for a traitor and locked him in the Tower. Maybe they will chop off his head."

My stomach heaves with fear but I refuse to let him see. I turn dispassionate eyes upon my brother and blink at him slowly.

"Don't be stupid, John," I say as if he is some loathsome toad. But, when I pick up my sampler again, I do not see a row of crooked flowers in a garden of stitches, I see my father chained in a fetid cell at the mercy of a heretic king.

I know my father favours the old ways. I have heard him mutter about the disgraceful manner in which the Lady Mary has been treated since her mother was set aside by the king. He was glad when they cut off Anne Boleyn's head and glad when Queen Jane married the king. She is known to be devout and to favour the old religion. Some even say she will guide the king back into the arms of Rome. The thing that confuses me is that the men downstairs, holding us hostage, threatening us with violence, are sworn to love the Pope also. How can they be good Christians? I cannot believe pious men would act like devils. Perhaps I am too young to understand, but although I try not to, I cannot stop thinking and trying to reason it all out.

***

At his knock, Dorothy pulls back the bolts and Layton's bulky body slides through the narrow gap. He twists his cap in his hands as she firmly replaces the locks, sealing us in again. Mother looks up from the fire, puts down her sewing.

"Master Layton," she beckons him forward. "What news? Has word come from Lord Latimer?"

"No, My Lady. I am sorry to say there is no news, but I thought I should warn you that the rebels have discovered the second wine store, the one that holds My Lord's most precious casks."

Mother gets up and moves toward the window, stops half way. "That is the least of my problems, Layton. Our own stores are running low. I am rationing the food but for how much longer can we hold out?" Her voice breaks, she lowers her head. I see a tear drop onto the back of her hand. I slide from my chair to stand close to her, clutching her skirt.

Layton swallows, shuffles his feet. "There is unrest all over the north, My Lady. The rebels suspect that your husband has betrayed them to the king, his delay in returning makes them ever more restive."

"For all they march in his name, these are not men of God! Only evil men and sinners make war on women and children ..." She sees my fear and stops mid-sentence, tries to smile, her hand reaching out to touch my cheek. Then she adds for my benefit, "It is fortunate we are so well protected."

I climb onto the window seat and look down into the yard, where a group of rebels are teasing a stable lad. Jeremy is a good boy. He looks after my pony, mixes poultices when she is lame, and has a special recipe that makes her coat gleam like satin. As I watch, they knock off his cap and each time he tries to retrieve it they kick it farther away. To them it is all a lark, but I can see Jeremy's misery in his hunched shoulders and the sorry droop of his head. I wish he would turn round and fight them but he is only a boy, half grown and puny.

He makes one more attempt to pick up his hat and, as he does so, one of the men kicks him from behind, sending him sprawling to the ground. Their rough laughter floats up to the window where I am standing. I know from experience the pain of falling on to the gravel. Last summer Dorothy spent an entire afternoon picking small stones out of my skinned knees and dabbing the bloody scars with stinging stuff.

I wish the rebels would go away. Why doesn't the king come and hang them all?

"They are not bad men," I recall Mother saying once. "They are frightened, angry men who urge the king to change his mind." But she was wrong. I think they have forgotten all about God and the king. I think they have all run mad.

As Layton quietly takes his leave of us, there is a great shout on the landing. A stampede of feet and the door is rudely thrust open. The steward is propelled backward into the room again. The women abandon their needles and run screaming toward the window. As the chamber fills with rebels, I stand transfixed and watch my world descend into chaos.

I see a rough, bearded fellow take hold of Mother's arm, drag her into the ante-chamber. I want to run after her but my feet will not move. The air is filled with screaming, the lower tones of hollering men. Everything seems to slow down and I observe every small detail of the unfolding horror.

Dorothy is battering a man with the warming pan, the words streaming from her lips the crudest I have ever heard. Betty from the kitchens opens her mouth to bawl in protest as she goes down beneath the onslaught. Our needlewomen, Tilly and Jane, run shrieking into a corner, huddling together against the wall, trying to evade their attackers for as long as they can.

And then I spy John, hiding on the bed, peering through the drawn curtains. I see his face crumple as he loses his self-control. He will hate it when he realises I am witness to his womanly tears and piss-wet hose. I open my mouth to call to him but as I do so a huge hairy hand clamps down upon my throat. I am dragged onto the floor, the rush matting scrapes my elbows, a great wet mouth smears across my cheeks, and stubble lacerates my skin. He fumbles at my skirts but I kick and bite and wriggle. My only instinct is to flee and if I have to kill him, I will.

But he is strong, too strong. His breath is foul, a stench of fish and dung, stale ale and ashes, his red lips fastening like a leech, his tongue deep in my throat, his filthy hands tearing aside my skirts, probing between my thighs. For a moment I break my face free, open my mouth and scream, my head crashing hard against the wainscot. I strain away but my body is trapped beneath him. Over his shoulder I see John standing upright on the bed, shouting in feeble protest, his face red and wet with tears. Tears he sheds for me.

A terrible pain, like a knife, and then a bang, an explosion, and my attacker slumps like a dead weight

14

across me. My throat fills with vomit, I battle to free myself but I am pinioned, I cannot move. A warm sweet scent tasting of copper engulfs me.

A great voice is shouting, swearing, cursing. Women are sobbing, weapons clashing. The burden shifts. I manage to free one leg and one arm and, with all my strength, I heave the rebel from my body and scramble to my feet. Gasping for breath, I look down to where he lies. His mouth is open, his eyes staring sightless at the ceiling, his beard sprouting blackly on his grimy face. A crimson stain is spreading across the floor beneath him.

I draw back my leg and swing it forward again, sinking my foot into his groin. He does not move. I make to kick him again but a hand gently clasps my arm, and I look up at Mother and a man I do not recognise at her side. The man is holding a smoking pistol; he rolls my attacker over with his foot and grunts in satisfaction.

Slowly I become aware of the ruin around us.

Broken windows, upset caskets, torn linen, a log from the fire smouldering on Mother's fine Turkey rug. "Are you harmed, Margaret?"

For a moment I do not answer. My female parts are stinging but I shake my head just once, and wipe the blood from my nose.

"Are you, Mother?"

"No, no, thank the Lord. But I fear some of the others ..."

"How did you get free, what happened?"

John appears from behind the bed hangings, climbs shakily from the mattress and wipes his face on his sleeve. "Soldiers," he says. "I think Father is back."

Downstairs, the sound of battle continues. Layton, a cloth tied around his wounded head, drags the corpses from our chamber and, as soon as we are able, we secure the door, eager for once to be locked safe inside. John, in a frenzy of fear, begins to pile every piece of moveable furniture against it, barricading us all in. Mother and I begin to comfort our women.

Several of them are wounded, violated, and all are traumatised. I give no thought to my own ordeal as I copy my mother. I try not to think of what has just happened but set to, bathing their eyes, cradling them in my arms, and feeling their tears soak into my gown.

All the time I work, I am aware of John silently watching me, his large round eyes unblinking as he waits for me to confess the truth. But that is a truth I will never disclose, a secret violation I will carry to my grave.

***

Father is different; thinner, older, more indecisive than ever. He constantly pats me, strokes my arm, holds my hand and tries to make me smile, but I have no smiles. He should have come sooner and prevented the attack. Then I might have been able to forgive him. Everything is spoiled now.

The rebels have gone and Father is pacing the parlour floor, explaining to us why he must ride straight back to London. The king doubts his loyalty. Cromwell is after his head, and his estates. Even the Duke of Norfolk has withdrawn his friendship. If Father is to salvage anything from this sorry mess he has to leave us again, immediately.

I do not care if he goes or stays, but I wish the castle were more secure. I am so fearful of a fresh assault that I no longer sleep at night. I can still smell the stench of my attacker's breath. I wake up weeping in the night, disgusted at my own violated body, but I cannot tell anyone. For some reason I do not try to analyse, it is imperative that they never know what happened to me.

As gentle as ever, Mother places her hand on Father's sleeve. "I understand that you must go," she says. "And in your absence I will do all in my power to restore order here. Perhaps we can join you in London soon. The children would like that, would you not, Margaret? John?"

She turns her attention to my brother, who wakes from his reverie and nods once. These days he displays a greater degree of anxiety than he has ever shown before. His eyes are restive and even now as we relax in the parlour he is poking a hole in the lace trim of his sleeve. I long to escape from Snape Castle. If I had my way I'd never return again. We are buried alive here and the need to escape the memories of the past few months is strong.

London; I imagine visiting the royal court. The rebels cannot hurt us there and perhaps one day I might have the chance of an appointment to the queen.

As a member of the queen's household I could delay my marriage to Ralph Bigod, remain free of a husband for much longer than if we tarry here. London, as wild and dangerous as the capital is, presents a much brighter future than Yorkshire. The promise of escape relaxes the tortuous memories. Mentally I begin selecting which gowns I will take with me, and which I shall leave behind.

April 1537 – Charterhouse, London

Our family is in disgrace and Father imprisoned in the Tower, but still Mother remains calm. Cromwell, the

17

king's secretary, believes we secretly supported the uprising. In truth, I have no clue as to where Father's loyalties lie, or what part he took in the Pilgrimage of Grace. We plead innocence and loyalty to the crown and, so far, there is nothing to prove otherwise.

The king and his henchmen have shown no mercy and the leaders of the rebellion have been hung. In the north of England rebel corpses hang like grisly flags in the rain, and they told me yesterday that, for his feeble part in the protest, Francis Bigod died too. My marriage to his son will not now take place. I don't know why. I try to imagine the grief the boy must feel to have lost his father in such a way, and hope that I won't soon have reason to share it. The death of Francis Bigod and the severing of my betrothal to his son has freed me, liberated me from a future I did not relish. It is one tiny thing to be thankful for as the world grows darker around us.

Every day, every bitter night that Father remains within the Tower, convinces me that they will hang him too. His brothers, my uncles, are also in trouble and to match my mood, every day is wet, and cold, and grey. The future is draped before me like a wet blanket, preventing the sun from shining. Once I was so happy, but everything altered on the day Father rode away to negotiate with the king on behalf of the rebels.

Whether he reached the king or not, I do not know; it is immaterial to me. All I do know is that he was away too long and returned to Snape too late to prevent the ruination of my world.

Katheryn visits him, takes him baskets of wholesome food, warm clothing. Each time she goes she asks me to accompany her, but I turn away and plead a headache or a sick stomach. While Father languishes, my

18

mother turns to the support of her brother, William Parr, who has maintained his high favour with the king. Mother's sister, Anne Herbert, whom I call Aunt Anne, is also on hand. She has a position in the queen's household and, at their contrivance, Mother and I find ourselves garbed in our finest for a visit to the royal court.

***

The queen is with child and everyone eagerly expects a boy, a lusty prince to follow his father. Our family does not go often to court but when I do, the things I witness there enthral me, and open my eyes to a new, exciting world.

Were it not for her finery I would describe Queen Jane as nondescript. She is sallow and meek, and according to Aunt Anne, behaves more like the lady-in-waiting she used to be than a queen. Her new status does not suit her and I get the impression she would rather be elsewhere. But when my aunt confides that Queen Jane is suffering from the most dreadful morning sickness, I sympathise a little more. Where any other woman could take to her bed, as queen she must do her duty and appear to be thriving.

She is overpowered by everyone; her husband, father, brothers. Aunt Anne tells me that the reformists are worried, for Queen Jane is an adherent of the old religion and Bishop Gardiner is rubbing his hands in gleeful anticipation.

The king, when he comes, draws all eyes, and when I look upon him it is as if the breath is sucked from my lungs. This is the man who felled the Pope, brought the church to its knees; the man who ordered the death of my betrothed. I examine him closely, taking in every detail.

Today he is amiable, a wide smile slashed across his face, his hearty chuckles filling every pause in the conversation. His clothes are exquisitely jewelled and trimmed, his cod-piece the biggest I have ever seen. Everything about him is impressive, huge, overwhelming, filling all who look upon him with awe.

He is accompanied by two men, whom I quickly discover are the queen's brothers, Edward and Thomas Seymour. Unlike the king, they are not at such ease in their splendour. Their clothes are not casually worn, they are a little too immaculate, their hair is a little too fragrant, their smiles brittle and wary, as if they have been painted on.

One of the queen's brothers spies Aunt Anne and, taking his leave of the king, bears down upon us, sweeping off his feathered cap to bend over Anne's hand. As he rises, the jewels on his doublet dazzle in the torchlight. Then he turns his attention to me, a benign expression on his face as his eyes sweep up and down my body. He doesn't appear to notice my youth, or the plainness of my gown. His hands are warm; my fingers tremble in his palm, my heart quailing beneath the power of his charm. It is the first time I have been noticed by a gentleman of court.

"I know your stepmother, Katheryn," he says. "Is she not here today?"

I rise from my polite curtsey, swallow my nerves and answer boldly. "She is at home, My Lord, bowed down with estate business in my father's absence."

He stands back, a smile hovering on the corner of his mouth, an unexpected dimple winking in his cheek.

"Ah, yes. Latimer. A sorry tale indeed. Cromwell is keeping him close, so he can watch who comes and who goes."

"I don't know, My Lord. I only hope he will soon be allowed home."

I have no intention of allowing Seymour to guess at my lack of parental love for my father. My eyes trail around the room as if I am a little bored with the present company and seek something new. A rakish-looking fellow wearing an embroidered eye-patch saunters over to join us. "Do you know my cousin, Sir Francis Bryan?" Seymour asks. "He also knows your mother. He was attached to her grandfather, William Parr's household."

My hand is taken by yet another stranger. I know of him, of course, everyone does. He is notorious, even the king refers to him as the 'vicar of hell.' I am not entirely sure what he has done to earn such a title but I am sure that twinkle in his eye can have nothing to do with hell. I find myself warming, and a smile tickles the side of my mouth. I try to hide it.

"Mistress Neville? I am delighted. Your mother is not with you?"

His voice is light and caressing, as if I am his close kin. He retains his hold for too long, his lips slow and moist on my fingers. My cheeks are burning as I sink into another curtsey, and stay there as if I am greeting a king.

It is a wonder that the knees of the court women are not riddled with rheumatism from so much bobbing and bending. Slowly I rise again, look at him, and snatch my eyes away. I don't know how to address this man. His one eye makes him menacing, but his lopsided smile and the way he carries himself is devastating to an untried girl like me. He smells of liquorice and pomander, with a hint of the stable; all three aromas are pleasing. I open my mouth to answer but he forestalls me.

"Thomas and I must call to pass an hour with Lady Katheryn soon. I hope we will see you also when we come."

Suddenly aware that my jaw is hanging open I snap my mouth closed, try to free my hand, but he holds on to it, his thumb stroking my knuckles, setting my insides atremble. I wonder if I am going down with a fever.

It is fortunate that Aunt Anne notices my confusion and swoops to my rescue. "You are a bad man, Francis," she teases, tapping him reprovingly with her fan. "What poor girl stands a chance when you two are on the prowl?" Francis Bryan is forced to relinquish my hand and exchange it for my aunt's.

We all laugh, Seymour's teeth flashing while Bryan rolls his eye at me and guffaws loudly. Something sinks in my nethers, a feeling of disappointment, humiliation. They were teasing me. I blush scarlet and turn away, once more a chastened child. How am I supposed to tell truth from lies in this place where nobody says what they mean, or means what they say?

Suddenly I am overwhelmed with longing for home and Mother's tranquil chambers where the fire burns brightly and the gossip is of homely, trivial things. I swallow tears, lift my chin and look across the glittering crowd, hearing but not listening to the chatter, the high-pitched laughter of the court as they enjoy the uproarious antics of the royal fools.

I want to go home.

London - June 1537

Cromwell, unable to find evidence that will allow him to send Father to the scaffold, reluctantly allows him to go free. He swears his fealty to the king, putting himself completely in his service. This means that although Father is at liberty, his every movement is watched and questioned by Cromwell. The king's secretary makes his enmity no secret and slowly, as if he is letting blood, he empties my father's fortune into his own coffers.

Poor Father is sent back north where the troubles continue with the Scots. John accompanies him, his sulky face leaving us in no doubt that he would rather stay at home. Father is rarely able to spend time with us, and Mother has to take control of his affairs in London. Just yesterday we learned that we have not paid enough recompense to satiate Cromwell and now, on top of everything else, he desires our favourite London home near Charterhouse. Within the week we must all move into lodgings to make way for him.

Mother has instructed the servants to pack up our things, and they scurry about, stuffing our possessions into crates and boxes while Mother and I sit for one last time in her parlour. I take up my sampler, consider the detested rows of crooked flowers. Why did I not make the border narrow and with less foliage and spare myself the torture?

"We must look about for a suitable husband for you, Margaret."

The needle I am using jabs into my skin and I pop the injured finger into my mouth, looking at Mother in alarm.

"Husband?" I stall. "I am in no hurry to be wed. I would rather see Father safely through his troubles first."

She smiles. "That is very thoughtful, my love, but do you not see that once you are safely wed it will be one more worry taken from his shoulders?"

"Burden, you mean." To avoid her shocked expression, I droop my head over my needlework.

"You could never be a burden, Margaret. We love you and want to see your future settled; that is all. I wasn't implying that you should be wed next week, just suggesting that perhaps you should cast your eye about for someone who meets your approval."

"Well, it isn't as if I can choose." I bite my lip, stab wildly with my needle, forming a row of untidy stitches far bigger than the rest. Tears begin to build behind my eyes. I sniff in an attempt to contain them.

"Is there no one at court who has taken your eye? You seem to attract plenty of partners in the dance."

As well as tears pricking at my eyelids, I now feel my cheeks burning with embarrassment. Surely she hasn't noticed my attraction for Francis Bryan? Since our first meeting he singles me out, pays me attentions that I have no idea how to deal with. He is a man in his prime with the reputation of a libertine. Even if Bryan were not already married, Father would never allow such a match. If he knew of my growing attachment he would be outraged. Francis' face might drift through my mind before I go to sleep each night, and I might recall every word he has ever spoken in my presence, but I realise that there can never be anything between us. Sir Bryan is toying with me. He sees me as a plaything in his courtly games. I am nothing but a 'Fair Geraldine' like the one from Surrey's love sonnet which is doing the rounds at court.

24

Before Father fell foul of the king I could have married well, a lord or an earl, but now I fear I will have to settle for some feeble, untried boy. Some second son with a paltry income and a tumble-down house. I am scowling over my artless stitching when the sound of horses' hooves on the gravel outside provides me with an excuse to put down my work. I hurry to the window.

"It is Uncle William," I announce with relief. Mother lays her sewing aside, smoothes out her skirts and signals for Dorothy to go and organise refreshment. Moments later the door is thrust open, Homer begins to yelp with excitement, and Uncle William enters. With him is Aunt Anne's husband, William Herbert, both of my Uncle Williams in one visit.

I beam a delighted welcome as they fill the chamber with the fragrance of the June day, a tang of horse and harness, cut grass and sunshine. I wonder why we have spent the afternoon indoors and suspect that Mother wanted to keep me closeted so that she might approach the subject of my marriage.

"Katheryn." He bends over and kisses Mother's cheek, before turning to me. Then Uncle William does the same. "Katheryn. Margaret. You are both looking well. I am surprised to find you indoors."

"I am waiting for the heat of the day to pass before we venture outside. The heat does not suit me."

"It is devilish hot," he says, mopping his forehead with his kerchief. "I've heard reports of plague. The king has cleared out of the palace and set up court at Windsor, refusing to let anyone from London join them."

"What of the queen? Is she with him?"

I know she is worrying about Aunt Anne, who is still with the queen. Seeing her concern, I begin to wonder if we are wise to stay so close to the contagion or if we too should run for safety. My thoughts are extinguished by my uncle's next words.

"Oh yes, you can be sure he will keep her on a short leash while she is in pup. Pray God she gets him a son, or we might have another Anne Boleyn on our hands."

"Hush, William. Watch what you say." Mother lowers her voice and looks sharply around the room, although every one of her servants is devoted to her.

Undisturbed by her displeasure William sits down, rests his feet on a low table and crosses his ankles, watches as Dorothy pours four cups of wine.

"How are things with you, William?" Mother asks her brother. In the pause that follows all eyes stray to my other uncle. William Herbert is teasing Homer by balancing a wafer on his nose and defying him to eat it. As Katheryn's brother's complaining tones continue, I watch in anticipation. Poor Homer shivers and drools but is too well behaved to snatch the treat before he is given permission. I smother a laugh and turn to my other uncle as if I am interested in his complaints.

"Things for me are as bad as you might imagine. I can't get the king to sanction my request for a divorce, for it seems divorce is for kings, not for commoners."

"King Henry's marriage to Catherine of Aragon was annulled, that is not the same as a divorce."

"Ha! If he wanted a divorce, he'd get one like that." He snaps his fingers, and Homer, mistaking it for a summons, abandons his game and rushes up to him, rolls onto his back, covering my uncle's hose with short white hairs. I stifle a laugh as Uncle William kicks the dog away, and Homer takes refuge in Mother's skirts.

Mother doesn't mind a few white hairs on her gown. She sits serenely and I know she is resisting the impulse to reprimand her brother for kicking her dog. She runs a soft white hand across Homer's back.

"Is there no way you can be reconciled?"

"NO!" Uncle William explodes. "She is a liar and a jade. I wish to God our mother had never arranged the match. It is a fiasco, a waste of my time and hers. I've been tied to the bitch since I was thirteen years old, and then denied her father's title after all. Since I cannot bring myself to share her bed, there will be no heir to follow after me – not of my getting anyway. You've heard she has taken a lover?"

Mother flushes as she gently replies, "But William, so do you. I am told you have more than one."

I am shocked at Mother for speaking out of turn. She has always taught me that women must turn a blind eye to male indiscretions. I turn a curious eye on my uncle, and the disturbing picture of him playing the part of an ardent lover sets my dinner curdling in my belly. His face grows dark with displeasure.

"That is different! It is not the same for men. I am not likely to foist some bastard off as hers, am I? I tell you I will not rest until our union is severed."

Mother picks up her embroidery again and continues to infill the border. I watch her deft fingers for a while, wishing my own needle was so obedient.

"Then I fear, Brother, you will wait a long time. The king is quite adamantly against it, I am told."

William slurps his wine, bangs the cup bad-temperedly on the table.

"Who told you that?"

She flushes even pinker.

"I believe it was Sir Thomas Seymour."

"Seymour? You've been discussing my affairs with Seymour? What possessed you to do such a thing?"

27

A look of annoyance passes over her face, impatience clearly perceptible in her tone.

"I believe we spoke of the question of divorce in general, and the king's piety and determination to rule by example."

"Example! If we all lived like Henry, the court would be littered with bastards."

"William." Mother's tone is sharp. "I will not tolerate such talk in my home. You know it is dangerous. Let us speak of other things. Why do we not take a turn about the garden since the heat of the sun is diminishing?"

Once outside, as we stroll among the flowers, I venture to quiz him. "Do you not love the king, Uncle?"

He looks at me askance.

"Not love the king? Who cannot love so virtuous a prince?" His expression denies the truth in his words and I smile as he ushers me past the fountain. I am aware that he has avoided my question, and perceive that my probing was inappropriate. For the first time I begin to understand that it is all very well to privately have no love for the king but imperative that none should know it, not even close kin.

Uncle William stops and plucks a rose bud. I look down and watch him fasten it with thick, strong fingers to my bodice.

"There," he says. "A rose for a rose."

Mother, who witnesses his action, laughs and waits for us to catch up with her. We link arms and move on together. Customs are so different in London. How is any girl able to recognise a genuine suitor when courtly games are played even between uncle and niece?

October 1537 – Hampton Court

The hot summer weather having deteriorated into rain and gales, people begin to flock back to London. The king is once more resident at Hampton Court, where Queen Jane has taken to her chamber. Since the middle of September she has been closeted away from the world to await the birth of her son.

On the morning, we wake to the news of midwives being summoned in the dead of night, and we are not the only ones to suddenly find excuses to be present at the palace the next day. Mother and I put on our best clothes and take the boat up river to confer with Aunt Anne when she is spared the time.

"Yes, she is in labour," she whispers when she slips out to see us. "The poor thing suffers so much. It is often the way with women who have a tiny frame."

Her eyes stray up and down my skirts, assessing the size of my hips, which are depressingly wide. Beside me, Mother emits a noise, indicating sympathy.

"And how is the king? Beside himself with worry, I should imagine."

"William says he is jubilant already, before the poor little thing is even born. God help us all if it's a girl."

She drops her voice as she nears the end of the sentence, clutches Mother's arm and turns her eyes up to heaven. We all know it is not a laughing matter, but we smile anyway.

"I must get back inside." Aunt Anne kisses Mother, cups my cheek in her hand and leaves us.

"We might as well return home." Mother looks out at the lowering sky. "It will soon be dark and we can't stay here all night. We will hear the news soon enough when it comes."

We begin to weave our way through the loitering crowd, her hand on my elbow guiding me ahead of her toward the courtyard. As we reach the door a voice calls out Mother's name, and we both turn, expecting to find Uncle William offering to see us safe home. Instead it is Thomas Seymour, the queen's brother. He squeezes through the crush and makes an elegant leg to Mother, sweeping off his hat with a flourish.

"Lady Latimer. I thought it was you." He is slightly breathless, colour in his cheeks as if he has just taken a gallop on a fiery horse.

"Have you just arrived?" Mother allows him to take her hand. He draws her close, kisses her lips, as is the way at court. When he withdraws I notice Mother is almost as flushed as he.

"No. I've been lurking in the palace for days waiting for Jane to let go her pup."

His casual reference to our hallowed soon-to-be-born prince startles me, but Mother gives a quiet laugh.

"Thomas, you dreadful man."

Something in her easy manner alerts me. I watch with increasing interest as he takes her arm and slowly leads her down the steps. I follow in their wake.

At first I had thought he was simply dressed, but outside, the dying daylight reveals that his white padded doublet is studded with tiny pearls that shine as we pass beneath the torches. His sleeves are slashed, peach-coloured satin spilling forth, his thickly lined cloak reaching his knees, his hose as white as the purest snow. As the brother of the queen, and soon-to-be uncle of England's heir, he has donned his most sumptuous clothes. I wonder if he is as good as he looks, or if it is all show.

"I will call on you both again soon," he says as he assists us into the waiting barge. "I enjoyed it so much last time."

"That will be lovely." Mother settles herself in the barge and, as I take my own seat, I strive but fail to be as elegant as she. I land with a plop in the cushions beside her. As the oarsmen prepare to move away, I struggle with my skirts that have somehow become tangled beneath me. Thomas Seymour lingers close to the stern, his eyes fast upon Mother's face.

"Perhaps I can bring you news, when the prince is born." He raises his hat, the fine fat feathers fluttering in the rising breeze.

"I shall look forward to it."

Mother lifts her hand, keeps it raised, her eyes fixed upon him, as the boat draws away from the river bank. The current takes us and the boat gathers speed before she realises I am watching. She gives herself a little shake and clasps her hands in her lap.

"Well," she says. "If he brings us the news it will save us the bother of going out in search of it."

Of course, we know the prince is born before Thomas Seymour returns. The bells ring out across London, and the peace is shattered by the two thousand gun salute that greets the Tudor heir. They say the king is beside himself, weeping with joy and kissing all within reach. Soon the world erupts in celebration; bonfires are lit in the streets, wine flows freely, and for days on end there are civic processions and banquets until the populace can take no more.

When he is three days old the Prince is christened Edward, after the king's Plantagenet grandfather. We do not attend the ceremony but Thomas, when he comes, describes it so well that we might as well have been present.

I glean from his words that Seymour is a little put out that he is not a godparent. That honour went to the Dukes of Norfolk, Suffolk, and Archbishop Cranmer, and to rub salt into the wound, his brother Edward is made the Earl of Hertford. Thomas is a little appeased when he is given a knighthood and promoted to the privy chamber, but it is easy to see how his brother's higher status rankles.

"That is good news, Sir Thomas," Mother soothes, using his new title. "Did you hear that my brother William is also honoured? I believe he will use the title Lord Parr."

Thomas rubs a fingertip along the line of his eyebrow. "Perhaps it will help him bear with his wife a little better."

Mother hides a smile, forces her face into feigned severity, but she cannot maintain it and they both collapse into laughter. Dorothy, entering with a heavy tray, raises her eyebrows in surprise. Her face is white and strained and I notice she is bursting with unspoken news. I stand up.

"What is it, Dorothy? What is the matter?"

She bends over and whispers in my ear. "It is the queen, My Lady. They are saying in the kitchen that she has been taken sick and is like to die."

Wildly, I look from Mother to Sir Thomas. Why me? I ask myself. Why is it left to me to tell him?

"It is the queen ..." Before the words have left my mouth Sir Thomas leaps from his place at the fireside, knocking over his cup. His wine spills and spreads like blood across Mother's skirt.

"I must go," he says, snatching up his hat and hurrying from the room. Mother watches open-mouthed, unable to speak or offer comfort.

The door bangs so hard behind him that the candles waver. The flames struggle for life, flickering desperately in a futile dance before they are extinguished forever.

October 1537 - London

London is plunged into mourning for the queen. Women weep in the streets for the pitiable motherless prince and his poor bereaved father. Forgetting the harsh rule of the last few years, the populace overlook the burnings, the disembowelling, the murdered monks, and their hearts fill with grief for their unlucky monarch. As Queen Jane's body is carried to Windsor, the crowd stand silent in the rain. The nobles follow in a bedraggled procession of damp velvet and dripping feathers. There is not a soul who doesn't weep for the queen who has given our king his greatest joy and his greatest sorrow.

Afterwards, the king locks himself away and no one sees him outside his privy chambers for weeks. Aunt Anne weeps, uncertain what she will do once the queen's household is disbanded. She tells us of how she found the king's fool, Will Somers, weeping outside his master's door, forbidden entry, refused the privilege of cheering his king's spirits.

For three long months the English courtiers creep around, the bleak cloak of death muffling all pleasure. Even Christmas is a sorry, sombre affair this year. Everything we do is tinged with the knowledge that our mighty king has been felled by personal loss. Now his presence is withdrawn, we miss the shrim of terror when he enters a room, the peculiar mix of joy and fear when he turns his small round eyes upon us.

And then, on a chilly day in February, like the sun appearing from behind a dark cloud, the king emerges. He is swathed head to toe in cloth of gold, and is as merry as a monarch can be.

Glad to put off our sombre clothes, Mother and I summon the seamstress and conjure new ones. I am given some fine new sleeves, two new hoods, and Mother allows me to wear her pearls on our next visit to court.

The hall is a crush, the heat from the hearth and the volume of bodies almost overwhelming. I am glad now that Mother reminded me to bring my pomander, for in February people do not wash as often as they do in June. I am forced to wave it beneath my nose very often as I surreptitiously search the crowd for Francis.

I hear him before I see him. He is laughing. The king's hand is on his shoulder, encouraging Francis to continue whatever risqué tale he is relating. From my safe distance I drink in his strange, rough beauty, and wonder if he will notice me tonight.

Mother falls straight into conversation with Uncle William and his party, giving me the freedom to let my eyes wander. Looking at the king today, you'd never imagine he has just emerged from three months of deep despair. He is magnificent, a head taller than any other man in the room. His doublet is just one shade lighter than the colour of his hair, and the gleam in his eye suggests that he is already in search of another wife, or mistress.

For a moment I imagine him noticing me, making me queen. I would be swathed head to toe in finery and jewels, and everyone at court would be falling over

34

themselves to please me. I forget the miseries of his last three wives and think only of the benefits. But then Francis turns around, his eyes straying about the room. When they fall upon me he pauses; a smile flickers at the edge of his mouth and my world hesitates, seems to falter, hiccough a little. In a flutter of panic I realise he has taken leave of the king and is weaving his way through the crowd toward me.

"Mistress Neville." He kisses my lips. My heart flips sickeningly as I try not to prolong the moment. A heartbeat later I remember to pull away and keep my eyes shyly on the floor. My mouth tingles from the contact. My fingers are burning in his palm. I cannot think of one intelligent thing to say.

"You look very fine." He indicates my silk gown, my fine new sleeves. "One would almost think you were out to catch a husband."

Beneath his penetrating gaze, I stammer and stutter like a fool, and it is not until he laughs that I realise he is teasing. I drop my head. I hate how he always mocks me.

"Come," he says. "Margaret. May I call you Margaret? Do not sulk and deprive me of your pretty smile."

I can do nothing else but obey. It reluctantly blossoms, spreading across my cheeks until I am beaming. I try to control it but it beats me, and a giggle splutters unbidden from my lips.

"That is better," he whispers.

The room is crushed and we are forced to stand close together. I am not sure if his hand is intentionally placed so near to my breast or not. I can appreciate each crease on his lips, each lash around his eyes, and each curl of his beard. I want to know what it feels like to be kissed properly, and to my surprise I find myself imagining myself crushed in his arms, his mouth on mine, our bodies merging, melding into one.

He is speaking. I haven't heard a word.

"I am sorry, Sir Francis. I misheard you."

He bends closer, speaks directly into my ear, his breath whispering on my skin, the fragrance of his body rising. I put my pomander away.

"I said; it is damnably hot in here. Shall I ask your mother if I can accompany you outside? I am sure you must feel faint."

I feel nothing of the sort but I let my head droop a little and try to look pathetic. "Yes, please," I whimper. "I do feel a little odd."

I am sure that if Mother wasn't so heavily engaged in conversation with Sir Thomas she would never allow me to go off unaccompanied with a man like Sir Francis Bryan. She turns reluctantly away from Seymour, flushed and laughing, and waves a careless hand.

"Yes, yes. Of course. Don't be long though, my dear."

My fingers caress the soft velvet of his sleeve as he leads me through the crowd. The people part and close around us again as we make our way from the hall. But, instead of leading me outside, he stops by a small antechamber and slips through the door, drawing me in after him. I pull away, but the instant my hand detaches from his sleeve I find myself bereft.

I am struck dumb with shyness, and have no idea what I should say, what I should do, so I just stand and stare into the flagging embers of the fire.

He comes up close behind me. "How old are you, Margaret?"

I turn toward him. He places a knuckle beneath my chin and lifts my face to his. My cheeks are burning and my lips begin to tingle in anticipation.

"I am old enough to be wed."

"But you've never been kissed?"

I shake my head but, of course, it isn't true. I have been horribly kissed, brutally violated, and I know things a maid should never know. But I cannot tell him that. I would be shunned.

Once I had thought I would never take a husband. Never want to be kissed again. I had imagined myself entering a nunnery, sacrificing my life to God. But that was before I laid eyes on Sir Francis Bryan, before I became acquainted with the 'vicar of hell.' Now my Judas body cries out for male contact and there is nothing I can do to govern it.

"You are ripe for a husband."

I open my eyes, look directly into his.

"So my mother tells me."

He reaches out. A finger traces a line of fire down my cheek, along my jaw, and his thumb rubs torment into my lips. I close my eyes again, and sense his face lowering to mine.

His lips are soft and warm, gentle. My heart is fluttering and leaping like a teeming pool of small, silver fish. He swallows my ecstatic sigh, draws me closer. His hands travel over my body. My skin heats and glows, and burns beneath his touch.

It is nothing like that other kiss. That was revolting and for a while had made me want to die. This kiss is different. This man makes me want to live as dangerously as he. It goes on and on. I don't want it to stop, yet I feel if it doesn't I will cease to breathe. I will die of passion.

We overbalance, fall against the wall, his hands begin to wrench my skirts to my knees. My breath issues in gasps. I have never wanted anything so much. But, just as I feel his hand on my naked thigh and my insides begin to melt, a great sound of crashing metal wrenches us apart. My skirts fall. I lean breathless against the wall while he stands alert and ready to run.

"What was that?" I gasp when I can find my voice. He draws the back of his hand across his wet mouth.

"I don't know; probably some idiot scullion dropping a tray." He turns back to me but makes no move to resume our passion His face is solemn. I smile, shamefaced but happy, while he runs his hands through his hair.

"Margaret," he says in a voice full of anguish, "I am a married man."

My heart drops like stone down a well.

"But ..."

"And I have to go away soon, very soon. The king is sending me on a mission to France."

I step forward, too close to be maidenly, and let him see the depth of my longing.

"But you will come back. You won't be gone forever."

He turns reluctantly away. "As I said; I am a married man."

"But, why did you ...? You do not love her..."

He laughs, his teeth glinting white in the light of the fire. "And what are you saying, Margaret? You will be my mistress? Become just another in a long line of women? Don't you know who I am? Don't you think I have earned my reputation?"

I want to cry. Suddenly I am no longer a fiery, red-blooded woman ready to give herself to a lover. I am a little girl again, deprived of my favourite doll. My lower lip trembles.

"I don't care."

He takes my hand, courteously. All sign of our former passion quenched.

"Margaret. I thought I could use you, as I have all the others, but I can't. I like you too much. Be glad of that. Come; let me take you back to your mother."

"I am not a child, sir."

He laughs a gentle laugh.

"Yes, you are. A maid who knows nothing of what you were offering me. And I am a cad who was ready to rob you of something irreplaceable. I refuse to do it. You see, I am not really happy with my reputation but sometimes, I feel obliged to live up to it."

He holds out his arm, and sulkily I lay my fingers on it and allow him to return me to Katheryn's side.

1540 – 41 - London

In a few short years the king has won himself another queen. She is called Anne, like his second wife. Fresh from Cleves, she rides through London in the cold to wed the king, but in a few short months is put aside. Aunt Anne says she does not please him. He finds her fat and offensive to his nose. All the court are talking of it, the poor woman must be eaten up with humiliation. I find it astonishing that one as unwieldy as the king should find it in himself to criticise another. When, in the privacy of our chambers, I voice this opinion to Mother, she hushes me.

"You must never say such things, Margaret. The king is to be revered. He is handsome and virile, and you must never think otherwise. People have died for less."

I look up, surprised. Of course, I would never be so silly as to speak openly before strangers, but I had thought us safe closeted together in our home.

King Henry is growing old. The golden prince is fading and emerging in his place is a tetchy old man. A man wracked with the pain of an ulcerated leg, and tortured with the knowledge that after a string of unsatisfactory wives, he has managed to produce just one legitimate son. There is no security in infants; the king needs a string of sons, sons who promise to grow into men. If he fails in this, the Tudor line will be extinguished.

Cromwell is to blame. It was he who pushed for the match with Cleves to strengthen England's position against Spain. While Henry storms about the palace in a ferocious mood, Cromwell skulks in corners. Wisely, he keeps his head down and his policies within bounds, but no one is very surprised when, a few weeks later, the council turns on him. They strip him of his privileges and titles, and cart him off to the Tower. Restrained for so long under his office, the noblemen of the king's council waste no opportunity to vent their spleen.

Thomas Cromwell does not make a brave prisoner. I cringe for him when I hear of how he rails against his fate, pleading with the king to show him mercy, revealing in gory clarity his lowly beginnings. But Henry is unforgiving. Escaped by the skin of his teeth from the unwholesome bed of Anne of Cleves, he is determined that someone will suffer for it. On the day he orders Cromwell's death, the nation holds its breath to see who will be the next to fall.

With Cromwell dead, our home at Charterhouse is back in our possession and, amid the flurry of moving back in, we discover that England has a new queen. Queen Katherine this time.

She is a Howard, a niece of the Duke of Norfolk, and is just a few years older than I. Aunt Anne describes her as a slip of unsubstantial prettiness who somehow manages to soothe and heal our ageing, malodorous king. Rather her than me.

Against all these great events, I spend a miserable few years. All I can think of or dream about is Francis Bryan, who is still abroad on the king's business. The tales of his debauchery in Paris fill me with grief; and the idea of him in another woman's arms is almost as abhorrent as the thought of bedding one of the many suitors Mother insists on parading before me. She assures me I will not be forced to take a man I do not favour, but I feel her patience is beginning to stretch.

My prospective husbands range from spotty youths to elderly gentlemen, and I like none of them. Luckily, Father is so often away on business that the question of my marriage is allowed to drift. But, in October, worn out by the harsh weather in the north and the trials of campaign, Father returns home and takes directly to his sick bed.

"What is wrong with him?" I cling to the door frame watching Mother calmly plump his pillow and smooth his sheet.

"He is just tired; worn out," she says, tiptoeing from the bed and ushering me out the door. "He is not as young as he used to be."

"Is he going to die?"

"Oh no, not if I have anything to do with it. He will soon rally with good nursing and wholesome food."

She shuts herself away in her still-room, preparing concoctions to soothe him, tonics to revitalise his flagging energy. In the downstairs parlour my brother John is waiting, and I steel myself to meet him. I pause on the threshold, at first not recognising the elegantly clad man in the shadows. He is staring from the window, unmoving; his frame taut, his shoulders braced. When he realises my presence he puts down his glass and moves into the light.

"Little sister." He comes forward to greet me formally, and all the while I can feel him assessing me: my face, my clothes, my posture. "Quite grown up."

He kisses my hand, laughs through his nose in a strange snuffling manner that reminds me of Father. John has grown; no longer the gangly boy but a sturdy, upright man. But I soon realise he is not as confident as he would have me believe. His palm is clammy. As quickly as is polite, I retract my hand and move to my favourite seat. Homer leaps onto my lap, turns circles, preparing to nest, and I let my fingers caress his soft short coat while John takes the opposite seat.

"Not married yet?" Something in his tone speaks of our unacknowledged secret and infers that I am soiled goods, unmarriageable and unwanted. I instantly bristle, preparing for a fight.

"Not yet." My hand trails along Homer's spine to his whip-like tail.

"But you've had suitors?"

"Of course."

"And not one of them pleased you? Perhaps you are too picky, Sister."

I do not intend to enter into an argument with him when our reunion is so fresh. Instead I turn the tables upon him.

"I understand you are betrothed to Lucy Somerset?"

"Hmm."

"And does that please you? She is maid of honour to Queen Katherine, is she not?"

"Yes."

"Is she pretty?"

"Pretty enough."

I look down at the rhythmic stroking of my hand. Homer is transported in bliss, his eyes half-open, or half-closed, his nose tilted upward in a contented manner.

Questions and answers. Questions and answers. I am aware that my brother desires to know just one thing. *Have I had a lover yet?* I wonder why it matters to him.

I look up suddenly, surprising his brooding eye upon me, and he looks away, a slight flush creeping up from his jaw.

"You will have to bring Lucy to meet us. It will be easier for her if she makes our acquaintance before you are wed. She is to be part of the family, after all."

"Hmm."

"I get quite lonely for female company of my own age. Aunt Anne has tried to get me a place in the queen's household but to no avail. She says I am on the list."

"You need a husband."

I stand up and Homer falls indignantly to my feet.

"I will take one when I meet a man I can abide."

I cannot keep the annoyance from my voice. John stands too. We are nose to nose before the fire, just like when we were in the nursery, squabbling over some toy.

"I knew it," he snarls. "It did affect you. You can't bear the thought of a man in your bed, can you?"

If only that were so. If only I could honestly swear that I hated all men. If only I wasn't committed to just one

43

and his name wasn't emblazoned on my heart. Tears prick behind my eyes. I try to blink them away. I look at the floor, the textures of the rush matting beneath my feet dissolving. I shake my head and John's hand clamps upon my wrist.

"Did you never tell *anyone* about it? Not even Mother?"

"She is the last person I would tell, and what was the point? My abuser was dead. The only person to suffer from making the fact known would have been me."

John says nothing. His former arrogance has melted away and I see now it was just a mask to hide his insecurities. I can see his face working as he tries to organise the thing he wants to say.

"I am glad you kept it a secret, if only for the sake of my own honour. I wanted to kill him, you know. I'm sorry I didn't."

"I know."

"But I did nothing. Do you know how I have suffered for that? I have lain awake of a night living it over and over. I was a coward. I should have killed him."

Do you think I have not suffered? The words are almost on my lips but somehow I suppress them. I reach out and touch his sleeve.

"You were just a boy."

"And you were a girl! When I think of it I ..."

"Then don't think of it. Shut it out. Move on, as I have done."

Our eyes meet. His are hooded, dark, rimmed in shadow.

"You have moved on, forgotten it? I thought you hated men?"

44

I laugh, as if I mean it, as if I really have forgotten. "That was your idea. I am not averse to marriage. I have other reasons for not following up Mother's proposals."

"What reasons?"

My cheeks grow hot. I lift my chin and look him squarely in the eye.

"I love another."

His face opens in surprise, his eyes round with curiosity.

"Love another? Who, for God's sake? Is he wed already?"

I shake my head and turn away.

"Is he beneath you? One of the servants? One of Mother's clerks?"

"John! No, of course not. He is just ... not for marrying."

"He doesn't love you? Is that what you mean? Margaret?" He takes hold of my elbows, gives me a little shake. "Answer me!"

Homer begins to paw at my skirts, thinking it a game. John pushes him down, kicks him away, and the dog skulks beneath the table.

"It is not your business. You are my brother, not my keeper. If there were any benefit to you knowing I would tell you, but there isn't."

At that moment the door opens and Mother sweeps into the room, her face breaking into smiles when she sees him.

"John. How lovely to see you." She holds out her hands and he is forced to leave my side to greet her.

"I will find out," he growls from the side of his mouth as he passes. I watch them embrace and when Dorothy comes in with a tray of cups, we take our places before the hearth.

As I watch my brother, I become aware of the signs of suffering on his face. The change in him began many years ago, before our mother died, before the events at Snape, but now, in the king's service, he has seen other bad things; things that have hardened him further. He looks unsettled, ill at ease, as if he expects to find an assassin behind every door.

"I was telling John he must bring Lucy to see us, so we can get to know her better."

Both heads turn toward me. "Yes," Mother smiles. "You must. She is with the king and queen on the Royal Progress, is she not?"

"I believe so." John shrugs. "And by the time they return I expect I will be back on the border, dealing with King James. But there is nothing to stop you from becoming acquainted in my absence."

October 1541 - London

Lucy and Aunt Anne arrive to take supper with us a few months later. Father, a little recovered, has accompanied John back to the Scottish border and we find ourselves a household of women again. Lucy is a pretty girl, about sixteen years old, and I know at once that we will be friends. She makes a great fuss of Homer and speaks enthusiastically of her own dog that she was forced to leave at her father's house when she came to serve the queen.

Lucy is a dainty little thing, her tiny wrists sparrow-like compared with my own. Beside her I feel clumsy and over-sized, but I like her despite that. She is everything I'd like to be.

Mother and Aunt Anne go into the next chamber to examine the new draperies for Katheryn's bed, leaving Lucy and I to become properly acquainted.

"What is the queen like?" I ask. "I've not seen her close up yet."

Lucy's eyes dart around the room, she leans closer.

"She is not what you'd expect at all. She is not at all grand, more like you and I, and she is very generous. Her rooms are full of presents from the king and she doesn't seem to value them at all, but showers them all on her favourites. She has made a great friend of the Lady Anne, you know, the king's last wife, and gave her two beautiful little spaniels. And she gave me this, look."

She holds out her hand and I take it, examine a small ring on her finger. A diamond surrounded with tiny pearls.

"Goodness, what a lovely thing. So you like her?"

"Oh yes." Lucy blushes. "But not just because of the gift. She is funny, full of laughter, and we spend all our days dancing or trying on new clothes. Her apartments are always full of young men."

I wonder what John would think about the blush that floods her cheeks when she tells me this. Has she set her heart on another? I make a note to probe her when I know her a little better, and turn the conversation back to the queen.

"I would love to see her properly. When I was at court last, the king seemed so much in love with her."

"Everyone is. Apart from those who worry about Gardiner and Norfolk's increasing influence; it was they who introduced her to the king in the first place."

Homer has shed hairs all over my hem and I absentmindedly begin to pick them off, one by one, and drop them on to the floor.

47

"Is Queen Katherine interested in state affairs? I'd have thought not, judging from all I've heard."

"No, not at all. She is all for pleasure. The only time I have seen her sad is when her monthly flux occurs and she knows she has failed to get with child again. She takes to her bed then, all crumpled with weeping, and doubled up with the cramps."

"Poor thing. It must be dreadful with all eyes upon her. I hope she falls soon. England needs another prince. You can't have too many princes."

"I could do with one myself," Lucy says with a wry grin.

"Hmm, my brother can be described in many ways, but 'princely?' I think not."

We fall into a fit of giggles that brings Mother and Aunt Anne back into the chamber. They join us by the hearth and, like a ball on a hoop, the conversation returns to the royal court.

"I can't wait to be introduced to the queen," I say. "I am so glad they are back from the progress now. I have a gown made from the same deep red shade as Mother's. I shall wear that."

"I shall look for you there." Lucy squeezes my hand and begins to describe a new hood she has had fashioned in a similar style to one of Queen Katherine's.

When they take their leave, there are kisses all round. They mount their horses amid much laughter. Lucy raises her gloved hand. "I can't wait to see you again," she calls as the party moves off, and I retire to the house knowing I have a new friend.

But before we can attend the festivities and I have my chance to be presented to the queen, dreadful news comes from Hampton Court. Queen Katherine is under arrest and her ladies are being questioned. Immediately our thoughts are with Aunt Anne and Lucy. It is only latterly that I consider the feelings of the doomed queen.

There is no question she is doomed. There are very few people who fall foul of King Henry and live to re-emerge from the Tower prison. Mother and I sit rigid, our dinner untouched. The servants creep around the perimeter of the room, as alarmed as we by the gossip and speculation.

"I can't help but think of Anne Boleyn." My voice is but a whisper but Katheryn raises her hand, silencing me before I speak further. I ignore her warning, too terrified to heed her.

"What about Aunt Anne and Lucy? What is happening to them? And Queen Katherine, she is so young. Suppose she ... you know what happened to Anne Boleyn ... in the Tower."

Mother's face is tight and pale, her lips bitten white. She jerks her head.

"They have not been taken to the Tower. The queen is at Syon. Lucy is with her. I don't know where Anne is ..." Her voice breaks on a sob and I remember that she and Aunt Anne are sisters, they shared the same nursery. I get up and do what I can to comfort her, but I am not skilled at intimacy. Awkwardly, I hold her close, pat her shoulder, make the proper noises, but all the time my mind is racing ahead, filling with images of another death, another burning, another beheading, another sacrificed queen.

Since my eleventh year there has been nothing but death, torture, mutilation and vengeance. Our religious foundation has crumbled and now no one feels secure. The English people creep in fear, never knowing who to champion, who to denigrate, who to venerate or how to pray. And all the while the king sits like a malicious spider, ready to inject his venom into those who fly too close to his web.

Uncle William comes in haste and Mother and I rush out to greet him when we hear his horse. "It is all right," he says before he has even dismounted. "She has been questioned and released. Since the queen, err, Mistress Howard, has only been allocated a few serving women, our sister has elected to return home. I have no doubt she will take to her bed and surround herself with her children."

"Oh, thank goodness, Will. I have been so worried. We both have ..."

"What about the queen?" I interrupt. "What is she accused of?"

Uncle William looks uncomfortable. "You'd not credit so sweet a child could be so foul." He shakes his head, ushers us indoors, keeping his voice low so that the servants cannot hear. "They are saying she is depraved, having had a score of lovers before she wed the king."

A score? I think before turning my attention back to Uncle Will's story. *She is just seventeen years old, there hasn't been time!*

"And it didn't stop when she married, either. She has been misbehaving with her own household staff, and Culpepper from the king's household has been taken into custody too. He won't live to see another sunrise; you can be assured of that."

I know Thomas Culpepper. He is the sort of fellow you don't forget; handsome, witty, the life and soul of any gathering. When I was at court the king made much of Culpepper, keeping him close to his side. His face was so fine that I enquired of Aunt Anne who he was and I learned he was a favourite of the king; the only one who could dress his wounded leg without making him scream.

If he is executed, King Henry will miss Thomas as much as he will miss his wife; after all, wives are more easily replaced than good servants.

December - April 1542 - London

So, with fear intensifying like a stifling fug over the royal court, Mother and I stay away. Father comes home again, this time on a litter, and I can see on his face that his days on this earth are now short. Once more he takes to his bed, but this time there is no talk of recovery, or of him returning to the war.

Christmas is a sombre affair. John doesn't come home. We have no clue what is happening to Lucy, and the dispossessed queen spends Yule in captivity.

Early one morning in February, they take her to the Tower and cut off her head. Lucy, who was with her to the end, comes to stay with us. She is a broken figure, a shadow of the bright girl I met before. Mother, whose skills at nursing have never been in such demand, opens her arms to yet another patient.

Although I am bursting with questions, I do not know how to phrase them and, hard as it is, I wait for Lucy to volunteer the information. I sit by her bed with my sewing while she lies quietly, her face almost as white as the pillow. From time to time she gives a massive sigh, guttering the candle that I sew by.

Downstairs, people come and go. Uncle William and Aunt Anne with her husband and children in tow. One by one, they make the pilgrimage upstairs to greet our stricken guest and try to make her smile.

While they are here, the house lights up a little. Homer wakes from his slumber and runs barking at the heels of the children until the din grows to such proportions that Uncle William sends them all into the garden. The dash of cheer in our lives at last tempts Lucy from her bed. She asks to be dressed for the first time in months and, a few weeks later, is mercifully much recovered when John arrives unexpectedly home.

I watch them together. He is stiff, almost unfriendly with her, yet she is as gentle and submissive as a lamb. It is as if he has no idea how to behave, how to be tender. In the end I take him to task.

"She has suffered so much," I scold him. "I thought your return would cheer her, yet you are as unfriendly as a snake."

He scowls, looks a little put out. "I am not comfortable with women. I have been at war too long, in the company of men. What am I supposed to say to her?"

I raise my eyes to heaven. "Take her round the garden. Discuss the weather, the flowers, or the birds on the lawn. Good heavens, she is going to be your wife, you must think of something!"

Later on I see them walking stiffly amid the flowers. Her hand is on his arm and he seems to be speaking to her. She looks startled, like a sparrow suddenly surprised by a tom-cat, but John doesn't seem to notice. He marches her on, waving his free arm in the air to punctuate his sentences.

When they return to the house, Lucy is chilled. I fetch a blanket and we sit close to the fire.

"What was John saying to you out there?" I ask, unable to contain my curiosity any longer. Her expression is bemused. She shrugs her shoulders, pulls a face.

"He was telling me how his horse was killed in battle and had to be replaced. He said the stallion he purchased was so unreliable he had to be gelded. He, err, your brother then went on to describe the procedure. It involved a knife and rather a lot of blood…"

I let out a little shriek of fury and, spinning on my heel, go in search of him. "John!" I march down the stairs and into Father's study where John is cleaning his weapons; a task he likes to undertake himself.

"Ah, it's you," he says when I burst in. "Well, I seem to be making headway with Lucy."

"What on earth were you thinking? Have you no sense at all? Women don't want to know about castration. Lucy needs gentleness. Don't you know what that is?"

He puts down his knife, leans back in his chair.

"No, I'm afraid I don't. That side of my education has been sadly lacking."

I watch him stare into the fire. He is right. We have known little softness, little security. And it must be worse for John, taken off to war when he was little more than a boy. He has learned survival, but that lesson has been at the expense of pleasure. I am sure he has known women, bad women and plenty of them, but he knows nothing of love, or life's joys.

None of us walk a safe path, but when I look back at our shared childhood I see a road littered with betrayal and fear. Our only constant has been Katheryn, who has been, and still is, there for us, like a soft cushion on a hard bench.

Summer 1542 - London

The king wastes little time mourning for his faithless queen. Instead he embarks upon a period of

53

what only can be described as levity. Determined to shake off the ill-effects of encroaching age, he dons his most splendid apparel and is seldom seen without a lady on his arm. He eats too much, laughs too much, but everyone knows his good humour is a mask for discontent. His single state gives rise to much gossip as the court falls to surmising who he will select to be his next queen.

Such is his reputation as a husband that I suspect there will be few to volunteer for the role. In the absence of a consort he invites his daughter, the Lady Mary, to preside over court. Mother has been friends with Lady Mary since they were children. In fact, she told me once that she was named in honour of Mary's mother, Queen Katherine of Aragon, or the Princess Dowager as we are now supposed to call her. In a great upheaval of excitement, we begin to order new gowns and trappings suitable for a short stay at the palace.

Lucy, reluctant to place herself in the way of the king again, tries to wriggle out of the visit but is ordered to accompany us by her furious father. She remains a shadow of her former self, a fearful look in her eye, but obediently she selects her plainest gowns and prepares to journey with us.

To my surprise, the atmosphere in Lady Mary's chambers is relaxed. The musicians play a lively tune while the assembled ladies and gentlemen exchange pleasantries. At first I do not notice the dazzlingly attired figure in the centre of the room but, when she turns and her eyes open in delight, I realise it is Lady Mary herself.

I have seen her once before, but on that occasion her face was dark, her skin sallow-looking, and her expression the very image of her royal father's. Today, she is happy and it shows.

"Katheryn, Lady Latimer! How happy I am to see you again." She grasps Mother's wrists and kisses her on the mouth while Mother blushes with pleasure. She tries to curtsey but Lady Mary prevents it. "No, you must not," I hear her warn. "I am just the Lady Mary now, remember that."

A look of pain flashes across Mother's face. "I will reluctantly bear that in mind, My Lady." She kisses the royal knuckles again and Lady Mary leads her away. I follow with my eyes lowered, playing the demure young woman as I have been instructed.

There are people missing from the royal court. Lady Rochford, who has been prominent for so many years, perished with Queen Katherine, and others who enjoyed the little queen's favour have drifted away or been banished from court. In the wake of the late queen's disgrace people tread with care, and think carefully before they speak. I miss the loud banter that went before, the laughter and the teasing.

But, truthfully, it is Francis Bryan whom I long to see. I learned quite recently that he returned from Paris in the spring upon the death of his wife. The news fills my foolish heart with hope.

"Mistress Neville. By God, you have blossomed."

I turn toward the familiar voice, my heart leaping, but it plummets instantly when I realise it isn't Francis. Thomas Seymour is grinning down at me. He is still enjoying high favour despite the demise of his sister, Queen Jane.

"Sir Thomas." I execute a dainty curtsey and allow him to kiss the side of my mouth.

"Your mother is here?" He stretches his neck, craning over the crowd in search of her.

"She is with the Lady Mary." I indicate the two women seated in a small alcove, their heads nodding, their hands embroidering their earnest conversation.

"Ah," he says. "I had better not interrupt." I watch him from the corner of my eye while he searches for something to say. He is a splendid-looking fellow. His embroidered black doublet is of the finest nap, the slashed sleeves revealing a splash of orange silk beneath. His beard, that waggles when he speaks, is neatly trimmed and scented with sandalwood, the kerchief that he clutches is of the best Holland.

Some say that, after the king, Seymour is the handsomest man at court. Were I not so loyal to my own true love, I would have to agree.

"Have you met my brother's betrothed, Lucy Somerset?" I draw Lucy into the circle of conversation.

"Of course. How do you, Mistress?"

When he leans in for a kiss, she turns her head a little so that his lips merely graze her cheek. I had hoped Lucy would help to break the awkward silence. She must know Seymour well, having been part of the queen's household for so long. But to my chagrin she flushes scarlet, bobs a curtsey and says nothing, leaving me to wrack my brains for something intelligent. Just as I am about to open my mouth to speak, Seymour asks a question.

"How is your father?"

I look at the floor, the exquisitely clad feet of the milling crowd, their sweeping gowns, and wrinkled hose. A mislaid kerchief floats like a feather to the ground.

"Not very well, actually," I hear myself saying. "Mother thinks he will not see out the year."

"I am sorry to hear that."

He doesn't sound it, and I notice that as he speaks his eyes constantly stray toward Mother and the Lady Mary. They have now clasped hands and Mary is leaning forward, speaking earnestly. Clearly they are discussing a matter of some urgency.

"The dancing will begin soon," Seymour says. "I will seek you both out then, if I may?" He executes a perfect bow and drifts away, leaving Lucy and I alone in the crush. She stands so close beside me I can feel her breath on my cheek.

"I hate it here, I want to go home," she whispers. "I feel everyone is staring. Come with me to an ante-chamber where it will be quieter."

"You used to enjoy court. What is so different now?"

She shrugs and her chin wobbles a little as she answers. "I keep expecting to see Katherine. I am listening for her voice, her step. It is so strange without her, and yet nobody else seems to notice her lack, or care."

It is true. Katherine's absence is unremarked. She was here, the highest woman in the land, now she is gone. Her life ended and no one is in the least affected.

A group of gentlemen come into the room, their faces a blur. When they halt before us I nudge Lucy, and we curtsey simultaneously as if we have been practising.

"Margaret." The voice I have heard so often in my dreams halts my breath. I look up and he is there, as if he has never been away.

Somehow, my hand is in his. He steps closer, I inhale the familiar scent, and his lips touch mine. Although the greeting means nothing, I never want it to stop.

"My Lord." I blink rapidly, trying to focus, engraving his image on my mind so that I can bring it out later and gloat at his beauty. "This is my soon-to-be sister-in-law, Lucy Somerset."

A dart of envy stabs at my heart as his lips brush hers, and I notice she does not instantly draw away. My eyes narrow. "Lucy and John will be married very soon," I add with intent. Francis bows again. I glimpse the back of his neck, the way his dark hair curls above his fine lawn collar. When he rises and begins to speak I devour his jaw, the fine chiselled shape of his lips. Lips I can still taste.

"I wish you happiness." He turns back to me. "And you, Margaret, are you not yet wed?"

I am so hot I can scarcely breathe. The blood is pounding in my ears, sweat breaking out beneath my arms, my heart fluttering like a moth in a jar. Any moment now, he will ask me the question that I never thought I should hear.

"Not yet, My Lord. I am waiting for the right candidate."

A dimple flickers in his cheek, his lips twitch.

"Good for you, Mistress. Life is a game of chance. It is best not to enter the fray until you have sized up the opposition carefully."

He bows and moves away. I want to scream for him to come back. Briefly I consider pretending to faint, placing my trust in his sense of chivalry to fly to my rescue and carry me outside. But the moment passes and instead of stalling him, I watch him leave, and desolation grows in my breast.

Suddenly the music stops, and a great clarion of trumpets announces the arrival of the king.

"Oh my God," breathes Lucy in my ear. "It is the king. I don't want to see him. Can we get out?"

It is too late. We cannot just leave the king's presence without a by-your-leave. I grab Lucy's hand and with the rest of the assembly, we sink to the floor in obeisance.

My corset digs into my ribs, depriving me of air, and Lucy is standing on my skirt. After what seems an age, at some unseen signal we all rise, and for the first time in years I look upon King Henry. The shock of it almost makes me cry out aloud.

He is still majestic, still splendidly royal. His clothes are the finest I have ever seen, his cod-piece just as prominent, but his dignity ends there. Our monarch has grown monstrously fat, and his tightly bandaged legs are splayed like saplings of oak. His gross velvet belly protrudes before him like the prow of a ship. The rings on his fingers are sunk into his flesh, and his once handsome face is heavily jowled, his eyes reduced to tiny spots of light that glimmer with suspicion.

No wonder Lucy doesn't want to see him. His presence, that used to ignite a room into cheer, now has the opposite effect. He signals for the festivities to continue and slowly, guardedly, the conversation starts up again.

The king passes among us, leaning heavily on a cane, his breath wheezing from his lungs at every step. As he comes closer, Lucy and I make way for him, sinking to our knees as we have been taught. I can feel her tremor as he passes by.

Mother, who has her back to him, is so engrossed with the charms of Sir Thomas Seymour that she is unaware of the king's approach. I can see her hands moving in a characteristic dance as she speaks. When the king draws near, Sir Thomas freezes and places a hand on her arm to halt her conversation and alert her to the royal presence. When she turns, her face is alight with suspended happiness.

The king pauses for a moment, his eyes narrow, and a smile is born on his sagging cheek, lifting him momentarily from gloom. He holds out his hand to be kissed.

"Lady Latimer, isn't it?" he says as Mother falls to her knees before him.

***

My father is dead. The knowledge rests like a rock against my heart. I had known his days were short, but what should be seen as a release for him still comes as a shock. John returns home, more brusque than ever, and seems to spare little time for Lucy. While he drinks too much, and I weep too much, Mother remains calm, organising Father's affairs and arranging for his burial at St Paul's.

Widowed for the second time, Katheryn seems small and sad as, swathed head to toe in black, she prays for Father's soul. And I, although I am almost a woman grown, am now an orphan.

To my great relief, Father has left my care in Katheryn's hands. I am confident that when the time comes, she will ensure I am wed to as honest a man as we can find. If only Sir Bryan were in that category. If only he did not carry the reputation of a rakehell.

Three months later, when the worst of the sorrow is passing, Mother looks up from a letter she is reading.

"It is from the Lady Mary. She invites me into her household, and offers you the appointment of maid of honour."

I put down my knife, push the plate away.

"Will you accept?"

We exchange anxious glances.

"Would you like me to?"

Rapidly, my mind assesses all the possibilities. Lucy was forcibly returned to court a few months ago, under stern orders from her father to pull herself together.

"We would be with Lucy again," I say, but I am also calculating that by spending each day at the palace, my chances of an encounter with Francis will increase ten-fold.

"Of course, we will need new clothes."

"And we all know how you dislike clothes, Mother."

She throws her head back, her laughter a welcome return after so many weeks of forced solemnity. I know she mourns Father as is her duty but, after witnessing her ecstatic joy when in the company of Sir Thomas Seymour, it is obvious to me that she never loved him. I find myself, in idle moments, wondering how long she has known Seymour and if there is anything between them.

A few weeks later, we leave mourning behind us and set off for the Lady Mary's apartments at Hampton Court. There we find the courtiers in fine spirits. The king orders entertainments and banquets. Although he can no longer dance, he likes to watch others. He sits at the top table after the feast has been removed, his hands on his knees, his eyes switching from one eligible woman to the next.

Speculation is rife among the court ladies as to who will be his next choice of wife. Some say it will be Anne

Basset, and if her mother's ambitions have anything to do with it, they may be right. Others say it will be Elizabeth Brooke, who has been seen in the king's company a lot lately.

Once these women would have been regarded with great envy but, these days, nobody desires the notice of the king. Therefore I am filled with great horror when he stops before me and, hampered as he is by his injured leg and walking cane, makes as elegant a greeting as he can manage.

Lucy and I drop to our knees. I am sick with dread. Surely not, surely not! I am plain, big boned and clumsy. The king prefers petite women, dainty dancers with great wit and a pretty smile. "Get up, get up," he laughs congenially and, exchanging terrified glances, Lucy and I rise from our knees.

"I find myself enchanted by your dancing, Mistress."

I open my mouth to reply but as I do so, I realise he has retained his hold on Lucy's hand. The king is addressing her, not me.

As he leans in to kiss her on the mouth, her face is like marble. She tucks her jaw into her shoulder and shudders a little but mercifully, the king laughs, mistaking her reluctance for modesty. He places a knuckle beneath her chin and forces her to look at him.

"Come, come, Mistress Lucy. There is no need to be shy with me. Come and join me in a game of chess; see if you can beat your king."

I watch in horrified relief as he leads her away. *Thank God*, I think. *Thank God*, but then my relief is quickly followed by compassion for Lucy. Poor, poor Lucy; her greatest terror is upon her.

She sits stiffly beside the king, dwarfed by his size, his majesty, his magnificence. A crowd builds up around the gaming table, and as always the king becomes the hub of much hilarity.

Lucy has little skill for strategy and no idea how to play chess. Each time it is her turn to make a move, one of the gentlemen leans in to assist her. With a great twist of jealousy I see Sir Bryan is among them. As he leans near he places a hand on Lucy's shoulder, his fingers are on her naked neck. He is too close, whispering which piece she should select, guiding her in her battle against the king.

She hesitates, looks up at him, their eyes wavering before she turns back to the board. My eyes are fixed on the hand on her shoulder and, as she reaches out to grasp the knight, I see him give her a little squeeze. I am the only one who notices when his littlest finger strays from the others to stroke where her skin is softest.

Something shifts in my heart; something that slashes, splintering my hopes. I bite down hard upon my own tongue. All I can taste is blood and bitterness. I cannot go on ...

Part Two
Katheryn: The Sixth Queen

March 1543 - Hampton court

Being widowed for the second time is very different to before. Last time I was just twenty years old. I had just lost my mother and the world was a vast and frightening place. I had little liking for my in-laws and so, with little money of my own, I turned to my friends and buried myself away in the north. But this time, I am comfortably left. I have influence. I have powerful friends and the ear of the king's daughter.

I also have the admiration and, I hope, the love of Thomas Seymour. He has been paying me illicit attentions for months now, and I had half expected he was dallying with me and would disappear when my husband John died. But instead, he continues to call regularly, treating me like an ornament that will shatter should he speak too loudly. But although I may appear fragile in my grief, inside I am dancing a jig. For the first time in my life I am independent and can follow my own directives.

When Margaret agrees we should join the Lady Mary's household, I am delighted. My life so far has been spent in relative obscurity, far from the delights of court, the gossip and the intrigue. The only time I knew myself to be fully alive was during the siege at Snape, when the danger and conflict made the blood course like a raging river through my veins. But the excitement was short

65

lived and as soon as it was over, life returned to its habitual tepid trickle of muddy ennui.

I love clothes; I love jewellery; I love to dance, and I have not yet fully enjoyed any of those things. I have kept my inner self repressed, my thoughts and beliefs hidden. Now, in Lady Mary's household, I can give my personality full rein – although perhaps, since Mary is so vigorously conservative, it will be as well to keep my views on church reform quiet.

But now, just a few weeks into our engagement at court, Margaret has fallen ill. I tuck her into bed, feel her brow which is cool and dry, and ask delicate questions about her female condition. She has no sign of fever. There is no rash, no pain, but she is pale and listless, constantly dissolving into tears for no reason at all. I mix a concoction of chervil and woodruff and wait while she drinks it. She pulls a face and hands me the empty cup.

"There." I tuck the blankets around her. "Try to rest. I will send for some books to divert your mind, but do not read for too long."

Homer is curled into a tight ball on the bed beside her, her fingertips move gently in his coat. Her tragic white face reminds me of when she was a child at Snape. As I close the door I pretend not to see her composure crumple as she subsides into tears again. I don't know what to do to help, perhaps weeping will relieve her.

Lady Mary will be waiting for me. I skim along the corridor, past the chapel where the choir is practicing, their soaring voices lifting spirits, infusing an ethereal peace throughout the palace. As I hurry through the outer chambers I spy Thomas, send him a fleeting smile as I pass. My heart beats a little faster but I cannot stop. I must wait until later when we have arranged to meet in the gardens.

"Ah, Lady Latimer." Mary puts her book on her lap as I join her at the fireside. "I was just finding the place where you left off." Her finger trails down the page, stops and taps three times on a red-lettered word. "Here we are. This is it."

She passes me the book and, still a little breathless from my haste, I begin to read. She lays her head on the back of her chair and closes her eyes. From time to time I look up to ensure she has not fallen asleep.

Although she is younger than I by a few years, she appears older. There is a perpetual crease between her eyes, making her seem cross and unapproachable but, in the company of friends, she is amiable and sweet-tempered. Poor Mary, she has been through so much, there is little wonder she is so cautious, so serious. Born a princess, for the first few years of her life she enjoyed adulation from everyone but, when the king began to seek a divorce from Catherine, Mary's life changed forever. Not only was she dispossessed as a princess, she was forced to bear the stigma of illegitimacy. The hand that was once sought by European princes is now spurned. No one is sure where she stands in the line of succession. It is doubtful if even the king himself remembers.

When the king and Catherine of Aragon parted, Mary was separated from her mother, never saw her again. While Anne Boleyn was queen, she was forced to act as an underling to the Princess Elizabeth. Mary being Mary of course, she came to adore her little half-sister and even now the girls keep up a correspondence.

It is only since the demise of the last queen, Katherine Howard, that Mary has regained some of her former standing. Until such time as her father remarries, she assumes the role of hostess at court, and she does it well. Elizabeth, now also stripped of her title of princess, remains at Hatfield, banished and out of favour with her father. No one at court knows Elizabeth very well, although we are all curious about the offspring of the queen we must not speak of.

Of all his children, in the king's eyes only Prince Edward can do no wrong. He is six years old now and a sweeter, more precocious child I never laid eyes upon. The king treats him like a child omnipotent, and I am informed that he leads Margaret Bryan, who has charge of him, a merry dance in the nursery. I know Lady Mary holds her brother in the greatest esteem, which says a lot about her, since many would resent him, a latecomer who stands so high in his father's reckoning.

While I read to Mary in her closet, the sounds of music and laughter drift in from the other chamber. She opens her eyes, lifts her head. With a deep sigh she rubs her forehead and straightens her headdress. A tight smile appears on her lips.

"I suppose you'd like to join them?"

"No, no, I am perfectly content to continue, My Lady." I keep my finger between the leaves of the book, my eye cocked to the door, waiting for her permission to escape.

"I suppose we should join them," she says as she stands and, with an internal frisson of excitement, I help her arrange her gown and straighten her hood before we join the company.

A hush settles on the room as we enter. I immediately spot Thomas lounging in the window seat watching his friend, Sir Francis Bryan, trying out the steps to a new dance with Lucy Somerset. Lucy blushes and dips her knee when she becomes aware of Mary's presence. After a moment, Lady Mary waves her hand

and the company resume their former jollity. I summon a page to bring my mistress a drink and prepare to settle beside her, but she leans forward, grasps my wrist warmly.

"I wish to speak to Lady Basset. You go and make merry with the others, Katheryn. You may be a widow but you're not dead yet."

Our eyes meet. Like a child caught with her hand in a bowl of sweetmeats, I feel my face grow hot beneath her eloquent smile. She knows my secret. She has guessed I have a sweetheart, I am sure of it. But she says nothing. When she turns away I begin to circumnavigate the room, slowly inching my way closer to Thomas' side.

He turns, as if he hasn't noticed my presence, his face breaking into smiles. "Lady Latimer." He kisses my mouth, grasps my hand and begins to talk of everyday things. Somehow, I respond as if the world is not dipping and swaying about me. Before moving on to greet another, he discreetly reconfirms our assignation in the garden and I promise to be there.

We part, for now, and the rest of the afternoon passes in an endless round of other people's enjoyment, other people's merriment. And all the time with one eye I am watching and tracking the sun as it journeys west outside the window. With the other I am aware of Thomas, his every move, his every smile.

It seems long in coming but at last my duties are done. I pause in the corridor, wondering whether I should run upstairs to check on Margaret or leave her for a short while longer. In the end Thomas has the greater pull, and I hurry toward the garden, down twisting stairs, along torch-lit corridors, my heart leaping like a rabbit in my chest.

The outer door is lit up with sunshine, casting the hall into almost pitch darkness. As I grow closer I can see outside to the garden, flooded with light. Thomas is lurking near the entrance to the knot garden. He has removed his cloak and draped it over his shoulder. I pick up my skirts and increase my pace. He sees me coming, lifts his hand in greeting, the effect of his smile is like warm honey pouring over my shoulders. I laugh aloud, and I'm about to dash forward when a figure looms from the darkness, obliterating the sun.

"Lady Latimer. Well, this is well met."

Abruptly, I fall to my knees before the king. The stench of his festering leg fills my head. I look at his shoes, his bulging feet pushing the velvet out of shape, his vast calves encased in tight white hose. His hand is gentle on my shoulder. "Get up, get up," he says. "Walk with me. Let us take a turn about the garden."

What can I say? What can I do? I rise, smile as widely as I can manage, and lay my hand on his proffered arm.

I blink in the sudden sunlight as we make halting progress. He leans heavily on my shoulder, overpowering me with his presence. "Good afternoon, Thomas." Henry pauses, waves his stick in the air in greeting as we draw close to my love. Somehow, Thomas manages to execute a perfect bow as, with my heart full of disappointed tears, the king and I walk by.

I can feel Thomas' eyes follow me all the way around the garden. He is still watching when we pause at the fountain where water cascades, the drops dancing with the evening light on the surface. Deep among the weed and slime, fishes are undulating in the murky depths. The king takes my hand, raises it to his mouth and kisses my fingers, and while he is distracted, I send Thomas a pulsing glance of regret.

"I am glad I bumped into you," the king is saying. "I would like to challenge you to another game of chess. You play so well. Quite remarkable in a woman..." As I watch Thomas quietly slip between the yew hedges that flank the path, the king's voice fades away. I give myself a little shake.

"Yes, Your Majesty. Of course, that will be my pleasure."

When the king begins to visit Mary's apartments two or three times a day, people start to speculate and notice his interest in me. My brother is delighted and doesn't hesitate to list the favours my influence can bestow. But, when he hears of it, Thomas scowls, muttering tight-lipped curses, and even Dorothy, the most discreet of servants, begins to ask probing questions. Only Margaret is disinterested. She remains in her chamber, hardly speaking. I have summoned the physicians to look at her but they all concur she is healthy, just lacking in spirit.

I am at my wits end with her, and her brother John is no less bothersome. He was a mischievous boy and a troublesome youth, who now seems bent on experimenting with all the temptations of adulthood. He drinks too much, loses money at the cockfights, and, I have heard, is a regular visitor to the stews. Has he no concern for the disease that is widespread there? Poor Lucy, no wonder she dallies with Francis Bryan when her betrothed neglects her so. I resolve to see what I can do for them. As their stepmother, I am responsible for their happiness. Perhaps, while it lasts, I can use my influence with the king to brighten their futures; it is high time Margaret was married.

May 1543

When evening falls and dinner is over, I find myself sitting with the king before the great hearth, a chess set on the table before us. I pick up my bishop; the king purses his lips, draws in his breath with a doubtful sucking sound. I know he is bent on undermining my confidence, and quite undeterred I make my move and pinion his knight. Henry lies back in his chair and surveys me good-humouredly.

"You are going to beat me again, Madam. I find myself at your mercy. There is nowhere for the poor king to turn."

I reach out to place his captured piece in a pile with the others, but he seizes my hand, turns it palm up. "Such beautiful hands, perfect fingers," he says quietly, caressing my skin with his stubby thumb. I raise my eyes to his and to my horror find they are filled with desire. *Surely not!*

I cannot withdraw my hand. I am forced to bear it. He pulls me closer, leans forward to whisper in my ear. "Come to my apartments later, Madam. I will send a page to guide you."

My belly rolls in rebellion, but already he is turning away, calling for our cups to be filled. It does not occur to him to wonder if I return his desire. I turn my head to where Thomas watches darkly from the corner and I cry out silently and helplessly for him to do something to stop this from happening.

***

Dorothy laces my gown, tucks a few stray hairs beneath my hood. "There, Madam. You are fit for a king now."

Her tone is eloquent with disapproval. I want to scream at her that I am defenceless. One simply does not refuse the king when invited to join him for a late supper. Scores of others have done the same. They are still regarded as decent women. Everyone knows Henry does not acknowledge refusal. I inhale deeply and smooth down my skirts, glance into the looking glass. The reflected face is pale and small, the eyes glimmering darkly.

"Have a care of Margaret," I say, as I pick up my pomander and fan. "She is so wan-looking. I had hoped to spend the night with her, to try to cheer her up, but the king ..."

"Don't worry, Madam," Dorothy smiles. "I will sleep with her in your stead. Just call if you need me when you return."

She doesn't add the words "If you return," but we both hear them as clearly as if they'd been spoken. I place a hand on her shoulder, gratitude tightening my throat, but my thanks are severed by a discreet knock at the outer door.

I feel like a whore as my escort leads me through the palace, but somehow I force my feet to follow. The corridors are silent; only the servants are awake now, clearing the debris, preparing the rooms for the following day. I wonder where I shall sleep tonight.

If I shall sleep tonight.

The king is alone. His supper table piled high with delicacies I know I will not be able to stomach. "Ah," he says, groping for his stick and rising to greet me. "Lady Latimer. I thought you would never come."

73

My instinct is to flee, every nerve in my body screams to run from his presence, but propriety propels me across the room. His mouth, wet and sloppy, is on mine, his hot hand on my neck, but he does not prolong the greeting. He pulls away, gestures to a chair, and I take my place at his table.

"Eat, eat." He picks up a napkin and begins to tear apart a roasted fowl, his fingers slick with grease. I am still full from dinner but I cannot politely refuse. Delicately I strip off a piece of meat and slip it between stiff lips, chewing only briefly before forcing it down my throat.

As we dine, the king talks expansively about his youth, his parents, his friends, many of whom have died at his command. It is as if he has forgotten their passing and speaks as if they are in the next room. Every so often he dabs his lips with a cloth, reaches out to touch my hand, my neck, my knee. Each time he does so I feel myself go rigid, and the food lodges in my throat.

Henry seems to forget he is no longer the youthful prince my mother knew. I am not certain how old he is but he must be thirty years my senior. His once golden hair is grey now; his once blue eyes are faded. The king laughs a lot, a great bellow that brings his servants creeping from wherever they have discreetly hidden themselves. Irritated at their presence he waves them away, pushes his plate aside and reaches again and again for the wine. I find I cannot empty my cup fast enough and he begins to chide me playfully, bidding me drink up and be merry.

"I am merry, Your Majesty," I assure him, although I have never been less joyful in my life. Very soon now I must give myself to a man who is not my husband, a man I do not and cannot love. My body longs only for Thomas.

I do not know what to do, or how to behave in circumstances such as this. I begin to worry that perhaps royal mistresses are supposed to know skills that are kept secret from decent women.

He is slumped in his chair, his red face glowing in the heat of the fire, his legs sprawled before him. Silence falls between us and the king grows thoughtful, his eyes fixed on the goblet he twirls in his fingers. The only sounds are the crackling flames and the gentle snores of his hounds that sleep beneath the table.

"You have been wife to two men, Lady Latimer." He speaks suddenly, making me jump. I dab spilled wine from my skirt and put down my cup.

"Yes, Your Majesty. Sir Edward Borough and Lord John Latimer, fine gentlemen both. I have been very fortunate."

He narrows his eyes. "Marriage suited you?"

"Oh yes." I look at my hands, my fingers laced in my lap, the skin on my knuckles white with tension.

"Yet, you provided them with no children, no sons to follow them…"

"To my great sorrow, Your Majesty."

Silence falls again, a flurry of rain patters against the window, the logs in the hearth slump, sending up a shower of bright sparks. Henry sighs, his chin sinks to his chest.

"A woman brings more benefits to a man than just sons."

My head jerks up in astonishment for I had never thought to hear words such as these from a man who desires sons more than anything on earth. The silence stretches on while desperately I fumble for something to say, but he forestalls me. "I am thinking of marrying again."

"That is good to hear, Your Majesty. You need a young woman to cheer you and fill your nursery with princes."

"NO." The word is short, harsh and cutting. "Not a young woman. I made that mistake last time ... with her, with Katherine." I look at my lap, my throat closing in panic at the intimate turn of the conversation. "Lady Latimer, I have it in mind to marry you."

Time seems to stop. Shock is ringing in my ears. My heart falters, sweat breaks out all over my body, trickling, cold and gruesome, between my breasts. I cannot speak. It is as if I am trapped at the end of a blind alley while a pack of hunting dogs relentlessly approaches to rend my body apart.

"Oh, you are overcome. My dear, how can you be so astounded at such happy news?"

He clambers from his chair, lumbers toward me and, in a trance I give him my hand, rise to meet him.

"Well, say something..." He doesn't notice my horror. He is laughing, amused by my astonishment, believing me to be speechless with joy.

"Your Majesty, I had thought you desired me as your mistress. I have given no thought to marriage..."

He pats my hand.

"It does you credit not to be too hasty, but I am growing old, Katheryn. I need a wife now."

"I would happily become your mistress now, Your Majesty. I am not ... I hadn't thought ... I am not long widowed, Your Majesty."

"It would not be seemly, my love. If you should conceive my child, I want him to be legitimate beyond doubt. I have had enough of my offspring being tainted with the hint of bastardy. I thought we could be wed in July."

Oh God. I had not foreseen this. The thought of being his mistress was bad enough, but then at least he would have tired of me, cast me off and left me free to marry Thomas. As queen I will lose Thomas forever and once more my life will not be my own. In fact, married to the king, I may find my life cut very short.

The king is still gripping my hand expectantly. I look up at him. His huge moon-like face is inches from mine, his foul breath tickling my cheek. I open my mouth and close it again, swallow mucus from my throat.

"It is an honour I have never dreamed of..."

"Is that a yes?" His grip tightens; his other arm slides about my waist. A despairing laugh escapes me as I realise I am lost.

"I suppose it is, Your Majesty. Yes."

"Oh! Wonderful! And I am Henry, call me Henry."

Before I have come to terms with what becoming his wife will mean, he drags me into his arms, engulfs my mouth with his so I cannot breathe, and I swoon in the arms of the king.

June 1543 - London

I am alone at Charterhouse, putting my affairs in order, when I hear a disturbance downstairs. Dorothy's voice, raised in outrage, is drowned by the gruffer tones of my steward. Footsteps on the stair, a thud as the door is thrown open.

"Thomas!"

I stand up at my desk as my visitor forces his way to the centre of the room. Dorothy barges in behind him bristling like cat.

"I am sorry, Madam; he just pushed his way in." She scowls her disapproval. The steward's bulk fills the doorway, ready to throw my caller out should I order it. For a few moments I stare at Tom, absorbing his dishevelled beauty, his red eyes, the ruined linen, his untrimmed beard.

"It is all right. You can leave us. We all know Sir Thomas is a gentleman."

I look without seeing at the paperwork strewn across my desk, tap a fingernail on the uppermost parchment.

"What do you want, Tom?" I ask quietly as Dorothy closes the door. He waits for her footsteps to fade before crossing the room in three strides. He grips my upper arms hard.

"Is it true, Kat?"

His eyes are blue, overflowing with desperation, wanting, and yet not wanting, to hear my answer. My eyes sting, his image blurs. My throat is closed, trapping my words. I nod my head.

"You're going to marry him? That … that *monster?*"

"Tom!" I put my hand over his mouth. "Don't ever say such things."

"I can't let you do it. You know what he is like, you saw what he did … to the others; to Anne and little Katherine."

My head is suddenly too heavy to hold aloft, it lolls on my chest as if my neck has snapped.

"How could I refuse him, Tom? How do I refuse the king?"

I don't tell him about the pressure from my brother William, who seeks to use my influence with the king for his own ends. I don't mention Anne's excitement that she will now be raised to the position of lady in waiting to the

78

queen. I am in a trap, a vice, squeezed from all sides by the silken pressure of those I love.

Family obligation.

"You should have married me when I first asked you, but no, you had to wait. You wanted your time at court. You should have listened to me, Kate!" His voice breaks. He thumps the table, the cups jumping, wine overspilling, trickling and pooling like blood on the tray.

"I know."

He walks away, stops, turns again, and ruffles his hair.

"He is sending me overseas. Clearing the board of opposition as if it is some … some game and you the prize."

"Oh, Tom." I cannot stop the tears. They well up from nowhere, flood my eyes, and spill down my cheeks, dripping from my chin, wetting my hands. He watches me helplessly. My chest heaves, my chin trembles. We both know there is nothing to be done. I am lost to him. We are lost to each other. The short breach between us may as well be miles wide. For a long moment we stand and stare, silent yet saying much. My heart is fit to burst.

I do not sense him move but somehow he is close to me again. I am in his arms, my cheek pressed against his heart, my head cradled in his hand. "Poor Kate," he murmurs. "Poor, poor Kate."

I raise my head and, as if I have silently requested it, his mouth descends to mine. My face is in his hands, his body tight against me as delight rushes in to replace despair.

I am no maid. I have known two husbands; I've been kissed by the king, kissed before by Thomas, but never have I known anything like this. He holds nothing back. My head swims, the world seems to tip. As my legs turn to string his doublet becomes my lifeline, but I kiss him back, returning his desire with every inch of my being. Colours and miracles swim about my mind and, when I can take no more, I wrench my mouth from his and look into his burning eyes.

There is no joy, no triumph, just a kind of inevitability; there is no help for it. Without a word he lifts me from my feet and carries me from the room to my inner chamber. He dumps me on the bed and turns to bolt the door.

I am almost thirty years old, yet never in my life have I known such pleasure. Although we both know we risk death to be so, I am naked in his arms, matching his passion with my own. I give myself to Thomas and he takes from me that which I have promised shall be the king's.

He rears above me, his face damp with sweat, and his beard moist with my kisses. As he watches my pleasure, I am not embarrassed. I twist and thrust and writhe beneath him before he gives in to his own delight.

When he is spent, he slumps across me, his torso heavy and hot, and the passage of his heart's blood pulsing in my ear. His love is crushing me but I have no wish to move, and when he rolls away I clutch at his hair, ask him to tarry.

Our heads are side by side on the pillow. He reaches out to tease a strand of hair from my eyes. I trace the movements of his mouth when he whispers to me. I crave words of endearment, promises of felicity, constancy but, instead, I hear something very different. As I digest the meaning behind his whispered words, my finger ceases its passage on his lips.

"Think of this, Katheryn, when you lay with the king. This is how it should be between a man and a woman. Think of this when you are in your dotard's bed."

And while the wounds of his words are still raw and bleeding, he rolls from my bed and quietly begins to put on his clothes.

12th July 1543 - Hampton Court

Although the wedding is still two days away, I am treated with deference. The king shows me my new apartments, close to his. The decoration is to be refreshed, Katherine Howard's initials, still entwined with Henry's, will be altered to mine. Katheryn Parr, the queen.

The other queens linger, engrained in the fabric of the building. I am given their jewels, and some of the gowns of Katherine Howard are altered to fit me. Their memory hangs in the air like a scent, their laughter echoing in the corridors, along with their tears ... their screams.

But I will be queen now. My personal wishes put aside, my heart locked securely in a wooden casket, entombed, never to be exhumed.

I stand like a statue while my women lace me into my bridal gown. My new shoes are too tight, the jewels hang heavy about my throat and my bodice compresses my lungs, hampering my breathing. Dorothy who, usurped by my sister, will soon be leaving me for Margaret's household, shows me a looking glass. A pale, thin woman looks back, the eyes large and darkly luminous.

Is that me? Can plain old Katheryn Parr really be about to wed the king? Mother would be pleased. If only she had lived to see it. She put such energy into marrying us all well, all but bankrupting herself to secure my brother the hand of the wife he now detests. Position is all that mattered to her; she had no time for love. Despite my black and aching heart, she would say I have done well.

I shut away the memory of Thomas' touch. I bury my Lutheran leanings and, almost in an instant, become another person. Katheryn Parr, the queen of England.

An intimate ceremony, Henry said. Just friends and family; yet the small room is bursting at the seams. From the corner of my eye I see both friend and foe have gathered to witness this most extraordinary match. The Lady Mary and her sister Elizabeth bend the knee as I pass by. Their smiles are warm and encouraging. I am stepmother to four now; Margaret and Elizabeth are of an age, and perhaps they will be friends. Margaret needs a friend.

While I try not to mind that the eyes of the entire court are upon me, Margaret and Lucy hover nearby. They seem unsure where they should stand, uncertain how to behave now they have been thrust to prominence by their relationship with me. I relax a little when I see Lady Mary beckon to them, and they take their places among her women. Elizabeth smiles warmly at Margaret, who flushes with pleasure.

Beside me, her eyes lowered respectfully, my sister Anne takes my prayer book. Her hand momentarily covers mine, offering comfort when she notices how my own trembles as I raise my face to Archbishop Cranmer.

His welcoming smile is genuine; it warms me. He is my long-time friend and favourite intellectual sparring partner. But there must be no more quiet meetings at Charterhouse with him and Miles Coverdale, and Hugh Latimer. The king wants only peace and so I must forget that part of me, ignore my craving for reform, and look to my own security. The past has shown too clearly what becomes of queens who meddle, or think too much. I must rein in my ambition and be merely a wife.

Gardiner, the most conservative of churchmen, is waiting at the altar. Henry and I stand before him. The king is massively splendid in cloth of gold that matches my gown. Sunlight slants through the latticed window, setting us both a glimmer. God creeps close, but as the Bishop of Winchester begins to speak, my body is bathed in the cold sweat of fear and regret.

Henry's fingers clamp down on mine; his hand is hot and damp. I long to pull away, but instead I breathe deeply and try to pretend I am somewhere else, somewhere safe and warm. Each time the shade of Thomas rears up in my mind I thrust him away, close my eyes to our dreams.

Our shared misery.

Henry repeats the words of the Bishop. "I, Henry, take thee, Katheryn, to my wedded wife, to have and to hold from this day forward ..."

I swallow sickness. Shove the memory of Thomas' love away. I bite my lip.

"... for better for worse, for richer for poorer, in sickness and in health, till death us do part ..."

Death. Only death can free me now.

And then it is my turn. I try to speak but my voice croaks. I cannot make my vow to the king sounding like a frog. I pause, put a hand to my mouth as I clear my throat, and raise my face to Henry, whose blue eyes are swimming with sentimental tears. It is a sentiment I do not share.

I lower my gaze and begin to speak quietly.

"I, Katheryn, take thee, Henry, to my wedded husband, to have and to hold from this day forward, for better for worse, for richer for poorer, in sickness and in health, to be Bonaire and buxom in bed ..."

His grip on my fingers tightens. I glance up at him and shrink internally from what I see there. Clear my throat again.

"...till death us do part, and thereto I plight unto thee my troth."

There, it is done. Henry engulfs me in his embrace, pulls away and holds our conjoined hands high for all to see. "Gentlemen," he cries. "Behold, your queen!"

A great cheer breaks out, deafening in its intensity. How many times has he presented the court with a new queen? How many wives has he celebrated? How many women has he grown weary of? How many more will there be before his time as king is done?

The rest of the day passes in a blur. I know I am surrounded by people. I am aware of them bowing, giving me their blessing, their good wishes, but my mind is elsewhere. All I can think of is the coming night and the horror that must come with it.

Henry is beside me, huge and amiable, his laughter louder than anyone else's. The room becomes a sea of smiling faces, the heat from the fire overwhelming, the food they place before me nauseating. For me, happiness is past, the future yawns like a vast hungry mouth. I will be swallowed up in it and never again allowed to simply be Katheryn. From this moment on, for every minute of every waking day, I will be The Queen. I want to run, as fast as I can. Run from Henry, run from Hampton Court, run from England, across the sea and into Thomas' arms. I should have listened. I should have ignored convention and wed him when he wished it. I should have listened ... *Why do I never listen?*

The chamber is almost dark. Despite the fine furnishings and fabrics, it smells of stale wine and piss, as if the windows have not been opened in years. I shiver in the gloom, uncertain until the embers slump in the grate, making me jump. Henry laughs gently and stretches a hand toward me.

He is resting like a shipwreck on a sheer cliff of pillows. His nightgown shines white in the moonlight, his bandaged leg protruding like a stricken mast. His feet are bare, his fat toes misshapen, the nails black. His small eyes gleam as wickedly as a pirate's.

He is disgusting.

Thomas, my mind cries, although I know it is no use. No one can help me now.

"Come, come ..." The king waggles his hand and I am forced to take it. He supports me as I clamber into the vast bed and settle stiffly at his side. His hand begins to pull at my nightclothes, his fingers hot on my thigh, his breath quickening, wheezing in his chest. When he first touches my naked flesh I jump involuntarily, making him laugh gently at my discomfiture. He begins to explore further. I close my eyes and force myself to turn dutifully into his body. One of his hands strays to my bottom, the other fumbles for my breast. I throw back my head and wish that I was dead.

"You will have to help me." His breath comes quickly, his words almost a gasp. "I am not as agile as I once was."

He shifts his bulk, throws aside the pillows until he is flat on his back. At first I do not understand his direction but as his desire becomes clear, with burning cheeks I climb up and sit astride as if I am mounted on a plough horse.

His belly undulates like a giant bowl of custard, his fat flaccid member squashed like a slug between us. At his insistence I wriggle and gyrate while he kneads my breasts, pinching my nipples until I squeal.

He takes this as a sign of pleasure, and gives throaty encouragement. I squeal again and try to smile while he flails and squirms like a great white fish beneath me.

I will never get a child by this man. He is not capable.

I think of Katherine Howard and her string of male friends, and wonder if perhaps her crimes were not due to lechery after all but desperation to get the king an heir. As the extent of the king's impotence becomes clear, so does the realisation that my own position is much worse than I had thought. If I displease him and do not fall pregnant, my life could be in jeopardy.

Eventually when he can thrust and writhe no more, Henry's body grows very still. I wait unmoving until his breathing regulates and I am sure he is asleep. Then I slide gingerly from his body, desperate not to wake him.

My nether regions are slick with sweat but I am certain he has spent no seed. He lies on his back, his mouth open, his great naked belly pointing skyward, the limp royal manhood curled like a worm in a nest of grey hair. I fumble on the floor for my nightgown and struggle into it, ripping the seam in my haste. Then I kneel on the floor hunting for my slippers, but I can find only one, so in the end I creep barefoot from his chamber and back to my own.

My new maid, Madge, is slumbering at the hearth. She leaps from her chair when my sobbing and shivering wake her and is instantly at my side, murmuring comfort.

"There, there, Madam," she whispers. "I have warm water waiting. Let me wash you and comb out your hair before I help you to bed. You poor, poor thing. There, there, Madam ..."

Her words are like honey for my soul. I curl into her caress like a child to its mother, and sob out my misery on her shoulder.

The morning after our wedding I expect Henry to be embarrassed by his failure of the night before, but he acts like a youth, boasting of his prowess by promising his closest friends I will be pregnant before the year is out. My heart sinks, my stomach turns. I look at the floor, my face hot.

Henry laughs, grasps my hand, and squeezes it. When I raise my eyes to his face, he is brimming with delight. Somehow, despite the horrid humiliation of our marriage bed, I have managed to please him.

As expected I appoint new ladies, honour my friends and family with advantageous positions. Having my nearest and dearest around me should make my household more comfortable, but they make constant demands on me. William pressures me to plead his case for a divorce. His wife, whom I have not appointed, is shaming us all by living openly with her lover. I soon learn that being queen is more about duty than pleasure and pretty things.

I am never alone now. There are always at least twenty people in attendance on me. Pages constantly come and go, lighting fires, replenishing the wine jugs, opening and closing the shutters. Dressmakers, statesmen, ambassadors bring good wishes from their masters overseas. There is no respite.

Even as I am made ready for bed I am not allowed privacy. A crowd stands watching, speculating on my relationship with the king, the possibility of another prince. Sometimes I want to scream.

I long for the solitude to sit and dream of Thomas. Thomas, who has gone from me, sailed across the sea, to another land, new adventures, other women.

I wonder if he thinks of me.

July and August are the hottest months and plague has broken out in London, throwing Henry into panic. One of my first actions as queen is to order the fine perfumes, juniper and civet, to freshen my bedchamber. The stench from the river creeps in through the open window, and cooking smells from the privy kitchens, which lay directly below my apartments, rise to such a degree that I grow queasy and irritable. I no longer want to eat. All I can smell is grease. All I can hear is the clash of pans. How have Henry's previous queens borne it?

When the king notices I am ailing, he is at once hopeful. He takes me to one side, places a hand upon my belly.

"Katheryn, is it ... are you? Could you be ...?" Swiftly I spare him the agony of hope. I cover his wrinkled hand with mine.

"Nay, Henry. I am sorry. It is the heat and the stench of the kitchens. The noise and the smell is interrupting my sleep ..."

"Noise? I had not realised you slept so ill. We must do something about that. We cannot have you inconvenienced. How are you to conceive a child if your sleep is disturbed?" He calls the steward, consults Denny, and plans are soon underway for new chambers to be made ready for me.

My rooms are on the east side of the inner court, adjacent to the king's. Anne Boleyn had disliked the modest lodgings she inherited and gave orders for redecoration she did not live to see. Jane Seymour, coming directly after, lived and died amid splendour conceived by Anne, as had Anne of Cleves and Katherine Howard. But I change all that. Within months I have moved to the southeast corner of the palace, into rooms that look across the pond gardens. There are pools and fountains that teem with golden fishes, and the paths are lined with gay heraldic poles topped with brightly painted beasts. The outlook and, more importantly, the aroma of these new rooms is far more suitable for the sort of queen I intend to be.

My mother always stressed that when one sets oneself a task, one should attend to it with the best of one's ability. Since I am queen I have decided to be the best, and hopefully the last, of Henry's wives. My chosen motto is 'To be useful in what I do,' and I am determined to be more than wife. More than queen. I will be his consort. I have influence and intend to use it. I begin to draw my friends closer and form new and forward thinking intimates.

Of course, I do not fall straight into my new role. At first I am uncertain, dressing as conservatively as I have always done. It is my new stepdaughter, the Lady Mary, who quietly informs me that such apparel is no longer appropriate.

"You are a Tudor now and must bear yourself like one. You must be seen in only the best, and that means the best gowns as well as the best jewels. My father has spent all his reign building up an image and now, as his wife, you must follow his example."

I need no second telling. My jewel coffers are already stuffed with gems, but within days I have summoned drapers from Italy, hat makers and embroiderers from France. Soon my closet is filled with the latest fashions from the continent. I have always taken great pleasure in clothes and fine fabrics, and I am so thrilled with the excuse to buy only the best that I go one better. I purchase gowns and hoods for Margaret and Lady Mary too.

As the treasures are unveiled Margaret and I squeal with delight, and even Mary is pleased enough to laugh properly for the first time in my presence. I embrace my new role to the full and soon find I enjoy it. I engage a company of players, minstrels and singers to fill my rooms with music and gaiety. The less pleasant demands of being Henry's queen, the duties that take place in private, are compensated by long hot baths in milk, steeped with rose water. Afterwards, when my skin is still wrinkled and pink, my women anoint it with almond oil and the scent of cloves.

But there is a serious side too. For the first time I am able to aid those less fortunate than myself. I give alms to the poor and assist the needy, endow seats of learning, schools and colleges. When word of my generosity gets out, my apartments are soon bursting with people begging for my favour. My influence with the king is talked about and I help where I can, but only if I think the cause is just.

Pleased with my popularity, Henry chuckles and squeezes my fingers a little too tight as he relates the praise of the Spanish ambassador, Chapuys, and the Duke of Najera whom we entertain in February with a display of our dancing.

"The Emperor will be envious," he crows. "I have myself a good wife at last." He kisses my fingers passionately. "Come to me later, I will dispense with my household early tonight. We must put ourselves to the task of making a son."

I curtsey low while he maintains his hold on my hand. When I rise, he kisses my knuckles in farewell before summoning his chair bearers. Lately Henry's leg has been bothering him and he has taken to moving around the castle in a portable seat. His spaniels run alongside, a crowd of servants in his wake. The court fall to their knees as their king passes.

As they disappear through the open door, Henry's fool, Will Somer, turns to me and makes a lewd gesture. The fool is permitted to cross boundaries others would not dare. I am supposed to laugh, so I smile and turn away, hiding my real feelings as I must hide so much else.

Spring 1544 - Hampton Court

This time, after I have tolerated Henry's husbandly attention, he does not fall asleep straight away. I lie beside him, trying to quell the nausea that close proximity to his wounded leg always induces. His left hand is hot upon my knee, his fingers exploring the contours of the joint. It strikes me as a singularly domestic situation. If only circumstances were otherwise, I might be lying in bed beside Thomas while he casually caressed my knee and spoke of trivial, homely things.

After a while Henry's conversation turns to politics. I am surprised when he asks my opinion on several state matters and I flounder a little, unsure if I should present my own opinion or give an answer that will please him. Before I speak I consider the question very carefully. He pats my knee again and I sigh with the relief of knowing I have answered well.

"Chapuys returns to Spain tomorrow," Henry announces, startling me from a drowsy stupor.

"Chapuys? The ambassador? Will he be gone for long?"

"For good." Henry shifts, the mattress dipping and the canopy swaying beneath his weight. "He is elderly now and ailing. He has been with us since I was little more than a boy. I will miss him, for all the annoyance he has caused me over the years."

"He must be growing old. Mary will miss him too."

"Mary?"

"Your daughter, the Lady Mary."

"Oh ... yes. Probably. He championed her mother's cause and always hated Anne ... But he is a good man, a fine ambassador."

I cannot help noting that this is the first time he has mentioned his second wife in my presence. Usually she is an unmentionable shadow, colouring every room, every moment of my life with the king. She is probably lingering in the darkness of our chamber this minute. After a while Henry becomes thoughtful, his fingers still lightly stroking my knee. I turn my head toward the window.

The light in the chamber has altered as dawn creeps into the east. In a wifely fashion I place my hand on Henry's chest and kiss his sagging cheek.

"We should sleep, Henry, or day will be upon us."

He yawns, revealing his coated tongue, his large yellow teeth.

"Yes," he says wearily. "Stay with me, wife. It is too cold for you to be running around the corridors at this time of night."

Obediently I sink further down the mattress, trying not to regret the comfort of my own fragrant sheets. Madge will have dosed off in her chair. She will be stiff and out of sorts in the morning.

"Good night, Henry."

"Good night, Ja … erm, Kate."

***

The gardens are lovely in May. Once the dew has dried, I go to my window where the call of the birds and the droning of the bees make me suddenly long to be outside. Courtiers are strolling among the flowers, and minstrels on the mead are tuning their instruments. Indoors, my ladies are about their tasks; Madge is folding linen, Anne is practising a new air on her lute, and Lucy and Margaret are sorting through a pile of sleeves. "Who would like to join me in the garden?" I ask.

Anne puts down her instrument and the other women run to fetch their wraps. Then there is a bustle as we change our shoes and call for a page to bring the dogs. At last we are ready but just as we are quitting the room, the doors are thrown open and Lady Mary is announced. She pauses on the threshold, her face dropping with disappointment.

"Oh. You are going somewhere." She sounds disheartened. I take her arm.

"We are only going to take Homer and Rig for a run in the gardens. It is such a lovely day. Why don't you join us?"

After a pause, during which her face suffuses with pleasure, she agrees, and we glide arm in arm from the chamber. She is less talkative than usual and I sense straightaway that something is on her mind. I am not yet comfortable enough with the shift in our status to enquire but, hopefully, the relative privacy of the garden will draw her out.

"The lavender is almost in flower." I pluck a stem and run it between my fingers, inhale the fragrance. "Soon the roses will be blooming too and the gardens full of scent."

Mary picks a spray of her own and holds it to her nose.

"Lovely. Lavender is so soothing."

The spaniels run ahead, barking, their curly ears flapping in their wake. Behind us, our women follow at a discreet distance, ready to attend us should we need them.

"Is there something troubling you?" I ask at last as we turn a corner and pass beneath a leafy arch. Mary looks at the sky, screwing up her eyes against the brilliance of the sun. I can see her mind working as she wrestles to form her words. Suddenly she reaches out and grips my hand.

"I – I have been a lonely girl. I expect you know that. Everybody knows the story. How I was kept apart from my mother because we refused to acknowledge my father's whore."

I flinch at the bad word. Try to smile. "I know something of it. I was far away in the north at the time, of course. So I wasn't here then. I wasn't at court."

"No. We were kept apart for years, Mother and I. It was hard, lonely, exiled as I was, and forced to attend upon Elizabeth as if I was of no account. But I wouldn't give in. I never said a kind word to the Bullen woman, and I never will."

Her voice breaks. She swallows. "It wasn't until she was gone and Father married Jane that I was allowed back to court. Jane was pleasant, quiet … timid, but she wasn't a mother. Anne of Cleves is pleasant enough. I still keep in contact with her but well, she is foreign, different. She doesn't fully understand, and as for Katherine, well. She was an embarrassment. I could barely look at her."

I don't know what to say, where to look, so I stand and wait for her to continue.

"What I want to say is this: I am glad you have married my father. You have long been my friend but I wasn't sure if it was a good thing when I heard you were to marry the king. But I have decided you are all I could wish for in a stepmother. I think you will do us all good. So thank you, and … and I'd like to welcome you."

Her cheeks are scarlet. Tears are balanced on her lashes, great round diamonds of emotion. Mary is not given to sentiment. It is the first time I have heard her make so long or so unguarded a speech. Her head is lowered, her lip trembling. I take her shaking hand again.

"Oh Mary, I am so glad you think so. I have not been blessed with children of my own, and have little cause to expect that to be so. But I am fortunate that I have Margaret and John, and now you and Elizabeth and little Edward to add to my family. I love you all like my own already."

We embrace clumsily, laughter breaking through the tears. When she pulls away, I offer her my kerchief and she dabs her cheeks, sniffs as she looks about the garden. She touches my arm.

"Look. Is that not Chapuys? I was hoping to speak to him before he leaves us."

Chapuys is being carried aloft in a chair rather like the king's own. I guess he is on his way to take his leave of Henry. Grabbing Mary's wrist I hurry unceremoniously along the path, my women panting in our wake. When the ambassador notices our approach, he signals his men to lower his chair and struggles to rise.

"No, no. Please, do not get up. I merely wanted to bid you farewell. The Lady Mary and I will miss you at court."

He sinks gratefully back onto his cushions.

"I am sorry to be leaving, Your Majesty. I have been here so long, England is almost like home." His eye switches to Mary. "And Lady Mary, I have known since she was this high." He pats the air at knee height and Mary steps forward.

"You served my mother and I well, Sir. I will never forget that ..."

I withdraw a few paces to allow them the privacy that their long relationship deserves. Mary is leaning forward slightly, speaking earnestly to the old man who stood for so long between her and the wrath of the king.

When it appears they are almost finished I rejoin them, take Chapuys by the hand and assure him of England's gratitude and our obligations to his master. When I take my leave he again struggles to rise, but I forbid it.

"The Lady Mary and I will continue our walk now, sir, and you must continue on your way to the king, who must not be kept waiting."

Still seated, he offers an awkward bow and grabs at the arms of his chair as it is lifted once more into the air.

"Farewell, Your Majesty. Farewell, Your Royal Highness."

Mary gasps at the illicit use of her old title and, pretending I don't see her grateful tears, I grip her arm tightly and turn her attention to Homer and Rig who are splashing with the king's spaniels in the shallow water of the fountain.

June 1544

Apart from John, whose bad behaviour continues, I am fortunate indeed in my stepchildren. But John is now a man grown and a soldier, gone to help the Duke of Hertford vent the king's fury on the Scottish border.

After the Scots had so rudely rejected Henry's plan to marry Prince Edward to the infant Scottish queen, war has broken out afresh. Henry knows that if we do not form an alliance with our nearest neighbour, they will range themselves against us with France. Scotland is far too close for comfort for that alliance to be borne.

But it is a relief both to myself and to Lucy, his long-suffering betrothed, that John's visits to court are now necessarily seldom and the letters he sends to his sister are brief and devoid of news.

Margaret is still sickly; ailing but not ill. Although I have brought forth the best physicians, they find nothing specific to be the matter with her. They suggest a holiday, a change of scenery, and since she and Elizabeth have quickly become such good friends, Margaret leaves court to join Elizabeth in rural exile at Ashridge. As she is bundled into the carriage I am still issuing instructions to care for her health, to eat heartily and to take as much fresh air as she can manage.

"Yes Mother, I promise. I am sure the visit will do me good." But, as the coachman whips up the horses I watch her sink back onto her pillows, and know in my heart that her words are just platitudes. She will continue to neglect herself regardless of what I say or do.

She writes to me regularly of her walks in the park. Her letters describe Elizabeth's home, Elizabeth's dogs, Elizabeth's insistence that she study hard. She writes:

"Elizabeth believes a woman to be just as capable of learning as a man and has a boundless capacity for study. Her dedication quite makes my head ache and I cannot hope to keep up with her."

I frown, hoping that Margaret doesn't tire herself out in competing with her stepsister. Learning shouldn't be a competition, but a pleasure. I pick up my pen and write back, warning her not to overdo things.

Elizabeth sends regular missives too, thanking me for my care of her and hoping that she will be allowed back at court soon. She does not set it down in writing but I do not miss her silent request that I use my influence with the king on her behalf. Perhaps, by Christmas, all the royal children will be welcome at court and we can enjoy the celebrations as a family.

Since I have taken my place as queen, Mary no longer presides over court, but she visits when she can and our relationship grows. I have hopes that in time she will see the benefits of accepting the new learning, but I do not pressure her. She is a little like her father in that she likes an idea to be her own. She will not be cajoled. I leave it to God; he will decide what is best for Mary.

By far the most startling of my stepchildren is little Edward. At just seven years old, he is self-assured and almost overwhelmingly regal. On our first meeting I expect dimples and mischief, but the child who receives me is quite different; his formal manner sitting strangely on an infant.

I watch in astonishment as he bows and lisps a pre-rehearsed greeting. Where I had hoped to scoop him onto my lap and smother him in kisses, I find myself sinking to my knees and kissing the royal hand. It is instantly apparent that this child does not require a 'mother' and I quickly realise I will need a different approach with Edward.

He is very aware of his exulted status and rarely descends from his pedestal. Instead of engaging him in play or laughter, I praise his scholarly achievements. He is currently under the tutoring of Richard Coxe, a progressive teacher who ensures his pupils enjoy their studies. I am pleased to note that Coxe is also a closet reformer, and hope that his influence will find fertile soil in the mind of our little prince.

Once I realise Edward's scholarly potential, I set about persuading Henry of the merits of Dr John Cheke, and he soon makes a welcome addition to Edward's schoolroom. As a result, it is only a matter of weeks before my youngest stepson is addressing me rather stiffly as 'Mother.'

I have come to love his open mind, his willingness to embrace new ideas. It is not something he has inherited from his father. Edward's letters are full of the new things he has learned, as well as admonishments as to how I should behave in my new state as queen. From any other child these instructions might seem precocious or repellent but, knowing Edward as I now do, I merely smile. Sometimes I even find myself considering his advice as if it comes from a man grown.

I feel I have brought new unity to Henry's family. In January the act of succession is drawn up afresh, naming Edward as heir and, should he die without issue, Mary. After her, should there be no living child to inherit,

Elizabeth and her heirs. It is a job well done and, contrary to all my expectations I am happy in my new role and satisfied with my achievements.

Amid all this I have also managed to compile a small book of psalms and prayers that is to be published under my own name. I am quietly proud of this and the small triumph adds to my general sense of contentment.

And, to my surprise, I am very content. Henry's visits to my chamber are less frequent now, perhaps once or twice a month, no more. I have learned to accept it and, on one or two occasions, he has even managed to perform the full act. I begin to cherish some hopes of presenting him with a child after all.

Surrounded as I am at court by the greatest thinkers of the age, I begin to turn my thoughts to setting my own ideas on paper. I turn my spare hours, the long nights when sleep evades me, to writing my own philosophies about the importance of God and prayer. I do not tell Henry about it. My thoughts and feelings are so wrapped up in reformist ideas that I know he will disapprove. He may have broken with Rome and allowed some adjustments to the way we worship in England, but at heart he is conservative, and I doubt that will ever change.

Just as I am settling happily into my life as mother to Henry's children, and queen to the people of England, everything changes. Henry, satisfied that Hertford has a firm hand over the disputes in the north, shatters domestic peace all over England and once more declares war on France.

***

As incapacitated and elderly as he is, Henry pictures himself as a prince of old, vanquishing the French with ease. He spreads a map across the table in my apartment and beckons me to examine it with him. "With Spain keeping Francis occupied on the opposite border, we will regain all our lost territories. Remember Agincourt, Kate?"

I nod enthusiastically. "Well, I wasn't born, Your Grace."

Henry laughs with delight.

"France remembers it too. How could they ever forget such defeat? I tell you we will have Montreuil and Boulogne under our control within the blink of an eye. See here?"

He pokes the map and I lean over his shoulder to follow his stubby finger along the ragged south coast of England. "The south coast is well fortified now; the new defences I've put up in the last few years will stand us in good stead. I'm not prepared to wait for France to come to us. We will invade just here, while Spain keeps them occupied over here. See? We will split the French forces in two. Norfolk will take Montreuil, and Suffolk and I will besiege Boulogne. The plans are all under way."

"Is Norfolk not a little old to lead an army now?"

"What? Norfolk? No, he is still in his prime."

The Duke of Norfolk must be close to seventy but I do not argue. My job is to amuse, to distract the king, not to cause extra concerns.

"What about the Scots? What will they do? Won't they join with France against us?"

"Hertford will keep them busy, don't you worry about that. And while I am gone I am trusting all else to you. You will be regent in my absence ..."

"Regent? Me?"

I sit down heavily as blood rushes to my head and my heart begins to thump loudly in my ears. "In charge of all England? To sit at council and make decisions?"

"Who else?" He pulls me from my seat and draws me onto his knee, barely wincing at my weight on his injured thigh. "In my youth I left the country in the hands of another Katherine, and I trust in you to do as well. Do you think you can, Kate?"

I don't know how to answer. I am only just feeling secure in my new position. To take the place of the king, however temporarily, and to undertake the governance of the realm is a terrifying honour indeed. The king is watching me. His flushed face is tense; his pale blue eyes intent on mine.

"I will try, Henry," I say at last. "I trust you will leave me sound advisors."

"Of course. I will form a council of five men, including your friend Cranmer, who should keep Gardiner and Wriothesley under control. But they must all adhere to your decisions. I will write, Kate, every day, and be assured my letters will be full of advice and instruction. We can beat France, Kate. You and I, we can do it together."

I smile gently, grateful for his faith in me. As I slide from his lap, Will Somer, who is never far from the king's side, creeps from a corner and begins to play the fool. His song is about a simpleton in charge of a sinking ship. As he sings he hunches over, performing a dance in the manner of a crab. Henry roars with laughter, but I see nothing funny. I dislike Somer's crude, irreverent brand of humour that seems to entertain the king so much. Excusing myself from his presence, I take my leave of Henry and return to my apartments to break the news to my sister.

"Regent? Good grief, Katheryn. That is an honour indeed. William will be astounded ..."

"I daresay the king has already discussed it with council. It is the men he has chosen to leave behind that bother me. Gardiner detests me and so does his crony Wriothesley, and as for Hertford ...well, let us pray he spends most of his time away from court. I just hope Henry will be back within the month, and we must pray that the strain of war doesn't prove too much for him. Despite his conviction otherwise, the king is growing old."

July 1544 - Greenwich

I join the king on the first part of his journey, stopping at Greenwich en route. My husband is in high spirits, almost boyish in his excitement to get to the heart of the action. That night, while the household is still settling, he comes to my chamber. I send my women away, trying not to notice Anne's look of compassion as she closes the door upon us, leaving us in privacy.

Henry is massive in his nightgown. He lumbers toward the bed and heaves himself onto the mattress. His breath sounds like the winter wind whistling down a chimney.

To give him time to recover from the exertion of climbing unaided into bed, I do not follow straight away. I linger at the hearth, finishing a cup of wine. He watches me, his legs splayed, his hands clasped on his belly, his scalp glinting through his close cropped hair. Reluctantly I put down my empty cup and, sending up a swift and silent prayer, approach the bed.

Henry's weight makes it impossible for us not to lie close together. I roll towards him, our bodies touching. He is hot, his gown already damp beneath the arms. As always, his lovemaking begins with an exploration of my knee and upper thigh. Then, unusually, he speaks into the gloom.

"If ... if anything should happen to me, you will be well cared for. I have willed that you shall be guardian to Edward after my passing. I trust you to ensure he learns all he needs to become a good king. He must never forget he is a Tudor."

I place my hand on his chest. "Henry ... don't even think such things ..."

"I must." He pats my fingers. "I must. Everything is left in readiness. It is up to you to govern fairly, and to do so with strength. You can't be gentle with them. They must learn to fear you as they do me. From now on you are my voice, until such time as I return or Edward is old enough to govern."

I nod. Fresh fears bubble up from my stomach.

"I will try, My Lord, and every spare moment, I shall pray for your safe and prompt return."

"Do that. Do that." His explorations take him higher, bunching up my clothes, his fingers find my core. Our faces are level on the pillow; he pierces me with his eye. "And pray I get you with child this night, Madam, and set the seal on all our good fortune."

I close my eyes as the trial begins. I try not to mind the progress of his stubby fingers, the trail of spittle he leaves on my skin. When the time is right, he hauls me up so I am seated across his loins. I feel him enter and my penance begins.

In the morning, hoisted like a sack of coal into the saddle, he rides away. He guides his horse through crowd-lined streets, raising a hand to greet his cheering subjects. I feel strangely bereft, like a ship that has cast its anchor, a crab without its shell. I am vulnerable and afraid. Although he cannot be more than four miles away, I sit down directly and compose a letter. I cannot confess to the feelings of cowardice that are overwhelming me so instead, seeking to comfort him as well as myself, I express a love that I do not feel.

...Although the distance of time and account of days neither is long nor many of your majesty's absence, yet the want of your presence, so much desired and beloved by me, maketh me that I cannot quietly pleasure in anything until I hear from your majesty ...

Henry has become my lord and protector; the warrior that stands between me and my enemies. It is imperative that he returns safely. The act of writing soothes and enables me to enter the fray of my regency with new courage.

Despite his promises, Henry does not write every day. In fact, the letters that do come are impersonal and directed to the council; orders for more troops, and more equipment. I crave an intimate word from him, some proof of his regard, some evidence of his faith in me. I have little conviction in my own ability.

From the outset, there is friction between myself and the men Henry has set beneath me. When, clad in a gown of masculine cut I arrive for the first meeting, Wriothesley is slouched in my chair. I recognise it as a challenge.

I wish my armour were thicker, the lance of my wit sharper. Straightening my shoulders, I position myself before him and, with a disdainful expression, wait for him to rise. After a long moment, during which my heart bangs sickeningly, he drags himself from my seat and takes one next to Gardiner. They begin to converse in whispers until Cranmer, his eyes crinkling encouragingly at the edges, calls the meeting to order and all attention is upon me.

Lord Hertford has a look of his brother, Thomas. I try not to notice the similarities of his dark-lashed eyes, the way he holds his head, the timbre of his voice. I am here to do a job, not to mourn the loss of a lover like some lovesick maid. I am queen now, in fact as well as name.

I deepen the tone of my voice, shorten my sentences and adopt a squarer pose to emphasise my substance. I am queen and regent of England. It is imperative that they know this and understand that they are now my servants.

We go over reports from the Earl of Shrewsbury in the north, and I issue orders for further weapons and provisions. Slowly, as we work our way through the agenda, my lethargic team of councillors begin to sit up and take note.

"I must be kept informed of events in France. We will write to the king asking for news. Verbal messages and scribbled notes are not enough. If the king is too busy to attend to it himself, then we must have more frequent updates from the king's council."

They nod, the murmur of several voices fighting to be heard. Eventually Cranmer hushes them.

"The queen is right. All must be set down on record, even the scrawled messages. There is no excuse for poor record keeping; even the king will know this."

A ship has foundered off the Scottish coast and letters discovered; letters containing secrets pertaining to the political stance of France and Scotland. I order them to be sent to Henry without delay, and this time there is no argument. I do not mince my words in these missives. Henry said I must make them fear me and gentle words will win me no battles. I scrawl my signature on several documents, a time is set for our next meeting, and it is over.

Afterwards, the men of the council trail from the room, yawning and stretching, and complaining audibly about missing supper. I remain at the desk and take up my pen to write once more to Henry. During meetings, I immerse myself fully in the position of Regent and it is only when I send word to Henry that I allow softness and vulnerability to creep into my words. I cannot think only of ruling. I have to think of my marriage, and a man like Henry likes to know that he is needed, and missed. At the end of the letter, as I take my leave of him, I inform him of the health of his children and beg him to write to me soon as I am in dire need of comfort.

It is true that I miss the king more than I had ever dreamed possible. With him gone, I am aware of those who resent me; they gather in groups, whispering. It is uncomfortable to be so hated, if only by a few.

Rumours that I am barren begin to circulate; I am a heretic, a traitor and I should be burned. A salacious play is performed in my presence, the leading character clearly intended to be me. I watch it, pretending I do not recognise the slur. I laugh and clap my hands, but every moment is a horror.

Each day I wade through duties that are becoming wearisome, fending off the resentment of the religious conservatives, while at the same time nurturing the love and respect of my new reformist friends. When I enter my apartments it is late, and I have not yet taken time for dinner. I am growing pale and tired, and Anne is increasingly concerned for my health.

"You are peaky-looking and not eating properly. You are not with child are you?"

I shake my head sharply, casting an eye about the chamber for fear that we are overheard.

"It is too soon to tell. I had hoped to greet the king with good news on his return, but there are no signs yet."

"But you've not bled. There is still hope?"

I nod as she presses a cup of warm wine into my hand. "There is still hope," I repeat, although I lost faith in ever becoming a mother many years ago.

"Drink that," she says like some bossy nursery maid. "It will fortify you."

I have recently upgraded my household, so now I am surrounded mostly by friends. My privy chamber has become a place of sanctuary, away from the critical eyes of my detractors, although I know there will always be spies.

I ease off my shoes. "The Lady Elizabeth joins us tomorrow."

"That will be nice. Margaret will be with her, I suppose. For once all your stepchildren will be under one roof ... barring John, of course. Is he still in the north?"

"Yes. His betrothed is here, though."

I have taken Lucy into my service. She fluctuates between radiant good health and the deepest gloom, and I have begun to suspect that this has something to do with Francis Bryan. I have observed them together, flirting and laughing beyond the bounds of courtly love. He is a notorious rake with the reputation of having an eye for young girls. I cannot have Lucy's character compromised. Once, I believe, Bryan set his sights on Margaret, and I was relieved when that attachment passed, but he cannot have Lucy either.

It is a relief that Bryan is now occupied with the war, perhaps in his absence we can bring Lucy to her senses. It will soon be time for her and John to wed. I must put more effort into seeking a husband for Margaret too; the promise of a family may be just what she needs to restore her verve.

Knowing Henry's horror of contagion, when the threat of plague raises its head again I issue a proclamation forbidding anyone to endanger the life of the Royal children. Anyone who has been in contact with the pestilence must stay away from court. It is a testing time for me, keeping the family safe, overseeing affairs at home and on the Scottish border, as well as keeping abreast of the situation in France.

I am in the process of recruiting four thousand foot soldiers to send to Henry when at last, a letter written in his own hand is delivered.

When the courier arrives, I barely take the time to listen to his verbal message. I snatch it from his hand as if it is a love letter and carry it to my bed, squinting in the dim light to decipher his scrawl. He thanks me for my letters, the venison I sent him, and excuses himself from not having written sooner.

...would have written unto you again a letter with our own hand, but that we be so occupied, and have so much to do in foreseeing and caring for everything ourself, as we have almost no manner rest or leisure to do any other thing.

I laugh through my tears. It is as if he were in the room, excusing himself for some small offence against me. In a rush of affection I stuff the parchment inside my bodice, promising myself to reply that very evening. I will urge him to come home, ask him how much longer this war will take. If nothing else it will soothe his ego to know I miss him. He swore he'd crush the French within a matter of weeks, but it is already September and still the town of Boulogne has not fallen.

Over supper I convey the contents of the letter to the children.

"Has there been hand to hand fighting yet?" Edward asks, keen to learn the details of the action. "Will Father fight himself or watch from afar?"

Elizabeth pauses with her spoon halfway to her mouth.

"Edward. Father will do as he sees fit. Why not listen to his letter instead of bombarding Mother with questions?"

He scowls at Elizabeth but subsides and allows me to continue with my news.

After supper we retire to my private chamber. Elizabeth is embroidering Henry some new gloves, each tiny stitch a mark of her love. Margaret, who hates needlework, grimaces at the mere thought of such a task. Her lack of needle skills is a long held joke between us. I remember her toiling over a grubby piece of linen when she was a little girl, her cockled, crooked stitches the cause of much heartbreak. Mary is playing with Rig, teasing him with a cushion, while Edward looks on with a mix of mirth and disdain. Margaret joins me quietly at the hearth.

I am pleased to note she is looking a little better. A faint trace of colour is in her cheek and I notice she enters the conversation more often, even if her comments are sometimes far too cynical for one so young.

The summer grows tired; the trees begin to give up their vegetation. Small yellow birch leaves litter the jewelled mead where we walk in the late afternoon sun. Elizabeth is relating a joke to Margaret; a risqué one for a girl. Every so often she glances in my direction to see if I am listening. I pause by the fountain and pretend to be distracted by the golden fish undulating just beneath the surface. My finger trails and the fish rise up to investigate with soft, gaping mouths.

"That's awful, Elizabeth!" Margaret's voice floats across the garden, half laughing, half disgusted at the punch line. "Where did you hear that?"

"I overheard Will Somers entertaining the guard. He is at a loose end without the king. It seems he keeps his crudest foolery for the lower orders."

I raise my eyebrows in Elizabeth's direction and she subsides, blushing. There is no need for a verbal reprimand, she knows she has displeased me and comes to sit at my side, takes my fingers in her palm. As she opens her mouth to speak, a shadow falls across the garden and we all look up, blinking into the dazzle of the setting sun.

"Will!" Anne leaps from the edge of the fountain to embrace him, but he holds his wife at bay and sinks to his knees before me.

"Your Majesty." My brother-in-law, Will Herbert, is still mired from the road. From his place in the dust he kisses the back of my hand. I stand up, suddenly full of fear.

"What is it?" I demand, forgetting the presence of the children. "The king? Is it Henry? Is he safe?"

"Nay, Katheryn, do not worry. I come with good news from His Majesty, who has lately taken hold of Boulogne. He sends you his good wishes, and this

111

message which tells of his triumphs. I have been five days on the road."

A gusty sigh of relief escapes me and, as Anne ushers William back toward the palace, the children gather round, clamouring for me to read the letter aloud.

Boulogne has fallen. I issue orders for praises to be read in the churches, for bonfires to be lit and for jubilation to ring out loud across the city. Delight fills me to the depths of my soul, not only that we are victorious but that the king will soon return. That night when sleep evades me, I call for paper and ink and pen a heartfelt prayer.

Our cause being now just, and being enforced to enter into war and battle, we most humbly beseech thee, O Lord God of hosts, so to turn the hearts of our enemies to the desire of peace, that no Christian blood be spilt; or else grant, O Lord, that with small effusion of blood and to the little hurt and damage of innocents, we may to thy glory obtain victory. And that the wars being soon ended, we may all with one heart and mind, knit together in concord and unity, laud and praise thee.

Although I am proud and delighted with the victory, I also long for the war to end so that Henry can return home to relieve me of the burden of rule. We are triumphant; Henry has gained his second Agincourt, won back Boulogne and Montreuil for England. Let that be enough for him. I can hardly wait to celebrate our great victory together. There were those who saw this war with France as folly, but Henry has proved himself a warrior king, like the kings of old.

But our delight is short-lived and word follows that Charles of Spain has betrayed us and formed a treaty with France. Now King Francis can send all his forces against ours on the northern front. We are isolated, our armies set against far greater numbers than before. For days I am left in limbo, unaware of what is happening or how Henry will act. My mind fills with images of those who have perished on the field of battle. I am not ready to be widowed again. I begin to muster reinforcements, determined to be ready should a summons arrive from France. But then I receive word that the king is coming home, and my heart floods with relief that my trial will soon be over.

At dawn I ride off at the head of a cavalcade to be reunited with my husband at Otford, where Henry will rest en route to Leeds Castle. I slide from the saddle and hurry inside to find Henry, looking larger and healthier than I have ever seen him.

"Kate!" he cries when he sees me. He slams his cup on the table and clambers to his feet, crosses the room to greet me. Although he still limps, he appears far more stable on his feet than when he left.

"Henry." I press my lips to his cheek, feel the tickle of his beard, and inhale the underlying reek of his bandage. "I had thought the war would tire you out, My Lord, but look at you, twice the man that rode away."

He is delighted by my flattering tongue and keeps hold of my hand as he ushers me toward the fire. "Bring refreshments, hurry. The queen is tired from her journey," he calls, his voice full of laughter as he winks at me. Someone takes my cloak and I begin to pull off my riding gloves, hand them to a nearby page.

"What made you decide to return so soon, Henry? I thought perhaps you were ailing. I have been worried every minute you've been gone."

"Do you think me some fragile maid? No, the air in France has done me good. I have spent too many months cooped up in the castle. In future I shall hunt more often, as I did in my youth. There was a time when I was in the saddle from dawn to dusk."

"I was sorry to hear of Charles' deceit. Were you very angry?"

"Furious! I knew I should never trust the Spanish. As soon as he was able, Francis turned his attention to us. The damned dauphin took Montreuil from Norfolk as if he was taking it from a baby, and sent him running for the hills. Boulogne is safe though. I thought it secure enough for me to come home."

I wonder how he will receive Norfolk when he returns. He has fought on Henry's side for years, sacrificing two nieces to the royal bed; surely Henry won't be too hard on him.

"And that Seymour fellow, The Admiral…"

My heart leaps at Thomas' name but I manage not to let it show. The table is piled with delicacies. I reach for a peach and begin to turn it in my fingers, looking for flaws as I wait for him to continue.

"The fleet was scuppered in a storm. His ships sustained considerable damage … it can only be due to incompetency, the fellow should be whipped."

He pretends to look toward the hearth but I know he is watching me. Careful not to let any emotion show, I begin to peel away the perfect skin of the peach. Slicing off a section I put it in my mouth, the sweet smooth flesh like heaven on my tongue.

Poor Thomas, exiled from court for so long, away from family, away from me, only to be summoned back to face a reprimand. When he comes I wonder if he will look the same, if he will see me altered.

114

Henry leans forward and plucks a handful of grapes from the bowl and begins to pop them into his mouth. Every so often, to supplement my peach, he holds one out between two fingers and obediently I part my lips and let him place it on my tongue. He watches me, making me blush as I chew delicately.

"I have missed you, wife." He speaks quietly, his words for me alone, and I realise that I have merely swapped one unpleasant chore for another. Yesterday I was regent, but now I am merely wife again, a brood mare that fails to breed. I could wish his words had not filled my head with memories of Thomas, for tonight I know I will not be sleeping alone.

Spring 1545 - Greenwich

With Henry once more at the helm, things swiftly return to normal. The few months he was away seemed long, but now it is as if he never left. While the king hunts with more vigour than he has for many years, the court continues to growl with discord. The gulf between Norfolk and Gardiner widens daily and the differences between them draws us all into the fray. We are divided into factions, those for reform against those opposed to it.

In the presence of the king we must pretend otherwise, but he is not fooled. He plays one subtly against the other. Like a small child with two beetles in a jar, he watches them circle and seethe, plucking them apart just in time, before any real damage is done. One day, I fear, they will find him off his guard and he will act too late to thwart the strike of a fatal blow.

The threat from France is not over. In fact the danger of war is greater than before. Not only are the forces of France and Scotland united, but Spain is now ranged against us too. I begin to wonder if we should ally ourselves with the Protestant Princes, but Henry remains staunchly Catholic in outlook, and no one since Cromwell has dared to suggest such a thing. We all know what happened to him.

Although Henry continues in relatively good health, he frets over the security of the channel ports. Three armies are on perpetual alert, with beacons ever at the ready should the alarm be raised.

Meanwhile, at court, Henry persists in his hope for a son. As often as he can manage it, he comes to my bed to do his duty by me. Afterwards, he lingers to hear my thoughts on the progress of his children, the state of his kingdom, my opinion of his latest composition. It is there, in the warmth of our marital bed, that I first begin to plant the seeds of an idea. By February, my most trusted servants are sent to Saxony and Antwerp to propose an alliance between Henry and the Kings of Denmark, the Duke of Holstein, and other German princes.

***

Amidst all the cares of the past months I have neglected to notice that Margaret is now far from well. She excused herself from duty, claiming a feminine indisposition, but when, after a few short weeks, I see her again, it is apparent she is very ill.

"Margaret." I rise from my chair, the dogs spilling to the floor, and put a hand to her forehead. "You are burning up."

"It is nothing." She shrugs from my touch, her voice deteriorating into a fit of coughing. I take her wrist, skin and bone, the veins on the back of her hand standing up, her knuckles prominent.

"How long have you been like this? Why wasn't I told?"

"It is a light chill; that is all. Dorothy said I should tell you but I thought you had enough to contend with."

"Margaret! Of course I should have been told. I am your mother; you are more precious to me than anything on earth. And it is clearly a good deal more than a 'light chill.' I will see to it that you have the best of care."

I order her to bed, putting her in the chamber next to mine, and assume the role I should never have relinquished, that of Margaret's mother. The doctors come, clucking doubtfully around the bed as they listen to her thin chest, examine her urine, and ask impertinent questions about her monthly flux.

Henry, when he hears it, disappears into his stillroom and emerges again half an hour later with a concoction of herbs that he swore cured him of a similar condition.

I have never known or heard of Henry's weight falling from his bones, or of him laid waste by a dry and racking cough. As far as I know, apart from his leg and occasional severe indigestion, he has always enjoyed the rudest health. But I take the offering gratefully and spoon it between her lips.

"There." Henry hovers uncertainly by the sickroom door. "You will soon be hale again, my dear." Having done his duty, he takes his leave as soon as he can. Poor Henry has always feared contagion and it is entirely for my peace of mind that he allows Margaret to stay. I know that I will not see him again until she is cured; he will occupy himself hunting, or bury himself in the steadily increasing pile of books that litter his private chamber.

It is a sorry time. I had expected Lucy and John's wedding to cheer her, but their marriage has little effect on her spirits. Daily, Margaret grows weaker. The catalogue of purges and potions they feed her have no effect. On a wet afternoon in March, we face the inevitable. She asks for paper and pen and together we set down her will. It is unusual for unmarried women to have anything of note to leave behind, but Margaret has estates left to her by her father, and a little money put aside. I am to be her chief beneficiary, but she also remembers Dorothy and her other servants.

I watch the passage of her thin, blue-veined hand as it travels across the paper setting her bequests in writing. A lump begins to form in my throat; a lump that grows bigger with each painfully written word, each laboured line. Soon my whole upper body is consumed with fear, grief and regret. I don't know how I can maintain my cheerful conviction that she will yet recover. I strive but fail to conceal my sorrow from her.

At last, she slumps back on her pillow, coughs pathetically. "I will sleep now," she says and before I have time to leave, she is slumbering. Instead of leaving I sit at her bedside and watch her breathe; the lace-trimmed bodice of her nightgown barely rising and falling.

She bears no resemblance to the pretty, plump child I first knew. In the early days she was an awkward, stubborn girl, and doggedly resistant to my presence. Those early years were difficult, fraught with rancour and resentment. I remember the first precious day, during the siege at Snape, when the last barrier between us fell and she at last allowed me to mother her, as I had so longed to do.

118

Now, the bones of her skull are visible, a network of blue veins at her temple, her once luxurious hair is thin and lank. I have failed. I promised John Neville to cherish her and yet, here she is, almost dead of neglect.

Guilt grabs me by the throat, choking grief for a life so easily lost. I send up a silent plea for forgiveness. I have been so caught up in my own life and my own trials that I have quite neglected to notice what was happening beneath my nose.

I sit there for a long time. Eventually, Dorothy appears to stoke the fire. She moves quietly across the room and sets a tray at the bedside. We speak in whispers.

"You should rest, Madam. It won't do to have you sicken too."

"Oh, Dorothy. I feel so culpable. I am entirely to blame."

She sniffs, shakes her head. "No, it isn't you, Madam. I think Margaret is one of those women who loves once only, and then wholeheartedly. There isn't any cure for that."

My head jerks up in surprise. Dorothy has always been perceptive. I search my mind for a possible candidate for Margaret's love.

"Who, Dorothy?" I ask at last. "Who do you think she loves?"

"Why Madam, who else but that one-eyed reprobate that is always sniffing around the young ladies; Francis Bryan."

She all but spits his name into the hearth. Tearing my eyes from Dorothy, I turn back to my daughter. She is frail, little more than a child. Francis Bryan is a man grown –he is middle-aged.

"No; surely not. She barely knows him. His attentions have all been for Lucy ... oh ..."

Realisation hits me low in the belly and rests there like a sickness. "Is this really true, Dorothy? Has she confided in you?"

Dorothy wipes her nose on the back of her hand. "Nay, Madam, she didn't need to. I have no proof, but I've seen her watching him as he flits from one girl to the next when he used to have eyes for no one but her. I've seen her come back after a feast and cry herself to sleep. I am not easily fooled, Madam."

Why didn't you tell me? I do not speak the words. Recriminations are no use now. While we dissect her private life Margaret lies like a corpse, the flickering shadow of the candle-light playing on her death-white skin.

"Can you die from want of love, do you think?" I whisper, thinking of myself and Thomas. He is my first and only love, but I would never let devotion kill me. Life is too precious; a gift to be enjoyed to the utmost no matter what fate might send your way.

"Oh, I reckon so, some of us anyway. Margaret's illness stems from the time we first came to court, the time she first met Bryan. There was a glow about her then. She was happy and joy flickered in her like a flame for a short while, and then was extinguished suddenly, like a light. She hasn't been the same since, Madam."

I know she is right. Margaret has willed herself to die, for want of a good-for-nothing. Dorothy circles the bed and pulls up a stool beside me.

"There's nothing more to be done, is there, Madam?"

There is no need for me to answer. I grope for her hand and hang on to it tightly.

Dorothy and I sit until night falls completely. When the candles fail we do not relight them. Darkness is a cloak. It disguises the moisture on our cheeks, the crumpling of our chins, and the furrowed pain upon our brows.

And when the morning comes, we emerge together from the darkest place and return to life. The pain of grief is hidden from view, but both of us will carry it forever, for it is carved deeply upon our souls.

Late spring 1545 – Greenwich

When I see him waiting in the shadows I pause, sure he can hear the thumping of my heart. He stands, hands clasped behind him, looking up at the half-completed portrait. I can scarcely believe he is there, in the flesh, before me.

Blinking back tears I move silently toward him, and without speaking, take my place at his side. His head turns slowly, his welcoming smile opening like a flower. In that moment I forgive him everything.

"It is a good likeness," he says at last.

I swallow, force myself to remain calm, remind myself I am a queen now and cannot fall into his arms. I turn my attention to the portrait.

"The king commissioned Master John to make my likeness as a sop to soothe the insult of the grand piece Master Holbein began."

"Master Holbein is dead, is he not?"

"Yes, but his apprentice is to complete it. I am mean-spirited enough to hope his brush is not too kind to Jane."

"She was his wife once too, and mother to Edward."

"I am queen now and have had more shaping of the prince than his mother ever had."

For a moment I forget we are speaking of Thomas' sister. I quash my resentment, lower my eyes. "Forgive me, Thomas. I misremembered she was your kin but I find the situation difficult, that is all. I have carried this country through the trials of war; I have reconciled the king with his children, raising them as if they are my own, yet I am not good enough to be painted as queen, alongside the king? Everyone is included: Henry, Edward, Jane, Elizabeth, Mary. Even the royal fools, Janet, and Will Somers have wormed their way into it ..."

"Shush, shush, I understand, but I must confess I find myself quite jealous of your jealousy."

I realise I am being ridiculous and a little of my ire drains away, but the sting of Henry's insult remains. I know Henry intends me no slight in commissioning a portrait of himself and his wife, Jane, with their children meekly beside them. It is the epitome of family unity and it hurts to be left out. More than I'd thought possible. They are my children. I've welcomed them, without hesitation, into my heart, into my household. His dead wife should stay in her grave where she belongs.

To ease me a little, the king has commissioned a full length painting of me, Katheryn the Queen, but still I feel excluded, segregated. I have been quietly sulking for a few weeks now but, as always, within minutes of his company, Tom has me laughing. He raises one quizzical eyebrow and instantly I see how petty and spiteful my behaviour is. For the first time since Margaret's death, my heart lifts just a little and I almost laugh.

It is strange being here with him like this, speaking of everyday things, as if nothing has happened. The image of our entwined bodies passes through my mind, the delight we shared. I wonder if he remembers it.

I continue to speak of triviality while my adulterous mind recalls a thousand instances of shared pleasure. The conversation falters, our eyes lock before he breaks away and his gaze trickles treasonously down my body. Eventually he realises the significance of my sombre-hued gown, and his eyes refocus and meet mine.

"I am sorry for your loss, Kate. Truly."

My name, spoken by his lips, is like a balm. I close my eyes for a moment as his voice continues. "Are you happy, apart from losing Margaret, I mean?"

As I ponder the question I look at the floor, the toe of my jewelled slipper peeping from beneath my kirtle.

"Not happy, Tom, but content. I have all I need."

I do not miss the flash of hurt in his eye and to cover the unintended slight, I continue quickly. "Did you hear my book is soon to be published?"

He steps back a little as if to regard me from a different perspective, and gives an ironic salute. "I did. You are to be congratulated. All over Europe people are talking about England's valiant and erudite queen. I am honoured to have *known* her."

I grow very hot under his praise, disliking the past tense of his sentiment. I open my mouth to utter a tart retort but, at the sound of approaching footsteps, my head jerks up. We both look toward the empty doorway, listen in dismay as the sound of laughter grows closer.

"I must go." He bends over my hand, his lips on my fingers, his beard tickling. And then he is gone, the hanging at the garden door undulating, his fragrance dissipating in the cool night air. My ladies spill into the room.

"There you are, Katheryn. We have been seeking you everywhere." Anne pauses, offers me my ostrich feather fan. "Are you quite well? You are terribly pale."

The spot on my hand where he placed his lips tingles. I turn back to the half-painted portrait of myself as queen. My image stares back, smug and serene amid the splendour that surrounds her. I do not recognise her; it does not seem remotely like myself.

"Evidently I am pale by nature," I say, gesturing to the likeness. "Master John apparently thinks so."

Master John, a newcomer to court, is working on a portrait of the Lady Mary also. Our images stand side by side, our faces complete, our nailless hands delicately hued, the sumptuousness of our gowns has only just begun to emerge from Master John's brush.

It is strange standing before one's own image. It is quite a different thing to looking in a glass. I observe the flaws, the characteristics that others see. For the first time I realise I am not plain after all, or at least, Master John sees me as pretty. Not beautiful, not handsome but, although I have passed my thirtieth year, my body is as slim as a girl's and my face is neat and unlined. I am not yet ageing. I am content with that.

***

To free my mind from the misery of losing Margaret, I immerse myself in study. When Mary shows an interest in my work, I persuade her to join me. She sets about translating Erasmus' paraphrases of the New Testament. I see it as a way of subliminally teaching the new religion and drawing her away from the old beliefs. Now I am freed from the restrictions of Rome, I am moving from Anglicanism and immersing myself in the teachings of Luther. I see now that I was blind before.

The new thinking helps me to overcome the great grief of Margaret's passing, and I am fuelled with the desire to open the eyes of others around me; including Henry, who remains determinedly orthodox in his religious thinking.

Sometimes when we are alone, or his leg is paining him, I distract him with articles I have read or discussions I have had. He is indulgent. He listens but he does not take the bait.

My new conviction makes me want to reach out and help others understand that the time we spend on earth is but a penance. I want to show them that a greater experience waits for us on the other side of sorrow.

When Wriothesley's wife, Jane Cheney, loses her infant son I am moved to write to her, to try to explain why she should not grieve. I urge her to understand that it, *'hath pleased God of late to disinherit your son of this world, or intend he should become partner and chosen heir of the everlasting inheritance, which calling and happy vocation ye may rejoice. For what is excessive sorrow but a plain evidence against you that your inward mind doth repine against God's sayings, and a declaration that you are not contented that God hath put your son by nature, but his by adoption, in possession of the heavenly kingdom."*

To my dismay I learn afterwards that, far from providing comfort, Jane is most distressed by my letter. She throws it down and subsides in a fit of weeping, taking to her bed for a week. She may think me hard but I know I am right. We can allow ourselves to become prostrate with grief, or we can accept it as a blessing. Only by picturing Margaret at God's right hand can I continue on earth, knowing that if I live my life righteously, my time will also come. I am living a penance; we all are, until God is ready to receive us into Heaven.

While I delve deeper into the minds of the great, Henry is occupied by more prosaic matters. The continuing threat from France and Scotland takes up most of his day. With our enemies united against us, England stands isolated. He tries to conceal it but I know Henry is angry at the turn of events. The war in France did little to advance us, and the coffers are empty. In the end, things become so bad that Henry is forced to debase the coinage. The merchants begin to speak out in retaliation against us, and the apprentices riot in the streets.

Mid- July 1545 – The Road to Portsmouth

Henry decides to travel to the south coast to oversee the preparations for war. Almost at the last moment he suggests I accompany him, and the servants bustle around making ready for the journey. It is a long but not an arduous ride, and we are all in high spirits as the cavalcade winds its way through the town and into the countryside. A recent rain shower has set the summer leaves aglimmer, and the scent of warm wet meadows rises in a mist. We pass fields of saturated sheep, their pungent oily aroma thick in the humid air.

Henry is mounted on a massive horse, his sore leg stuck out like a thick white lance before him. Despite his discomfort he is full of enthusiasm for the week ahead, and rides at my side as full of bounce as a small boy on a Sunday outing.

"You just wait until you see the ships, Kate. There is nothing like the royal fleet on the brink of sailing. The French will turn and run when they see us bearing down on them."

The French navy is reported to be nearing our shores. At first we believed their target to be Boulogne, but for some reason they have changed course and are headed for England. Our ships are manned and battle ready. I smile at Henry's brave talk and dig my heels into my mount's sides so that she keeps up with the longer stride of the king's horse.

"I am told that the French fleet is far bigger than ours, Henry. My brother says they have three hundred ships while we have scarce half that number."

He waves his arm in the air, dismissing my womanly concern. "That will make no difference. Remember Agincourt? Were we not outnumbered there too? Rest assured, my dear, one good Englishman is a match for five Frenchies."

We pass a cluster of hovels and a pair of flea-bitten dogs come rushing out to bark at our heels. One of them is limping; he gives up the chase and falls back behind his fellows to watch us go. A band of ragged children appear to add their cheers to the dogs' fury. Henry waves his plump hand in their direction and they stand barefoot and open mouthed, awed by his notice.

A little farther on we pass a homestead, a more prosperous looking place. A woman is spreading laundry to dry on the hedgerow. She straightens up with a hand to her back, tucks her straggling hair beneath her linen cap, and attempts a clumsy curtsey. As we ride on by she turns on her heel and, ducking her head, hurries into the house. I imagine her telling whoever is inside that she just saw the king and queen ride by. I imagine their disbelief, their derision of her story.

The king spurs his horse forward to catch up with the men, while I fall back into the company of my ladies. Anne and Lady Carew ride side by side, gossiping amiably. They draw apart so that I can ride between them.

"You must be eager to see your husband, Lady Carew. It must be hard to have him so far from home for so long."

"Indeed, Your Majesty. I have not seen him since the Spring. He tells me in his letters that he is delighted to be given this new commission."

"I am sure he is." I regard Lady Carew from the corner of my eye. We have met before but she is reserved, nervous, neither friendly nor unfriendly. I don't really know what to make of her. She is not part of my household but I invited her along on the romantic notion that she might be missing her husband. But she has shown little excitement and offers little in the way of conversation.

I decide she is sad. Although it is never mentioned, her father, Henry Norris, was executed along with my predecessor, Anne Boleyn. He was accused of adultery with the queen and some say he was the father of Elizabeth. I don't believe this, of course. Elizabeth is far too much like the king, both in looks and temperament, to be sprung from any but Tudor loins.

Mary Carew must know I am watching and thinking about her, but she gives no sign of it. She holds her head high, her lips are pinched and her eye is fixed on the road ahead. I give up the attempt to befriend her and turn my attention to Anne, who is soon chattering away, describing her latest additions to her wardrobe.

I am not greatly interested but I listen and wonder idly when the new scarlet kirtle and sleeves I ordered from the dressmaker will be ready. Of all the colours, scarlet is my favourite. It is such a brave, royal colour. I much prefer it to purple. I imagine my new red gown embroidered all over with gold thread, and the thought of wearing it paints a little smile on my lips.

Henry raises a hand and we slow our mounts. Ahead on the road are a troop of soldiers, heading for the wars. The king sends a rider ahead and the troop move aside, lining the road to let us pass. They are a grubby, tired-looking bunch, but raise a ragged cheer as we draw near.

We pass so close I can smell the sweat of their bodies, see their dirt-engrained pores, and when they snatch off their caps, their sweaty hair is plastered to their scalps as if stuck with glue. At the sight of their weariness I cease to mind the ache of my loins from the long ride, the soreness of my buttocks, the chaffing of the reins. My saddle is suddenly a luxury. Perhaps I should purchase the army some new boots. I decide to make a point of doing so when I return to the palace.

The next day we arrive at Southsea and discover that the fortification is barely finished. Our apartments have been made ready but lack the finishing touches to which I have become accustomed.

"Oh, my lord." Dorothy, who has re-entered my household after Margaret's death, looks around the chamber. She dumps her bundle on the settle. "Don't worry, Madam, I will set it right in a jiffy."

I am longing to call for a bath to be drawn, to soak my aching bones in warm water while my women pour scented oil over my head, but that will have to wait.

I sit close to the hearth and hold out my hands to the sulky flame. Although it is July, the sun cannot penetrate the thick walls of the castle. The air is frigid since the tiny windows let in very little light or warmth. Dorothy lights the torches. Anne helps me remove my shoes and outer clothes and, clad only in my shift, I retire to the bed which at least has been made up in readiness.

"I daresay they weren't expecting me. It was a last minute decision that I came."

Dorothy looks up from the hearth where she is vigorously pumping the bellows, encouraging the flames to greater warmth. "Well, I hope the king is properly housed," she says. "An old man like that can't be expected to make do..."

She stops suddenly mid-sentence when she realises she is in danger of speaking treason. One must never refer to the king as either old or ailing. It is tantamount to imagining him dead, and for that crime, the punishment is death.

I sigh and reach out for a cup of wine. "I will pretend I didn't hear that, Dorothy," I say. "Now, why not run down to the kitchens and discover the arrangements for supper."

Left alone, I lie back on the pillow, close my eyes and listen to the sound of the sea. It is strange to know the French fleet is just a few leagues distant but, judging from the hubbub of soldiery in town, we are well defended here. I have never seen so many guns, or so many masts bristling in the harbour. Today I have inhaled stenches and seen sights I thought I should never see, and hardships and a way of life I have never imagined. Perhaps it is better to be queen and live a sort of half-life than to be free and at the mercy of want and poverty.

19th July 1545

It is a bright morning; the sun is warm and welcoming. It is the sort of day that can only promise victory. We climb the twisting stair to the battlement and look out across the bay.

The sound of jingling horse harness rises from the street, pennants snap in the sharp Solent breeze, and from far off comes a shouted command from the royal fleet. We watch as the ships prepare to do battle against the much larger invading French. They are close now.

Slowly, led by the flagship, The Great Harry, and the Mary Rose, our ships manoeuvre into battle position and the guns begin to sound. I cannot help but jump involuntarily when the first shots are fired. Anne and Mary Carew and my other women cower beside me, smiling and laughing in feigned girlish fear. A sharp acrid smell of gunpowder floats inland.

When the noise subsides, Mary leans over the battlement hoping to catch a glimpse of George. Last night at supper she was reunited with her husband. I saw a pink flush rise from her throat to transform her stiff, unhappy face into something else, something extraordinary. I know what she was feeling, for I have felt it too. I have been in the arms of the man I love, and experienced all-consuming desire. I will never forget it.

To my shame, I find myself wondering what passed between them when they retired to their quarters. I wonder if he loved her as thoroughly as Thomas once made love to me. I shake myself, dispelling the inappropriate thoughts, and turn my eyes back to the action.

The ensuing engagement is not something I would choose to watch. I don't like to think of the men that

131

could die today while I take pleasure from the safety of the shore. But Henry desires me to be at his side, and at his side I must be.

The Mary Rose fires first from the starboard side, making me flinch again. Mary covers her ears, her eyes brimming, her face creased in a grimace. "That was very loud!" I exclaim and she manages a shaky laugh. She is warming to me, slowly the barriers are breaking down and we are becoming friends.

Forgetting I am now her queen, Anne is hanging onto my arm. I can feel her excited laughter vibrating along my side. I clutch her hand and turn to see Henry, who stands a little behind us with the men of his privy household.

The king points a finger, indicating where the ships should go next. Beside him, ignoring the squeals of the women, Charles Brandon nods. It is as if the men are witnessing a life-sized game of chess, as if real lives, real husbands aren't at risk. I remember Henry explaining that there are more than four hundred and fifty men aboard each ship. I try to imagine the squash, the stench and the squalor. It must be like hell on earth.

The king stands proud, hands on hips, his demeanour belying his failing breath, his crippled leg, his lack of virility. He looks out across the sea, his papery cheeks growing pink in the sea air, the white feather in his cap fluttering like a stricken gull. Slowly, the pride of the English navy turns to offer a broadside attack.

It is one of those briny coastal days when the wind is sporadic with intermittent breezes that extinguish the warmth of the sun. A sudden gust, seemingly from nowhere, lifts the king's cloak, making him shudder.

"Someone walking over my grave," he laughs as he wraps it closer to his bulk. He glances at me and I smile dutifully, convincing him of my adoration. And, engaged as we are in this moment of marital insincerity, we both miss the precise moment when the Mary Rose falters.

When we turn back to the panoramic scene, the action is stilled; the flags on the great ship snap and flutter. Like a painting the scene is frozen momentarily, the great ship balanced on the cusp of fate. As if in premonition the king holds his breath, grabs my arm as my heart falters and I send up a prayer.

But, in a heartbeat, the ship is heeling over, cries of terror as her open gun ports fill with water. We stand appalled as the first sailors fall from the rigging to splash into the sea. On the snapping breeze the screams of the stricken men are borne toward us, and my husband's prowess instantly shrinks. His breath whistles from his lungs, his grip is tight and painful on my wrist.

We watch transfixed as the massive cannon break free, bursting through the sides of the ship, surging into the waves. All around us people are screaming, shouting orders; a crowd surges toward the dockside, the air clamouring with terrified voices.

On board The Mary Rose, the tilting deck is a chaos of fleeing men. They are screaming, leaping from assured death to certain drowning. As they run, they cast off their clothing, kick off their shoes in the futile hope that, although they cannot swim, they will float when the swiftly swelling sea engulfs them.

The end is quick. Henry and I watch in horrified silence while around us on the battlement, women are weeping, wailing, praying. Charles Brandon and Anthony Browne are shouting, waving their arms. Below us in the precinct men are fighting to mount terrified horses, although it is too late for fruitful action; there is nothing to be done.

It is far too late to prevent disaster. Henry knows it in his heart. I know it in my own. Now, so quickly, the only visible sign of Henry's favourite ship is the top of the mast jutting from the water. Like a great white jellyfish the mainsail is foundering in the waves and only a few survivors are left, clinging to the fighting tops. The balmy sea is littered with the wreckage, and the remnants of his fighting crew are flotsam.

I am suddenly aware of someone sobbing, and slowly I turn in a daze to find Mary Carew fallen to her knees. It is only then that I remember her husband is on board. Before I can move to comfort her Henry stumps forward and, throwing down his stick, he lifts her up and draws her into his arms.

He wraps his arms about her, and over the top of her head his eyes meet mine. There are great shining tears on his lashes, dropping onto his white and sagging cheeks.

"There, there," he croaks, caressing her shoulder awkwardly with his jewelled hand. "There, there."

What else can he say?

Henry rages. Henry storms. Weeping one moment for the loss of life, and the next he is cursing, demanding to know who is to blame. He cuffs any servant unwise enough to creep too close. Even though Lord Lisle bravely defends our shores and prevents an invasion, Henry takes no comfort. He wants vengeance.

"I will crush the French. I will see every one of their ships on the bottom of the ocean." He clenches his fists, red-faced with fury. And then, like a turning tide, his rage recedes as he descends into self-pity again.

"My ship," he mourns, "my lovely ship. For thirty-four years she has defended our shores, steered us from

134

danger. I always preferred her to The Great Harry ... such wonderful lines ..."

He subsides into sentimental reminiscence. I bend my head over my needlework and allow him to vent his emotion. There is little I can do to ease it.

He recovers, of course, but his confidence has taken a heavy blow. As the months pass he becomes ever more suspicious, ever more vindictive towards those who cross him. Everyone at the palace, be they high or low, treads with caution.

January 1546 –Westminster Palace

January blows in hard. Wrapped in furs in the warmth of my apartments, I am well enough. Henry spends much of his time in his own chambers, for the first time leaving much of the day to day running of the state to Sir Anthony Denny. With just his fool for company, Henry positions his spectacles firmly on the bridge of his nose and hunches over his books. Sometimes I hear him strumming a sad tune and I know he is very low.

To ease his sorrow, I have taken to visiting his chamber several times a day to help him pass the time. I like to read to him and would prefer to read from the Bible but, since the act was passed prohibiting women from doing so, he is uncomfortable with that. Instead I select theological texts and try to divert his mind from his aches and pains. With a roaring fire and a table of delicacies, Henry and I are quite cosy, but I am all too aware that those outside the palace know little of such comfort.

As winter melts into spring, they tell me the poor are struggling. Incessant rain, insufficient bread, and a rise in sickness is taking its toll. In some quarters there are beggars on every corner, and the bad women are abandoning the stews and come spilling across the river, straying into the nicer parts of the town. Henry is determined to stamp out vice, but I have little hope of him succeeding. When he walks among us the devil takes on many forms, and sometimes I fear he infiltrates the palace too.

The devil in my happiness is Stephen Gardiner. He and his pack of dogs are in full cry, and his quarry tremble. I am watched constantly and there is nothing I can do about it. He waits to take me down, as he has dethroned other queens before me.

I order new locks for my coffers, smuggle papers to the safety of my uncle's house, and conduct myself with even more prudence than is my usual habit. When Thomas Howard, the son of Norfolk, is arrested, I know that all those with Lutheran leanings must look to their safety. None of us are untouchable.

One outspoken supporter of reform, Anne Askew, has been taken up again. She was arrested and reluctantly freed several months ago, but now they have her once more. Anne and I are not acquainted but I know of her, several of my closest companions are friends of hers. If Gardiner can forge a link between us, I know he will not hesitate.

Although July approaches, it is too chilly to go outside and I hug the hearth. My sister Anne slides through the door and hurries to my side. She whispers in my ear. I put down my sewing and the blood begins to pulse in my head. I get up and, taking Anne with me,

136

retire to my closet. We stand close, our voices scarcely audible even to each other.

"Sir George Blagge? Are you sure? Does the king know?"

She shrugs, her wide eyes blank with shock.

"I must tell him. I am sure he will want it stopped."

George Blagge is Henry's friend; a rotund, merry-faced fellow of extraordinary wit. He has earned himself the nickname Piggy, and Henry, no lightweight himself, loves to tease him about his girth. Sir George takes it in much better humour than his king would were the same appellation ever applied. Despite his comedic appearance, Blagge is keen for reform, but he keeps a low profile, his primary concern being loyalty to the king.

Later that day, when I am sure Henry is not too distracted, I whisper the news into his ear. At once he is on the alert.

"Piggy? In the Tower?" He searches for the truth in my eyes before fumbling for his stick and struggling to rise. "Denny," he hollers. "Fetch Gardiner: send for Wriothesley."

As his attendants come running, I melt into the shadows, unwilling to be identified as the bearer of the tidings. I sleep badly that night, afraid for Sir George, afraid that Gardiner will talk the king round and he will be led to destroy another friend.

The next day I sit bleary-eyed from lack of sleep beside Henry, and together we look across the throng of subjects. I have a headache that is impairing my vision and the rich array of velvet and feathers merges into one. I press a finger to the centre of my forehead and, closing my eyes, massage my brow. I wish myself a thousand miles away. When the babble of conversation is suddenly

137

severed, I look up from my reverie to find Henry leaning forward in his chair. He slaps his own knee in delight.

"Ah, my pig!" he cries. "I see you are safe again?"

George Blagge steps from the crowd, his red face glowing in the overheated hall. He extends a chubby leg and bows extravagantly low. "Yes, Sire. And if Your Majesty had not been better to me than your bishops, your pig would have been roasted 'ere this."

Henry throws back his head and roars with laughter, glad he has saved his friend, and glad to have thwarted Gardiner. He throws the Bishop a smirk of triumph but Gardiner keeps his eye averted, pretending indifference.

Several times of late I have heard Henry complain that Gardiner is getting above himself. I hope the king's intervention will serve as a deterrent, a warning as to the limits his victimisation can reach. It would make us all a little safer.

But I am wrong; it is as if nothing will stop this most determined bishop, not even the displeasure of the king. My friends are afraid to meet, afraid to discuss the subject closest to our hearts. When we are together we are so fearful that we speak loudly of harmless things; the flowers that are burgeoning in the garden, the litter of pups born to Catherine Willoughby's dog.

Cheekily, when times were safer, she named one of her spaniels Gardiner, and took great pleasure in exclaiming, "Gardiner, stop it at once or I shall spank you." There was a time when we'd roll with laughter whenever she did this in the bishop's presence. But, these days, she is less outspoken and merely clicks her fingers to summon her dog whenever she desires him to come to her side.

The whisper is that Anne Askew is in great danger in the Tower and likely to be executed. She has friends among my household, some of whom send her money and clothing. For her sake I am glad of this but, even though I have no part in it, I greatly fear their actions will bring trouble down upon my own head. I am certain Gardiner and Wriothesley seek to incriminate me.

I am with Henry in the solar. His leg is paining him and he has it propped upon a stool. Much to the fool's chagrin he has sent Will Somer away, and I am reading psalms from Henry's book of hours. Henry lays his head on the back of his chair and closes his eyes. I know he will soon drift off to sleep but I continue to read, for should the sound of my voice cease, his snores will stop and he will declare he was listening. But on this occasion, it is not my tiring voice that wakes him but a great kerfuffle that breaks out in the corridor.

"What the devil ...?" Henry jumps awake, blinks at me stupidly before turning in his chair. I put down the book, fearing to find an assassin or the palace guard with a warrant for my arrest. "Find out what it is," Henry orders, and, with halberds raised, his guards throw open the doors to discover the commotion.

A few moments later they reappear with Sir Anthony Knevet, the lieutenant of the Tower, held firmly between them. "Knevet!" Henry exclaims. "What is going on? Let him go!"

"Your Majesty." The guards release him. Knevet throws them a furious look and tries to snatch off his hat, but discovers he has already lost it in the scuffle. His thin hair is standing up wildly, sweat trickling down his temple. "I am sorry to disturb your majesties but I must have urgent speech with you, Sire. They tried to keep me from you..." He glares at the guard again before turning his eyes back to the king. A small crowd of courtiers have clustered about the privy chamber door. Henry waves a hand.

"Get out the rest of you. I will speak with Knevet alone."

The men shuffle from his presence, the chamber doors are sealed, and Knevet falls to his knees before us.

"I have come straight from the Tower, Your Majesty, where Gardiner, Wriothesly, and Rich are questioning the heretic, Anne Askew. They have her on the rack, Sire."

I leap to my feet, a gasp escaping before I can prevent it. Henry narrows his eyes and leans forward, his penetrating gaze making Knevet squirm.

"A woman? On the rack?"

The man stands taller. "They bade me order her strapped to it. At first, I obeyed them. I thought they merely meant to scare her a little but when they told me to stretch her, I refused. I mean, a pinch wouldn't hurt but I was not prepared to make a full turn and torture a woman. It is illegal under your law, Sire."

"I know my own law," Henry growls. He thinks for a while, his breath wheezing. "For how long did they turn the screw? Does she still breathe?"

"She was breathing when I left, Sire. I cannot vouch for it now. When I refused to give the order, Wriothesley and Rich took control of the ropes themselves."

I cannot stop tears from spilling over. Knevet glances at me before turning his eyes back to the king. "I left some time ago, came by way of the river from the Tower to here, before fighting my way through the palace to reach you. We may be too late to stop it."

Knevet and I flinch when Henry's fist thumps down hard on the arm of his chair. He lets out a roar and, almost immediately, the door opens and Denny pokes his head into the chamber. "Your Majesty?"

Henry beckons him forward and Denny inches a little nearer.

"Call a scribe to bring parchment and pen and bring me that dog, Gardiner, and his bloodsuckers. This time he has gone too far."

July 1546

In some perverse way, although poor Anne Askew is not released from the Tower, Henry thinks he has done her a service. I suppose she might see it like that. At least her present torment is eased. They throw her back into her cell, continue to question her, to try to trick her, until her guilt is confirmed and she is condemned to die.

My spies bring me news of it. I hear how Gardiner and Wriothesley crept late last night into the king's closet and were with him for hours. They emerge in the early morning, looking pleased and rubbing their hands. A short time later I hear they are forgiven, allowed the grace to continue their hunt for other heretics.

Catherine Willoughby comes to see me, her white face and anxious, fidgeting hands reveal at once that her news is not good. She breaks down as she speaks of what she has witnessed at Smithfield.

"They had clearly been tortured," she weeps. "John Lascelles could hardly stand, he and his friends were dragged to the pyre, and as for poor, dear Anne, she was so crippled from the rack that they had to carry her there on a chair."

I don't know what I can say. There is nothing I can do but I feel deep, deep shame that my husband has allowed this to happen ... "They bound her so tight to keep her upright that she cried out in pain, and when you think of the agony she must already have suffered ..."

Catherine sobs into her kerchief while I helplessly pat her shoulder. My chest feels as if a tight band is constricting it, but I do not cry. For weeks following the incident I am put off my food, I cannot swallow, cannot smile. Although I am not in any way culpable, I feel it and wish I had been bolder and stood more strongly against it.

Although these terrible things have always happened, it is never easy for me to ignore the punishments my husband inflicts upon his people. Usually I tell myself they are traitors, men who would do us harm, but this time it comes too close. Unable to do anything to prevent it, my futility as queen is suddenly, blindingly clear. I can do nothing to help my fellow believers, nothing at all.

They tell me Anne's end is quick, thanks to a friend throwing a bag of gunpowder onto the smouldering flame. I suspect that friend has links with my own circle, but I do not want to know. I shut myself away in my chamber and refuse access to anyone save my sister. If the king requests my company, my ladies are to plead I have a headache.

I cannot face him.

I cannot believe he has let this happen.

Years ago, when I was no one of any import and wed to Lord Borough, I think I may have met Anne Askew. I don't recall ever speaking to her for she was a child and beneath my notice. But my husband knew her family, and I was probably in her company once or twice. I search my memories and conjure up a small, dark child with fervent eyes and fidgety hands. Even this slight acquaintance makes her death, and the manner of her dying, somehow worse.

I know her martyrdom won't be the last.

Sleep evades me for days and I grow hollow-eyed and sallow. Henry, when I finally face him, cannot fathom the reason for it and suspects I am with child. I have to disappoint him again but he cannot be surprised; we have not managed a full relationship for a few months now.

I visit him as often as I am allowed, but sometimes his chamberer tells me the king is unwell, or resting, or busy with state affairs. On these occasions I take a walk in the palace garden, or occupy myself with my ladies, sewing or dancing. I try to avoid religious debate, although the matter is close to my heart and forever whirling about my mind. When I am allowed access to the king, I divert him with snippets of gossip, letters from his children, and praise of Prince Edward. Sometimes I read to him; sometimes we discuss theology and history. His leg has been bad of late. I hate to see him suffer and wonder if it is due to his diet and suggest he eat a little less.

"Don't be stupid, Kate," he says. "How can what I put in my mouth affect my health? I eat as well as I ever have."

I am offended at being labelled 'stupid', but I say nothing. I change the subject, turning to religion and how blessed I feel to have access to material refused to other more lowly women. Henry remains silent but he continues to stroke my fingers and, thus encouraged, I wonder, as if in passing, if it would be so harmful to allow other women to read it too. "Would it not improve their minds, Henry, drive out their ignorance, and instruct them in piety and devotion?"

He growls something under his breath and, realising he is becoming tetchy, I change the subject yet again. "Mary is sick once more, the poor thing. She is troubled monthly by her womanly state. I suppose it is a cross all women must bear ..."

In this manner I chatter on until an usher informs us that Gardiner requests an audience. I have no wish to be in his company and, as he enters, I rise to my feet, kiss the top of Henry's head and tell him I will be back later. I eye the man coldly as I sweep past without acknowledging his ironic bow.

There is still plenty of time before dusk, so I gather a few ladies and we take a stroll around the privy garden. The evening is warm; the bees are busy in the buds and the birds foraging in the undergrowth. A minstrel begins to play on the greensward, and the sound of my ladies' laughter wafts pleasantly on the breeze.

It is a short time of respite from the pressure of the court, the needs of the king, and the suspicion of my enemies. Anne and I link arms as if we are children, and she tells me the latest news of brother William's marital exploits. By the time we return to my apartments I am relaxed and happier than I've been for some time. Perhaps the bad times are passing now; maybe the worst of my fears have been of my own making.

It is late and I am just getting ready for bed when Anne hurries into my chamber. She jerks her head and, after I affirm her silent command, my attendants curtsey and leave us alone.

144

"What is it Anne?" I ask. She hurries to my side and kneels at my feet. The flames of the fire throw shadows about her face, making her gaunt and pretty in turns. For the first time I notice she has a sheet of paper crumpled in her fist.

"You are in danger," she whispers, smoothing the letter out on my red velvet kirtle. Her hands are shaking as I take it from her and scan the words of the hastily scrawled message. There are a few words only; words that immediately impress themselves like a brand against my soul. I can almost smell burning.

Your Majesty is in peril. A warrant has been issued for your arrest. Gardiner has been instructed to discover the extent of your heresy.

Alarm rings somewhere in the far reaches of my mind. I turn the paper over and back again. It is unsigned but it appears to be written by the hand of a friend.

"Where did you get this, Anne?" My voice does not shake. It does not betray the utter terror that is shrieking in my breast.

"A servant dropped it as he was passing my door, as if by chance. I think it was George Blagge's man but I cannot be certain. It was dark."

Lately a law was passed forbidding the possession of heretical books. Henry knows I have some in my possession. There is little time to do anything about that now.

I look at the note again as if the content may have altered in the short time I have looked away. The pen strokes stand out starkly against the white page.

The extent of your heresy.

My inner calm begins to slip. My hand shakes. I drop the letter, and begin to whimper. Homer and Rig look up from their basket. Anne grips my wrist.

"Don't Kate. You must be strong." Her eyes glitter intently in the firelight. "If you are to survive this you must keep a clear head. You can reason your way out of it; you are the cleverest woman I know, far cleverer than the king and all his minions."

But I cannot stop it. It is as if someone has removed a bung from a barrel. Panic surges forth in an unstoppable flow. Strength abandons me and I drop suddenly to my knees.

"I must burn this." Anne shoves the note into the fire and vigorously stirs the embers. Slowly I turn my head, watch the edges blacken and curl. The paper grows dark, the letters shrivelling like a heretic as the flames take it.

I am sobbing now.

My ladies come running. "What is it? What is it?" I hear them murmur. "What is it that ails the queen?"

They bear me to my bed chamber, strip away my gown, and pull off my cap. My hair cascades, covering my upper torso like silk against my naked skin. I shiver in the half light as they pull off my chemise and help me into my nightgown, and all the time I am wailing and sobbing like a woman run mad.

I roll into bed, bury myself in cold white sheets. Grip the pillow, twisting it in my hands. Involuntarily my knees rise to my chest as my heart fills with despair. "Oh God," I wail. "Help me, dear God."

I cannot stop myself. My prayers go on and on, my tears soaking into the bed linen. My women hover uncertainly in my chamber. As if in some half-waking dream, I am aware of the exchange of wary looks. From a distance I see myself writhing like a crazed woman. I see the door open, see my attendants fall to the ground as my husband is borne into the room. They place his chair on

146

the floor near my bed and silently everyone creeps from the chamber, leaving us alone.

Henry watches me.

I sit up, sniffing inelegantly, wiping my nose on my sleeve. I know my appearance must be offensive to every one of Henry's fancies. I risk a glance at him. He is in his night clothes, leaning forward in his seat, his brow creased with concern. I sniff again, and smothering terror, cough to clear my throat. I swallow phlegm.

"I am sorry you should find me like this, Sire," I croak. Henry shifts in his chair, fumbling for his sticks. Shakily he gains his feet and shuffles toward me. "I am sorry I have inconvenienced you," I add as he grows closer to the bed.

The mattress dips beneath his bulk. He fumbles with the torn and knotted sheet, his hand warm upon my naked knee.

"What ails you, Kate?" he asks, full of concern. "Are you sick? Have you miscarried?"

I shake my head; pull myself farther up the pillow. "No, My Lord. I – I have heard a rumour that I have displeased you." I blink through tears, trying to focus on his face. The realisation that I am on to his schemes races across his countenance. He frowns, seems confused, and runs his tongue across his front teeth.

"I am not displeased with you, Madam. Not enough to warrant this … display."

A hiccup escapes me. I try to smile, wipe away a tear. "Then I am glad, My Lord."

Henry straightens up. "If you are feeling better I will return to my night time preparations. Come to me later if you've the mind. You can read to me."

He clambers back into his chair and calls for his servants to bear him back to bed. When he has left me, my ladies fuss and fumble around, clucking like hens around a damaged chick. I slide from the mattress.

"Come," I say wearily. "Make me ready for the king. He desires my company." I take a deep breath, stand before the fire while they anoint my skin with fragrant oil, bathe my sore eyes and brush out my copper-coloured hair.

The trial is not yet over but I see a glimmer of hope. When I am ready, Lady Lane holds aloft a candle and accompanies Anne and I to the royal bedchamber. As the door is thrown open and I prepare to enter, Anne sends me a look meant to bolster my resolve. I feel like a Christian entering the lion's den.

After Henry has tried and failed to love me, I lay my head on his shoulder. I can hear his heart beating, slow and loud. He fiddles with the end of my hair, his voice rumbling in my ear. To my horror he is talking, not of love as I had expected, but of religious things. As he waits for my reply, I shift a little in the bed.

"I do not know, Henry. It is not for women such as I to know these things." My heart is beating so hard I am afraid he may hear it and guess at my duplicity.

"You knew such things the other day, when last we spoke of it. You had become quite the theologian."

I take a deep breath, turn onto my stomach and begin to twiddle his chest hair round my forefinger. I smile a slow beguiling smile in the hope that wantonness will divert him.

"Oh Henry, I was pretending knowledge so as to distract you from your pain. I would never presume to instruct you, but I confess that, in such discussions, I profit greatly from Your Majesty's learned discourse."

I can feel him relax beneath the combined comfort of my words and my busy finger. He stretches and smiles, his grip on my shoulder becoming firmer.

"I am glad to hear it, Kate. Then we are perfect friends again." His hand slides across my skin, discovers and begins to squeeze my breast. I close my eyes and hope his attention will be brief.

I wake in his bed to find a bright and cheerful sun hovering just a little above the windowsill. Beside me Henry is snoring. His mouth is open, his cheeks slack. Each breath he takes blasts foully in my face. I turn on the pillow and watch the morning for a while before easing myself from the mattress. I grope for my nightgown, slide it over my head but, as I reach the foot of the bed, he stirs and opens his eyes.

"Are you leaving me, Sweetheart? Is it time to rise?" He blinks at the bright light streaming in through the casement. "It is a lovely morning. Meet me after breakfast for a turn around the garden."

I hasten back to the bedside, plant my lips on his forehead, and take my leave of him.

Much later we are seated in the shelter of the laurels, watching Rig pestering Homer, who is trying to sleep in the sun. Rig has no desire to lay down; he darts around, every so often rushing back to his friend to snatch at his long ears. "Look Henry," I say, drawing his attention to their antics, "Rig is such a pest."

Henry chuckles and squeezes my knee and I try to savour the moment. At least I can feel a little secure again, and sure of his affection.

The sun is deceptive and a lively wind ripples the surface of the fountain, bringing with it the scent of roses

149

and honeysuckle. Anne and Lady Tyrwhit are laughing at some joke, their heads close together and their brightly coloured kirtles merging. Courtiers stroll together; some are lovers, some are friends, some are probably conspiring against their foe.

My hand is clasped in Henry's and after a while it grows hot and clammy. I long to remove it, wipe my palm on my gown, but I tolerate it. I remind myself that I am lucky to be here, back in his favour.

After his efforts last night he once more holds hopes of a son, but I am less convinced of success. I try to turn my mind from the indelicate procedure required to stir the king to perform the required act. I try to just be grateful for my freedom. I may have drawn further away from the heretical fires but recent close proximity to them has made sleeping with Henry seem not so great a penance after all.

Henry is telling me a story about a day in his youth when he jousted incognito and astounded everyone with his prowess. I smile at the picture his words evoke. Had I known him when he was in his prime I might have loved him in earnest, but the days he is talking of were before I was even born.

Henry ceases suddenly, cocks his ear, alerting me to the sound of tramping feet approaching along the gravel path.

When Wriothesley and a company of the guard emerge from an archway cut into the yew hedge I give a little scream. My security has fled. I leap to my feet, darting behind Henry's back as if he will jump up and lay about him with a sword in my defence.

"What the devil ...?" Henry lumbers to his feet, stands wavering, leaning heavily on his stick. "What is the meaning of this?"

150

I remain behind the king, his velvet bulk protecting me from the worst of the chancellor's ire.

"I have a warrant for the queen's arrest," Wriothesley booms. "And have come to take her for questioning."

Henry wavers. I increase my grip. He could change his mind. He could hand me over: discover the truth. My hand slides up the back of his doublet and comes to rest on his shoulder. To my great relief, after a few heartbeats Henry covers my hand with his.

"Get from my sight, Wriothesley. What are you about, you knave! You are a beast and a fool!" He makes to cuff the chancellor around the head, but the man ducks away, backs off.

The rumpus has drawn the attention of the courtiers and one my ladies titters behind her hand. At the sound of her amusement the party relaxes, one of the gentlemen guffaws and soon they are all laughing. Henry and I remain unsmiling as a scarlet-faced Wriothesley recovers his hat from the path, bows low before the king, and makes humble apology.

I hold my breath as he flees the scene and when he has gone, release it slowly. My women cluster about us, exclaiming and laughing in relief while my heart resumes its normal process. Gratefully, I squeeze my husband's hand and he draws me close to his shoulder, kisses the top of my head. But despite the hilarity of our courtiers the day is spoiled, the sun suddenly not so warm. I suppress a shudder.

"Come along, my love," says the king. "Accompany me back to the palace."

<u>March - November 1547 – Windsor</u>

Henry's health is deteriorating. He takes to his bed with a fever while the physicians whisper in corners, knowing that they must lance the build-up of noxious matter in his thigh. His long-suffering physician, Doctor Butts, died last year and his replacements are not so accomplished at dealing with a difficult, pain-wracked monarch.

Such times are always hard for Henry. He has suffered these bouts of extreme pain since an accident at the joust long ago. I have often heard of the fearful day when the court believed him dead. They say he lay unconscious for two hours while all around him despaired. In those days, Anne Boleyn was queen. I wonder how she felt as she waited anxiously to discover if he would live or die.

There was a time, when our marriage was young, that I longed for an end to Henry's life. This is treason I know, but in those days my mind was with Thomas and I believed our time would come. Now I am older, and more sensible, I realise that without Henry I will be a prime target for my enemies. If Henry dies and Gardiner still has the upper hand, he will pounce on me like a cat. Regent or not, he will wave his flag of religious conservatism high and do all he can to bring me down. I am powerless to stop him.

Henry knows of my fear. He cannot but be aware of Gardiner's hatred for me. "Don't worry," he says. "When the time comes we will have him. William Paget has certain papers that will see an end to our greedy bishop ..." He places his finger against the side of his nose, closes one eye and leaves it at that. I itch to discover what hold Henry has over Gardiner, but I know better than to press him. I can do nothing but trust him.

This latest bout of illness leaves the king low. He is vulnerable and he knows it. He takes more and more to his private apartments, becoming ever more unpredictable. He strikes out at those who serve him. Like a spoiled child he sets his ministers running to and fro, chasing one whim or another, and even I am not immune to his spite.

He tries his best to be kind to me but sometimes, when he is at his lowest ebb, his cruel words bite deep. In the privacy of the royal chambers he compares me with his other wives. I listen resentfully as their shadows creep from the darkened corners to listen. I can almost see them gathered about our marriage bed, gloating.

I am not as young and fair as Catherine when she was a bride, nor as witty and bright as Anne. I have failed to produce a son as Jane did. He doesn't mention Anna of Cleves or Katherine Howard, but I know of old that even I compare favourably to them. In his latter days, dead as they are, it is Anne and Jane that become my chief rivals. I try not to mind. I know that tomorrow, full of remorse, he will shower me with extravagant gifts by way of apology.

It is a difficult time. I constantly bolster myself with the knowledge that I am named regent in his will. If I can navigate myself free of Gardiner and Wriothesley, after Henry has gone I can continue to guide and mentor Edward. I am determined to ensure he rules justly, and produce both a king and a man to be proud of. The boy favours reform and perhaps, if I am cunning, between us Edward and I can bring down Gardiner and free England once and for all from the Roman church. I set my heart on turning the whole of England to the new faith, and embracing all that is new and better in the world.

But that is the future. I must think of the present too. In the meantime I must tread a careful path through Henry's mood swings, bear the stench of his rotting flesh, and try not to compare too badly against the other wives. Sometimes I ponder on how I will be regarded in years to come. Catherine of Aragon will no doubt be remembered as pious and stubborn. Anne Boleyn will probably be remembered, quite unjustly, as the whore. Jane will become the blessed mother of the heir, and Anna of Cleves the lucky one, the one who got away. And Katherine Howard, although barely more than a child, will forever be the harlot. But what will I be? Katheryn the last? The boring one?

I laugh suddenly at the absurd path my thoughts have taken, and Anne looks up from her needlework.

"What amuses you?" she smiles, resting her work on her lap.

"Oh, nothing really. I was just thinking of the future and what people might say of us when we are long dead."

Her eyebrows hurry toward her cap. "And that makes you smile? Can you not dwell on happier things?"

I turn a placid face toward her. "Like what, Anne?"

"Oh, the coming summer when there will be pageants; jousts; a summer progress. A turn about the hall with a handsome young partner ... there are lots of things to look forward to."

I look down at my linked hands. The tips of my fingers are white because they are clenched so hard. All those things she mentions have no part of my present state. I am the wife of a dying king. I have enemies all around, and as such I walk a slippery path.

But for now, I am Henry's darling. As he begins to recover, he showers me with so many jewels and furs that my coffers cannot hold them and I have to order more. I bestow gifts upon my ladies, and upon Elizabeth and Mary too.

It is while I am sorting through my belongings that I stumble upon a piece of crumpled linen. My breath falters a little as I reach out to take it from its wrapping. It smells of lavender, and long-passed days of contentment. I smooth away creases to reveal Margaret's sampler; a piece of work she toiled long and hard over. Her lack of skill was the despair of her sewing mistress. As I trace my fingertip along the line of crooked stitches, those days float back to me. I can almost hear her voice.

"Must I really begin it again, Mother? Does it really matter if I cannot sew? I am sure I must have other talents?"

I am sorry now I made her persevere. She was right. Needlecraft was a skill not hers to master. I should have let her play more while she was a child. She was always escaping her duties and running off into the woods. Had I known her life would be cut so short, I would have let her run and run. We are infants for such a short time and, looking back, it seems as if Margaret's childhood was severed. Between leaving Snape and coming to court she became a sad and burdened soul, although I never discovered why until it was too late.

"Shall I throw that away, Your Majesty?" I look up and discover Madge waiting for reply. She is carrying a pile of garments to give to the needy. She holds out her hand but I clasp the linen to my breast.

"No, no. I shall keep it in memory of someone, someone very special."

She sniffs and turns away, puts down her bundle and begins to sort another pile. Someone lets the dogs in and, seeing me kneeling on the floor, they launch themselves upon me. I am engulfed in fur and muddy paws, licking tongues warm and smelly on my cheek.

Laughing, I try to fend them off. "Down Homer; down Rig. Help!"

I am still laughing when I realise I have company and see my brother William is watching from the doorway, an eyebrow raised in surprise at my lack of poise.

Spying the newcomer, the dogs abandon me to leap and grovel at his feet. Ignoring their enthusiastic greeting, William comes forward, makes his bow and holds out his hand to help me rise. I brush my hair from my eyes and look up at him, hoping for some sign of amusement but I am disappointed. Sometime during his humiliating quest for a divorce he mislaid his sense of humour. Anne Bourchier, his wife, shocked the world when she openly took a lover, and shocked us all over again by producing a litter of bastards.

I doubt my brother will ever retrieve his smiles after the humiliation that followed. The last few years have left him stiff and humourless. But, rumour has it that since the annulment he has begun to court Elizabeth Brooke. I hope with all my heart this marriage will be a success. But his newfound respectability spurs him on in his attempt to seek political advancement, and he looks to me to provide it. These days my heart sinks a little each time he visits.

It would never do to let him know how tiresome he has become, so I usher him toward the hearth, and he takes a chair opposite mine. As we sit and converse politely, I notice how he has aged. Harsh parallel lines balance on the bridge of his nose and deep grooves of disappointment flank either side of his mouth. He is a discontented man who has no expectation of the world ever being kind.

"I hear the king is ailing again."

I incline my head. "Yes, he is a little out of sorts but should be recovered before the week is out."

He leans closer, drops his voice. "One day he will not recover, you know. Are you certain you are to be regent over Edward?"

I look away. "One should not speak of the king's demise, Brother. We should pray for his recovery."

"I do, of course, I do. We all do." He straightens up, his discomfort increasing. "All the same, it is as well to know where we stand should events go against our most earnest wishes."

I look down at my linked fingers. "When last the king and I spoke of it, then yes, he indicated I was to guide Edward in the early years of his reign."

"Good. Good." He clears his throat, licks his lips. "Boys, even princes, need a firm hand. I will be close by to assist you in this, in any way I can."

"I am sure you will."

After that I turn the conversation to other, less dangerous things. I summon Anne and she joins us, her uninhibited chatter breaching the gap between William and I. Since I married the king, he has always been far too conscious of my status for us to be easy friends. It is different with Anne. She often forgets to treat me in the manner expected and acts as she always has; she hugs me, teases me and, should I offend her, she does not hesitate to let me know of it. I find her company restful. I don't know where I would have been without her during these trying years.

Henry, enjoying a burst of sudden energy, spends the summer hunting. He cannot ride for as long or as hard as he used to, so a special ramp is constructed from which he can shoot at the passing game. I am quite certain the kills he makes are more down to the skill of his beaters than any hunting prowess on his part, but I praise him just the same. After each such foray he returns to the palace exhausted, and retires to bed shortly after dining. I think he should desist; it will not do to undermine his already failing strength but, of course, I do not tell him so. It would never do to let the king realise he is growing old.

As I had feared, a summer chill puts paid to this burst of good health and he takes to his bed again. His physicians scratch their heads and try to come up with a suitable cure but nothing seems to fully restore him. In November when he succumbs to fever once more, he takes himself to London for restorative baths that have cured him in the past.

I find myself left behind, my time very much my own and, since Gardiner is now in disgrace and not as intrusive at court as he used to be, I dare to get out my books again. In the seclusion of my privy chamber, I resume my studies.

To my delight, I discover that the men who are filling the shoes of Gardiner and his cronies are my friends and fellow reformists. It is a great relief to find the tide is turning again, and those for the new learning are taking precedence over the old.

The Duke of Norfolk and his son, Surrey, have also found Henry's disfavour and are taken prisoner. They now languish in the Tower. They are no friends of mine, but Norfolk has served Henry long and well. If Henry were feeling better, I might speak to him and beg him to show leniency, but the matter will have to wait. While he is so ill I can do nothing. In the meantime my own life takes on a strange sort of stasis where nothing happens, nothing alters, and each day is just the same.

December 1546 – Oatlands Palace

Henry, being much recovered, decides to go hunting. "Come with me, Kate," he says, much as he did when we were first wed. He clasps my hands, gives me a small encouraging shake.

"I am sorry, Henry. I would love to, truly I would, but I have the headache and need to rest quietly in my chamber until your return."

"Very well," he growls, after examining me for signs of fever. "It is well not to overdo things. I will be back in time for supper. I expect you will be better by then."

They haul him onto a horse and he rides away. I watch him go, raise a hand in case he should turn in search of me, but he does not look back. I stand and wait until his figure is no more than a bright regal spot against the otherwise dismal countryside.

"Come, Anne. I will take a bath. Summon the women. An hour or two soaking in a tub will restore my spirits and chase the megrim away."

Judging from his high spirits I expect that, after his return, I will be summoned to the royal bed. I call for milk to be added to my bath to soften and sweeten my skin. Behind a screen, a musician strums a lute. I lie back, letting the warmth seep into my bones, relax my tired muscles, and the headache begins to recede.

When all the heat has dissipated from the water I step onto warm towels, and my women begin to pat me dry. They brush the knots from my hair, smooth it to a shine before oils and perfumes are applied to my skin. My women's hands are gentle and soothing. By late afternoon I am ready. I smell delicious, my cheeks are rosy and my hair burnished to crackling gold. I send the women away and sit at the hearth to await my husband's return.

The shadows grow long, and the sun sinks into the west and I am still waiting. It is almost dark when the servant comes to draw the shutters closed.

"Shall I bring supper, Your Majesty?"

I look up from my reverie. "No, no thank you. I shall dine with the king tonight, I think."

I am swamped with a strange detachment and, closing my eyes, I drift off to sleep. It is not until well into the evening that anyone thinks to inform me that the king has been taken ill.

I stand up too quickly, making myself dizzy in my haste. I am suddenly afraid.

"What ails him? He did not fall?"

"No, no, Your Majesty. He just came over tired while he was out. He says he feels sickly. The king returned some while ago and has taken to his bed."

Still clad in my nightgown, I hurry to his bedside, and when his servants try to keep me from him, I dismiss their protests. I push open the door and enter the dark room. The shutters are closed, the fire low in the grate and the torches have been extinguished. The high bed seems as big as a battleship in a sea of blackness. I move across the floor.

Henry is sleeping, his belly jutting toward the ceiling, his nightgown white against crimson covers. For a moment I examine his sagging parchment cheeks, the droop of his mouth. Then, tentatively, I take his hand and he stirs, turns his head toward me. "Kate?"

"Are you all right, Henry? I have been so worried."

"I asked for you earlier but they said you were resting. I am glad you have come."

I wonder who told him I was resting. Why did they not deliver his message? Are they purposely trying to keep us apart? Why would they? I am paranoid. Or am I?

"How do you feel, My Lord? What is the trouble?"

He tries to laugh but it ends in a cough. "You sound like a doctor, Sweetheart."

"Well," I say primly. "Let us hope I know the cure."

His grip on my hand tightens. "Kate. You, you know I must leave you soon, don't you? I cannot stay forever. Even kings must ..." He cannot say the word and I don't want him to. Suddenly he is the most precious person in my life; the axis upon which it all turns. All the years he has kept me unwillingly at his side disappear. He has been a good husband to me and I cannot help but feel sorrow.

"Henry." I lean over the bed to stroke his brow, finding it clammy and cold. "You will not die just yet. You are strong. You just need rest. By tomorrow, or the next day, you will be up and about again and we will laugh at your fears."

He makes a noise, something between a grunt and a sigh, such as a small boy would make. I continue to stroke his hair, my other hand clasped in his.

"There will be ructions when I do go," he murmurs as sleep takes him again.

161

In the days that follow, Henry is seldom fully awake. He drops in and out of sleep like a baby. He is forced to postpone an audience with the French envoy. Denny continues to issue day-to-day matters, the stamp he uses bearing Henry's authorisation is kept busy.

I visit the king several times a day, sometimes staying for the whole afternoon although the room is noxious. His bedside is cluttered with pills and blisters, plasters and tonics, none of which seem to have much effect.

"I am in a purgatory of pain," he complains during a period of lucidity. "What have I done to deserve this?"

I refrain from reminding him of the suffering he has allowed to be inflicted on others. I hope God isn't wreaking vengeance for the innocents he has had executed, the friends he has forsaken. To me, who knows him so well, Henry is a good man who has sometimes taken the wrong path. His intentions have been good but, tormented by the need for a son, fear and paranoia took control. If ever a man needed lasting love to guide him, it is Henry. But whenever he came close to discovering love, he destroyed it. I don't believe he ever found love, not true love; not even in me.

But, just as I am despairing, the sickness eases. He spends a few days in his chair, castigating us all for our neglect in his hour of need, and accusing us of wishing for his death. A day or so later he is close to his former self and once more terrorising us all from his seat.

The court moves to Nonsuch Palace where the king takes up the reins of government again, meeting with the Scottish ambassador in the quest for peace. But, as the end of December approaches, he regresses and grows weak again. He calls me to his side and tells me he is going to Whitehall. He tries to hide his discomfort as he takes his leave of me.

"Can't I come with you, Henry? Spend Christmas together?"

"Nay Sweetheart; not this time." He squeezes my hand. "Next year though, we will make a point of being together; you, me and all the children at Greenwich. We must look forward to that."

He kisses my cheek. My throat aches. I don't believe him. I don't believe I will ever see him again. He is preparing to leave me, whether for another woman or for the next world makes no difference, but I am certain this will be our last goodbye.

January 1547 - Greenwich

It is a drear Christmas season this year. Mary spends it with me; we huddle at the hearth like two old maids and worry for the health of the king. In the end, unable to stand not knowing any longer, early in January Mary and I take the decision to move our households to Whitehall. But still they keep me from my husband.

While he is closeted away, I fear that Hertford, Dudley, and Denny are working against me. They will not want a woman in control. They proved while I was regent that taking orders from me was against their nature. I pray, both for the king's health and for my own future. I feel vulnerable and afraid, and I think Mary does too. She prays for the king in her own way, a way that is so alien to mine. But despite our differences in religion she is, as ever, a good companion and empathises with me at this difficult time.

I am never sure of Mary's real opinion of Henry. She never speaks against him and professes love for him but surely … surely she must have some resentment for the suffering he caused both her and her mother. His involvement of her in his divorce from Catherine destroyed Mary's youth; when he declared her illegitimate, it took away her chances of a dynastic marriage. I would like to strip away the bonds of propriety and ask her outright what she really thinks. Honesty would bring us closer.

Sometimes I feel like tearing off my bonnet, throwing it to the floor and crying, 'I never truly loved your father, not in a romantic way, but I will mourn him still. He was my companion and guardian and it is killing me that they keep me from him." Mary must be sharing these chaotic emotions; a mix of duty, resentment and fear.

Of course, I don't say anything of the sort. I remain outwardly calm, inwardly seething. To maintain appearances I send Edward and Elizabeth the customary New Year's gifts, a tiny depiction of Henry and I, and with it I enclose a letter with my love.

A week or so later I receive a gift in return from our future king with a message professing his love and gratitude to me, his mother. I am very touched and wipe away a tear before I tuck the precious items in my coffer.

Elizabeth sends a translation of a poem by Margaret of Angoulême, 'Le miroir de l'âme pércheresse.' Although her accompanying letter begs me to forgive the inaccuracies and mistakes, I am astounded by the fine job she has made of it. Her craving for perfection makes me smile. She is not an easy child to reach but I seem to have succeeded, as I have with all three of Henry's unhappy children.

On the twenty-first day of January, Henry Howard, the Earl of Surrey, is beheaded, his father still languishing in the Tower. It is a sad time. I remember reading his poetry, the elegant turn of phrase, the deep seated sentiment. Poor, foolish man. Henry, conscious of his failing health, is nervous for his heir. Surrey should have known he was too close to the throne for the king's peace of mind. I suppose nothing could have saved him. I make a note to write to his mother, Elizabeth, and send her my condolence.

I seem to be writing so many letters in these sad times. Daily I send word to the king, asking for news, begging to be allowed to see him, but I receive no reply. I pace the floor of my apartments, chewing my nails, furious with circumstance that places me in such a helpless position.

William calls once a week to ascertain my state and discover my news. He is still full of plans for the future and almost desires the death of the king. He rails at me, irate that I have allowed myself to become so powerless.

"You are the queen," he cries. "You have rights."

It seems that William has at last forgotten my inflated status and, piqued into anger, I reply more sharply than is my usual habit. "I am a woman, William. Queen or not, I have only as much right as a man allows. The king is in the hands of his ministers. There is nothing to be done."

"Maybe there is … maybe there is…" He narrows his eyes, staring into the flames. "Seymour is back at court."

I frown, confused for a moment, thinking he means Edward, the king's uncle. But then I realise he is speaking of Thomas.

"Thomas? Is he … back in England?"

I don't know how much William knows or what he is implying, so I wait for him to continue.

"He returned about a month ago. Has he not asked to see you?"

I shake my head very firmly. "He has not."

"Good. Good. We don't want rumours breaking out again." I can feel the blood surging in my skull as I am consumed with embarrassment, my ears begin to ring. He will try to see me, I know it, but I have no idea how I will receive him, or how I even feel about him now.

"Perhaps we can get him elected onto the new king's council. It is his right, after all, as the boy's uncle. He would support your regency, I should think, hey?"

Drawing my lips into a prim knot, I blush even hotter. "I have no idea."

"So, you've given up hope of the regency?"

"No!" I stand up, my fists clenched, my fingernails stabbing my palms. "William, please. I am about to be widowed. My head is pounding. We must let things take their course. We can take no action until then."

He stands up also. "I must go. If Seymour tries to see you, refuse him entry. Let me deal with him. You are, or will be, the dowager queen and far above the likes of him. You must avoid a scandal."

I am so tired of being told what to do but, before I can show him the rough edge of my tongue, he has gone. He leaves the door swinging open and my ladies surge into the chamber in a rainbow of coloured brocade.

27ᵗʰ January 1547

I wake suddenly in the early hours, certain that something is wrong. It is as if something has shifted, irreversibly altered, and my sense of danger increases. Sliding from the bed, I tread carefully across the floor, making as little noise as I can to avoid waking my woman. Carefully I open the shutter and the moonlight floods into the room.

The moon floats benignly in the night sky, leavening the dark, painting the slumbering, snow-laced garden a silvery blue. I shiver, hug myself, and turn away. A jug of wine stands on the night table and I fill a cup, the liquid cool from the chilly nocturnal air. As I grope my way back to bed, my woman stirs and yawns, her long bare arms pale in the moonlight.

"Are you all right, Your Majesty? Can I get you anything?"

"Not unless you can bring me peace of mind." It is a poor attempt at a joke. She stumbles from her truckle bed and helps me settle, tucking the sheets tightly around me.

"I am sure the king will recover, Your Majesty. He always has before."

She is young; so young that she has never yet been wed, let alone known the trials of widowhood or the vulnerability of being a woman alone.

Obediently, I relax on the pillow and appease her with a hollow smile. "You get some sleep," she says and, forgetting that she is here to do my bidding, I close my eyes.

Her bed creaks as she climbs back in. She turns over, thumps her pillow a few times and within moments is snoring again. Wide awake in the darkness, I listen to her laboured breathing and think of Henry's passing.

167

What will his death mean to me, and where will life take me next?

As soon as I am dressed in the morning I hurry along to Henry's apartment, but once more they halt me at the door.

"I need to see my husband," I demand with as much authority as I can muster. But I am met with a steely refusal. I press my lips together, suppressing my fury. "Then send Denny out. I will speak with him."

After being kept waiting for too long, the door opens a crack and Denny slips out. Reluctantly he pulls off his cap and makes a sketchy bow. I have always hated people who refuse to look me squarely in the eye.

"This is outrageous, Denny. I would speak to my husband. If he is likely to die then I want to say goodbye. Surely, I can just sit quietly and hold his hand?"

"He is too sick for visitors, Your Majesty. His physicians have advised against it."

We draw aside as a troop of servants appear bearing trays of food; the King's taster comes hurrying along behind.

I watch them disappear unchallenged into the chamber.

"I see he is well enough to eat, so why is he too sick to see me?"

Denny inclines his head, infuriatingly calm in the face of my simmering rage. I bury the urge to slap him.

"The king must keep his strength up. I shall send for you the moment he asks to see you."

"You will send for me the moment he wakes up."

Denny closes his eyes and bows his head in silent agreement. I swallow the snub, turn on my heel and march back to my own apartments where, safe in the company of friends, I give way to a storm of weeping.

For three days I continue in a sort of void. My household continues much as usual, but I am detached from it. I cannot join in with the dancing, nor laugh at the antics of the fools. I curl in the window seat with Homer and Rig, let my fingers travel through their warm coats and look out across the frigid garden. There is nowhere warm in the world, my very existence lacks comfort. I will find no security or safety in this world. Not without Henry.

Through green distorted glass I see the fountain where Henry and I walked so often. It is stilled now, the water frozen in a thick wave at the rim; the usually rippled surface solidified. Stopped.

Flanking the path, naked shrubs cast skeletal fingers to heaven and birds forage fruitlessly in the fallen leaves beneath the bare hedge. With a heavy sigh I turn back to my book which is open on the sill beside me, but it does not hold my interest. Nothing does.

My ladies are sorting silks on the table ready for a new project. Respecting my mood, even if they do not understand it, they keep their voices low. Rig wakes and stretches, shows me his pink tongue and sharp white teeth. He stands up, his entire body stiff, then he shakes himself, scattering hair over me, before sitting down and proceeding to lick his nethers.

Homer growls suddenly.

Footsteps, voices at the door, and Cranmer is announced. My face begins to relax into a smile as he inches toward me, but then I notice his face is white, his eyes are pink-rimmed.

"Your Majesty." He bows formally low and I know his tidings before he speaks of it.

"He is dead, isn't he? The king is dead!" My words end in a sob, born of fear and a huge sense of loss.

169

"Yes, Your Majesty. Three days hence."

Shock and anger replaces the burgeoning of my grief.

"Three days? But … but, he can't have been dead that long. He was alive when I tried to see him yesterday. Denny said he would summon me when he woke … I-I have been deceived, haven't I, Thomas? They lied to me."

The realisation of their deceit sickens me as Cranmer regretfully closes his eyes, slowly inclines his head.

"But … why?"

"The council thought it best, Your Majesty, to get things in order …"

"Council? What are you talking about? Why wasn't I summoned at once? As Edward's guardian, I am to be regent. Henry told me so."

"Alas, Your Majesty, during the last days of his life the late king made certain changes to his will. Instead of a regent or a protector, he elected a council."

So that is what they were doing. That is why they kept me from him. I look into Cranmer's eyes. They are full of regret, sorrow that he has to speak words that will injure me.

"What other changes did he make?" My lips are tight. I know the answer already; he has no need to give voice to it. I am dismissed. My regency and my stepson are stolen from me. I am powerless and, if this newly-formed council have anything to do with it, probably destitute.

16th February 1547

I am dressed in a blue velvet gown, a widow's ring is pushed onto my finger and my head is covered in a veil. It is cold; so very cold in the Queen's closet from where I observe the internment of Henry's body in St George's Chapel at Windsor, beside his third wife, Jane.

It is not easy to listen to the droning Latin rites of the old religion. It is as if Henry never questioned the old faith, never moved away from Rome and all its heresy. My heavy heart is full of anger as I hear but do not engage with the ceremony.

The people cannot see me. I am not part of the rite. It is as if I no longer exist. As Queen Jane steps from the dark to reclaim her husband, I am rejected. Yet Henry *loved* me. I eased him through his last years; distracted him from his pain, and did my best to bear his child. He would not want me to be so meanly treated.

The court has become a friendless place. Hertford's wife, Anne Stanhope, who has ever hated me, snubs me at every turn. No longer constrained to pretend to love me, she promises to be trouble in the future. Her new powers, or those of her husband who has claimed the protection of the new king, will ensure that others follow her lead. My future looks very bleak.

Henry has not left me penniless. I still have many houses and could retire from court altogether. Perhaps I will repair to Chelsea or Hanworth, and hold a small court there, inviting only those who love me. But I am still queen and will remain so until my death, if only I can persuade someone to acknowledge that fact. I begin to observe those around me and count my real friends on my fingers.

Once the service is done, with a heavy heart I take a private way back to my apartments. I am glad to reach the solitude of my own rooms. Full of sorrow and lacking any hope for a bright future, I pull off my veil and throw my prayer book on the bed.

As Anne and Dorothy help me from the heavy clothes and into a loose gown, I stand dejected. I have no idea what to do, or where life will lead me now. The women are hovering by the door. "Leave me for a while," I say. "I would like to be alone."

Anne frowns. "It isn't good for you to be on your own. Shall I sit with you? I promise not to talk."

"No. No, thank you." I try to soothe the rejection with a smile and reluctantly she backs away, follows the other women from the room and closes the door.

I sink onto the floor before the fire and click my fingers for the dogs, but they are nowhere to be seen. I suspect one of the women has taken them into the garden but even so I feel Homer and Rig have deserted me too.

With a ragged sigh, I rest my cheek on my palm and gaze into the fire. There are dragons and sprites in the flames. It is another world; a world I visited as a child. A realm without rules, or kings, or queens.

A rush of wind as the door opens and swiftly closes again, a footstep sounds behind me. I raise my head.

"Kate?"

I scramble to my feet and stand in disbelief that he has been so bold as to come. My voice is unfriendly and defensive.

"How did you get in here?"

"Anne let me in."

He hesitates, uncertain of his welcome. We regard each other for a long moment, both unsure of what this meeting means. Uncertainty does not sit well on him but on the outside at least, he has not altered. He is still tall and strong, still handsome. As he draws nearer I catch the remembered fragrance, and the years tumble away, as if they have never been.

I try to fight it but grief and loneliness make me weak. I should send him away at once, call the guard and have him thrown from my presence. But he is a friend, in a friendless world. I fumble to remind myself I am queen and he is far beneath me.

"I gave orders I was not to be disturbed…"

"Perhaps your sister knows you better than you know yourself."

At the glimmer of his old bravado, I step away, increasing the gap between us, and turn toward the fire. But he catches my wrist, takes my hand to his mouth and kisses my fingers … and at his touch my toes curl.

Part Three
The Lord High Admiral

<u>February 1547</u>

Kate hasn't changed. She is still the beautiful, complex, contradictory woman I remember. When she married the king, I was jealous and angry. I left the court and sought solace with other women, more women than I can count. I have barely seen her since. I thought I had forgotten her but, after an encounter with her brother William, something drew me back.

I don't think it is love; I am not given to sentiment. It is more a case of finishing what was begun all those years ago. I have never forgotten that hour in her bed. She was a widow when I took her for the first time; she is a widow now, and close to the young king. If I can possess the queen, I will stand a better chance of gaining control of the boy.

When I steal into her apartment, she stands like a statue and allows me to kiss her fingers in a gentlemanly salute. Even when I linger and let my tongue play upon her wrist, she does not move. I glance up at her face. She shows no emotion but a small vein is throbbing in her temple. I can almost hear her heart beating.

My hand slides about her waist and still she does not speak, does not move. I inch closer. Our breath entwines. She tilts back her head and slowly, and softly, I kiss her lips. Katheryn is still as sweet as strawberries.

One kiss is all it takes. Starved of my touch for so long, she clings to me like a limpet. I drag the stupid cap from her head and her hair envelopes us. It swamps us like a bag of red snakes, tangling beneath my arms, caught between our frantic, searching mouths. Impatiently, roughly, I drop her to her feet again, bunch her wild golden mane into a ball and thrust it behind her. Clamping a palm either side of her face I look at her, and she looks back, contemplating sin. She breathes short and fast, as if she has been running. Her eyes are glittering, her teeth glimmering white against kiss-reddened lips.

Irresistible.

Taking her pert little chin between finger and thumb, I push back her head and seek with my tongue the ticklish place between her neck and shoulder. She squirms against me. "Thomas!"

It is not really a protest. I do not stop. Her body is flat against mine; I trace every curve and contour, feel her heart hammering against my palm. Her body is tight and firm, like a virgin's and I cannot fight such charms. Hell, why should I fight it? She is almost begging.

Without a word I carry her to the bed as I have done once before. She scrambles back toward the pillow, a wanton thing with snarled hair and sparkling eyes. With one hand I wrench open her gown and, still fully clothed, cast myself upon her.

***

It is late when I finally buckle my sword belt and fumble for my cloak. Kate is huddled in the bed, weeping. I can't cope with female tears so, pretending not to notice them, I do not remark on it. I kiss the top of her head. "I will come again soon, sweetheart."

176

She cries harder. With an impatient sigh I quit the room. Anne Herbert is hovering close to the door, preventing the entry of Kate's companions. I jerk my head and, recognising my silent communication, she scratches on the door and disappears into her sister's chamber.

I do not leave at once but tarry a while to pass the time with Kate's attendants. They vary in age from twelve to forty and in each one there is something intriguing, something worth pursuing. All women are fascinating; a challenge, whether they know it or not.

But Kate, my Kate, has something they lack and I haven't visited her today just to bed her. Until I saw her I wasn't even aware I still wanted her. I came to talk to her about my nephew, Edward; about the regency. I want to discover a way for us both to get our feet beneath the council table. It was business but, as I take my leave of her women and quit her queen's apartments, I realise I have quite forgotten to raise the matter. I will have to come again.

They have closed ranks against us, ousting Kate from the regency, and tried to appease me with a barony and a seat on the privy-council. I am appointed Lord Admiral as well, but that is paltry next to my brother's self-aggrandisement. He has dubbed himself Duke of Somerset and, even worse, paid off the council to elect him as Protector to the king. My brother now has total power over our nephew, leaving me the scraps. This is not what our sister Jane gave up her life for. The king is my nephew too and as such should be a benefit to both his uncles.

Over the next few weeks I give the matter much thought, and decide it might be safer to hedge my bets. It is imperative that I remain close to the king; he must think well of me. As well as wooing Kate, of whom young Edward is very fond, I set my cap at his sisters too.

I have known Elizabeth since she was a sprat. Indeed, she is still but a girl and yet to blossom into the beauty that her mother was. She has already shown herself favourable to my certain brand of charm, and I look forward to the challenge. When she is ripe for it, perhaps I shall offer her my protection and my love, and take some joy in it. Her sister Mary however is a different kettle of fish.

Already past thirty, she is sallow-skinned and as pious as her mother was. She will, I am sure, prove a harder nut to crack. I rub my fingers through my beard and give the matter my deepest consideration.

As the elder sister, Mary is Edward's heir. Should anything happen to the king (God forbid, but children often die), Mary would be my safest bet. Married to the queen, I would be as good as king. I sit back and imagine it, picture the power. A smile stretches across my face at the thought of putting my brother's long ugly nose out of joint.

But I cannot admire Mary; she does not share her sister's promise and holds no charm for me. It is her sister I have a fancy for. It is a great shame that Elizabeth was not born first. Bedding the red-haired shoot of Anne Boleyn would be sport indeed. I can woo the plain, prim Mary who is closer to the throne, or her pretty sister who is unlikely to ever wield any real power. My choice is not an easy one and in the end I write to them both, professing to each my devotion and support.

A message arrives from Kate and I drop everything and hurry to her house at Chelsea where she continues to mourn the loss of her husband. I leave my horse on the small track that flanks the garden wall and come to her secretly.

She said she would wait by the fountain in the garden, and as I approach, I find her leaning over the pool. She is tracing circles on the surface of the water with her finger and the ends of her veil are in danger of a wetting. She makes a sad but pretty picture in her widow's weeds and the dogs snuffling in the grass at her feet.

After a quick glance about the garden to ensure we are alone, I quicken my pace. One of the hounds wags its tail but the other growls, making Katheryn look up. By the time I reach her side she is waiting, standing stiff and upright, her head level with my chin. "Thomas," she whispers as I make my elegant bow.

I take her fingers, draw off her glove and my lips find her skin. Her face is flushed. She takes back her hand. "I hope you are well," she says as we begin to stroll.

Realising that the visit is not immediately to be the illicit romp I had hoped for, I take my lead from her and begin to regale her with news from court. But despite my best efforts she remains listless and sad. At the end of the garden where the path forks, we hesitate, deciding whether to turn left toward the rose gardens, or right toward the wood. I choose the latter and she follows meekly.

We pass beneath the skeletal canopy and walk for a while in dappled shade; as it grows darker she shudders a little and gallantly I offer her my cloak. My fingers brush her cheek as I position it around her shoulders but she draws away, follows the path that leads deeper into the covert. My spirits rise a little.

"Thomas, I have heard from the king," she says. "He writes very affectionately. He says he is well and assures

179

me he is keeping up with his studies. He says he means to be a wise ruler. I am pleased he continues to address me as 'Mother.' Look." She offers me the letter she has drawn from her sleeve.

"Hmmm." I hand it back non-committal, hoping she will continue to chat so I can just enjoy looking at her. A tree has fallen across the path, I extend my hand to help her over it but, once safely on the other side, she releases my fingers at the first opportunity.

"I am glad Elizabeth is with me now. She is quiet about Henry's death, but poor Mary is the opposite. She is really suffering and seems to have taken it very badly. I believe she regrets all those years that she defied him, as if she feels she let him down in some way. I've tried to bolster her by praising the loyalty she showed her mother but well, you know Mary. She doesn't feel things lightly."

"No. I imagine she would be loud in her grief." The path begins to run down the hill, a trickle of rain water in the centre, the rising aroma of damp decay. The sound of the stream clattering over small rocks and stones draws us forward. We pause on the bank where a mass of celandine forms a carpet dotted by a few lingering snowdrops and clumps of pale primroses. The scene captures her attention.

"So pretty," she murmurs. I glance back up the hill, the way we have come. Apart from birdsong the woodland is silent and, unable to help myself, I grab for her hand.

"Not as pretty as you, my Kate."

She stops, and looks down at our joined fingers.

"We can't keep doing this, Thomas. What if I should get with child?"

"You never did before." I am kissing each cold finger in turn; they quiver beneath my lips.

"Fortunately no, I didn't. But if I had done I at least had a husband to conceal our sin."

"Sin? Is that how you see it? I thought you loved me."

She snatches away her hand. "That is beside the point, Thomas. What we have done is wrong outside of wedlock. The king is not yet cold in his grave, and … and since you've not been forthcoming with a proposal, we must stop; before it is too late."

She is angry, the blood hot in her cheeks, her eyes glinting dangerously. I grope for her hand, try to placate her but she slaps it away. "I am serious, Tom. I didn't ask you to come here for that."

I laugh cruelly, as my anger rises to match hers. "So what do you want? You asked me to come, lured me into the wood and then once I try to take what is clearly on offer, you push me away. You are a tease, Madam."

She turns coldly away, refusing to rise to my bait. I have the sudden urge to argue with her, to get her to slap me again, wrestle her to the ground and muddy her carefully applied majesty. Having sampled the tart sweetness of her body, I am loath to sever our connection.

"Come," I back down, smother my annoyance and try to placate her by reaching for her hand again. She jerks it away, spins around to face me and for the first time I notice the misery on her pinched features.

She is cold and sad, and I am adding to her desolation. "Kate." Searching for a way to bring her round, I stand up, grasp her shoulders and force her to look up at me. "Of course we shall be wed. I didn't think I had to ask. We've been betrothed for years, haven't we?"

It is as if I have been bewitched. *Whatever possessed me to say that?* But I cannot retract it. Her pink and white face opens into a smile that would melt any heart.

She falls into my arms.

"Oh Thomas," she squeals, smothering my beard in tiny kisses. "I am so happy, so happy." I tolerate the tickling caresses for a few moments and then, gripping her head in my hands, I hold her still so I can kiss her properly.

Her mouth opens beneath mine, her tongue tentatively probing, and my heated response knocks her hood askew. Lust stabs through my body, making me groan aloud, and she whimpers in reply. Feverishly, I begin to wrench up her skirts, cursing the amount of winter petticoats she is wearing. Her thick woollen stockings cling maddeningly to my rough fingertips but I explore further until mercifully, I discover flesh; hot, silk-smooth flesh.

Kate hangs limply in my arms; her eyes close as I begin to love her, and she grows moist at my touch. Sinking to my knees I lay her down among the celandine, trailing her russet hair in the shining yellow flowers.

She lays at my feet, her long lean legs part and I throw off my sword, fumble with the lacing of my codpiece. Kate reaches for me and I sink into her embrace; plunge into the wonder of her warm arms.

***

It is as well that Elizabeth rejects my proposal for I am now well and truly betrothed to Kate. It is our secret as yet, for the council will want to postpone any marriage

182

until they ascertain she is not carrying the late king's child.

She has told me of her life with Henry, the indignities of his bed, and I am confident that, if anyone's seed has taken root in her, it is mine. Since the day in the woods I cannot keep away, and have visited her nightly. I ride with great stealth to Chelsea at dusk and leave her before dawn. Sleep is a thing of the past and I am as weary from loving her as I have ever been. We both grow heavy-eyed from lack of rest. Her ladies begin to count their fingers, working out how long it is since she last bled.

For all her prim looks, Kate has the instincts of a slut. She found it hard to be tied for so long to an impotent man, and now she gives her desires full rein. It is a joy for me to discover that she revels in bed-sport as much as I. Often, she takes the lead and her vigorous libido delights me. I am reconciled to the idea of marriage now. If I have to marry, then it is as well to wed a woman who is buxom in bed.

But for now we must exercise caution, and Kate insists we keep our correspondence to a minimum. "I will send to you once every fourteen days she says. "And no more." But no sooner has she made this rule than she breaks it by sending word to me. My eyes quickly scan the contents of her letter. Anne and William Herbert are in residence at Chelsea and she urges me to come to her after midnight, and be gone again by dawn.

That night, as I ride the shadowy path to my sweetheart's arms, I encounter a fellow on the road. At first I do not know him. He raises his cap, whistling as he passes by without a word but, as I grow closer to Chelsea, I realise he is the manservant of William Parr, Kate's brother. If he recognised me he will not bite his tongue. I know we cannot keep our secret long, and if we are discovered they will separate us and do all they can to prevent our union. I decide the marriage must take place without delay, although I keep my reasons from her.

"We must not tarry any longer, Kate. I cannot wait. Let us wed in secret. They will be powerless against us then. I want you in my bed, and I want the world to know you as my wife."

She hums and haws for so long that I have to increase my persuasion. "We can retire to my castle at Sudeley and you can help me with the improvements I have planned. You will love it there; it is by far the prettiest of all my properties. Elizabeth can come with us, and my ward little Jane Grey also."

"We would face so much trouble. We'll likely be banished from court."

"Only for a while. They'll soon forgive us. I am Edward's uncle; you are his mother. I am his friend; his ally. I furnish him with pocket money and ensure he is not shamed by poverty when my brother keeps him short of coin. He owes me a little leniency."

I lie back on her pillow, put my arms behind my head and admire the way the dawning day is tinting her breasts with a rosy hue. Her nipples are proud in the chill of the morning. I reach for her again.

She pulls a worried face and I soothe it with kisses, suck her lower lip as I hitch my knee across her thighs and slide my right hand up her ribs toward her breast. We are both sore from loving but I can't help but take her once more before I have to ride away.

June 1547

Barely two weeks after our closeted marriage Katheryn begins to worry. "You must visit the king," she says, "get him on our side. If he condones our union, then so will everyone else." She frets about the furtive way our vows were exchanged, and fears that we have affronted God, that we have risked our standing at court.

"Don't worry," I assure her as I watch her gather up her rich red hair and tuck it back beneath her cap. She turns to me, grips my fingers, no more the feverish lover, she is now a strait-laced, rebuking wife.

"I will worry, Thomas. If I am already carrying your child the world must know that it is your child, begat in wedlock, and not Henry's. Speak to the king. He loves us both, and perhaps he will be forgiving. The sooner done the better."

She drops my hand, stands up and smoothes her skirts. As she walks away, I smother a sigh. There is nothing I hate more than being instructed by a woman.

In truth I am uneasy. The news that I have wed the queen so soon into her widowhood will not sit well with either the king or his council. My brother will be livid. I scratch my beard as I consider how to approach them. In the end I write to Mary. If I can get her on our side, she could intervene on our behalf; her approval may ease the precarious path that lies ahead.

I am not a man given to writing letters with ease but as evening stretches across the gardens, I take up my pen. The first two attempts end up in the fire. I can think of no easy way to confess to a marriage that, to some, is next to treason. I am forced to employ a little cunning and pretend to be seeking her support for a proposed marriage rather than a union that is already signed and sealed.

Katheryn, when she hears of my deception is displeased, and her distress increases when we receive Mary's prompt reply.

...My Lord, in this case I trust your wisdom doth consider that if it were for my nearest kinsman and dearest friend ..., of all other creatures in the world, it standeth least with my poor honour to be a meddler in this matter, considering whose wife her grace was of late and besides that if she be minded to grant you suit, my letters shall do you but small pleasure. On the other side, if the remembrance of the King's Majesty my father (whose soul God pardon) will not suffer her to grant your suit, I am nothing able to persuade her to forget the loss of him ...wherefore I shall most earnestly require you (the premises considered) to think none unkindness in me, though I refuse to be a meddler in anyways in this matter, assuring that (wooing matters set apart, wherein I being a maid am nothing cunning) if otherwise it shall lie in my little power to do you pleasure, I shall be as glad to do it as you require it, both for his blood's sake that you be of, and also for the gentleness which I have always found in you

Your assured friend to my power,
Marye

Katheryn pales when she reads it, the letter flutters to the floor. "I was so sure of her support in this ..." Her voice trails away, her head droops. "Yet she shames me for unseemly haste."

"Mary knows nothing of love, Kate. She is a maid and thinks passions can be governed, but a love like ours cannot be contained. It cannot be ruled."

She looks up, tries to smile through her tears, and I drag out my kerchief and dab her cheeks dry. Kate sniffs a little and looks at the letter again.

"I am sorry to have wounded her. She has been my friend since ... Lord, I don't know, forever. It hurts that she thinks ill of me, and we were less than truthful. If Mary discovers we are wed already, I am not sure she will ever forgive me."

"Then we must ensure she does not discover it."

Kate looks at me, her eyes wide with disapproval. "That isn't the answer Thomas. Deception is wrong, especially if it is for self-preservation. I am not sure I can forgive myself, let alone expect others to."

She may be overflowing with guilt, but such pious philosophy confounds me. A fellow must do what a fellow can to keep himself from harm's way. A few lapses of truth never hurt anyone. Kate looks like a smacked puppy, she dabs her eyes again.

"Don't worry." I draw her close, kiss the top of her head, and inhale the lavender and juniper of her laundered cap. My fingers are on her neck, she lifts a shoulder and I trace the line of her collarbone, feel her skin thrill at my touch. She turns, without prompting, into my arms, lifts her face so I can kiss away her sorrows, her uncertainties and doubts.

Afterwards I help Kate dress, lacing the back of her gown crookedly, her stockings wrinkled about her ankles. She laughs up at me through her dishevelled hair. "I will do it, Thomas. Your skills as a lady's maid are sadly lacking."

I am glad to be freed from the task, since my pleasure lies in the disrobing rather than the redressing. Pulling on my doublet I move to the open window, look out across the garden. "Perhaps I should see the king after all and put my trust in him."

She straightens up, pushes her skirts down to cover her limbs. "Perhaps you should. I can see no path but an honest one."

"It is a little late for that," I quip as I blow her a kiss and slip from her chamber.

The court is crowded. People from far and wide have come to seek an audience with the new king. Those who had Henry's good will come to ensure it continues with his son, and those who had fallen from the old king's favour come to redeem themselves with the new.

The outer chamber is crowded. I hold a pomander to my nose and push through the throng, looking for friends. Allies are few and far between since my brother, Dudley and their ilk closed ranks against me. The new religion binds them and, although Kate is hot for Protestantism, all religion leaves me cold. I pray if and when I have to, but God rarely intrudes into my personal life. Neither for the new church nor the old, I am in solitary limbo, alone in a world of heaving piety.

A hand falls lightly on my arm and I turn to greet Lucy Somerset and Katheryn's stepson, John, now Baron Latimer, back from the wars. I bow stiffly, reflecting that, although he does not yet know it, he is now my kin in the eyes of the law. John is a rogue and a villain but I greet him cordially before spending a pleasurable moment tasting the sweetness of his wife's lips. She murmurs something and as I lean closer to hear her words, I notice how faded she has become. "I have been so long from court, Sir Thomas; it is good to see a familiar face."

"It is ever a joy to see yours," I reply, kissing her again, although I am itching to leave her company.

"I miss court so much and I miss the queen too. I was loath not to go with her to Chelsea and have no ambition to join the household of the Lady Protector, even if I was asked. Tell me, have you seen the queen, Sir Thomas? Do you know how she is finding widowhood?"

While I pretend to scan the room I watch her from the corner of my eye, searching her words for an ulterior motive.

"No, not recently," I lie. "Please excuse me; I have an audience with the king. I must not keep him waiting."

I kiss her wrist, bow frostily to Latimer and melt into the crowd. The first person I bump into is John Fowler, a friend of mine from the privy chamber.

"John!" Genuinely pleased, I slap him familiarly on the shoulder. "It is good to see you."

His beam is as wide as my own. "Where have you been hiding?" he asks. "Breaking the heart of some wench, I'll warrant."

I pretend to be offended for a moment but I cannot maintain it and we break into laughter. When we've both sobered, I look about the hall, hear the clambering noise, high pitched laughter, and inhale the overpowering odour of too many close pressed bodies. "Have you seen the king today? How is the boy enjoying being lord over all of us?"

"His majesty is well. Still studying hard, doing his best to outwit his uncle, Somerset."

"Ha! A monkey could outwit my brother." We both laugh again. John raises his cup and we fall silent while he drinks. "I wonder if the king ever wonders why I have never married."

Fowler lowers his cup again. "Married, Seymour? Why should he wonder such a thing?"

I shrug and try to look innocent. "They will be urging the boy to think of a match for himself soon, I daresay. The council will lose no time trying to marry him off, poor fellow. They'll expect him to produce an heir before his balls have dropped. I pray you, the next time you see him, ask his grace whom he would choose to be my wife."

John Fowler bows, his mouth twitching in amusement. "What is up your sleeve, Tom? Have you been hooked? I never thought I'd live to see the day."

"Not hooked, John. Just curious, shall we say."

"That's what killed the cat you know, Tom. I'd tread warily if you don't want to be caught."

We part on laughing terms after agreeing to meet in a few days.

But my scheme does not go to plan. Instead of Katheryn, as I had hoped, Edward suggests I marry Anna of Cleves, or Princess Mary. My hopes sink as I cast about for a way of making my marriage to Kate seem like it was the king's idea all along.

"Damn me, Fowler. Anna of Cleves? I don't think so, and as for the princess, she would have none of me, I know that. What about the queen? Katheryn and I have always rubbed along nicely. Ask his majesty if he would vouch for me if I pressed my suit with her."

Fowler rubs his eyebrow with an ink-stained forefinger and looks at me quizzically.

"Am I missing something, Tom? There were rumours she was sweet on you years ago but I dismissed all that as back stairs gossip. You've not been dallying with the queen all along have you?"

This time there is no need to pretend shock. "Do you take me for an idiot? I value my head and would never trifle with a queen." As he grunts approval I add wickedly, "not so long as the king was still breathing."

As luck would have it I am granted an audience with the king before Fowler has time to press my suit further. I enter the royal apartments well-armed with gifts and bribes for my nephew.

"Uncle!" The boy looks up from his book, dismisses his companions with a jerk of his chin, and climbs from the window seat. "It is good to see you, sir. I am kept very busy by the Protector and have little time for good company."

I can sense no resentment in his words so say nothing in disparagement of my brother.

"I have brought you presents," I announce as I delve into my bag. First I toss him a bag of coin. "This should keep you from the embarrassment of an empty purse for a while." When he feels the weight of coin his coolness melts away. He gets up and comes closer, leaning over my shoulder as I bring forth some books, suggested by Katheryn; dry, dusty stuff about religion and philosophy. He turns the pages carefully, looks up with a wide smile that reminds me fleetingly of his mother. With a surge of guilt I realise I seldom think of Jane except in terms of the son she has left behind. The quietly pious girl that grew up in the midst of our noisy family at Wulfhall is almost forgotten.

With a surge of irritation I realise I should look after Edward better. The boy is too pale, too bruised beneath the eye. He should read less and be outside more. My brother is too careful of him. A boy needs fresh air and hunting; his life shouldn't be all study and inactivity. If we are not careful we will create a milksop king. "We should go hunting, Your Majesty, just you and I and a few of your retainers."

"Uncle Somerset would never allow it. He keeps me closeted, safe from assassins, but I'd like to, if we could arrange it."

"You are the king." Without waiting or asking for permission I sit beside him and crane over his shoulder at the picture he is studying. It is an image of the flayed man; a grisly thing for a boy to ponder. "You should instruct your council, not the other way round."

He says nothing but his sigh is lofty. I sit up straighter, hand him a packet of sweetmeats. "I have something else for you. Shall I call my man to bring it in?"

In an instant he forgets he is king and becomes a boy again. "Oh yes; what is it, Uncle?"

His cheek bulges with a sugared comfit, his eyes alight with speculation. I clap my hands and the doors open to admit my man, who has a monkey clinging to his head. Edward's face opens in surprise, his high pitched laughter carefree, as it should be. "Is that it? Is the beast for me?"

"It is, Your Majesty, but be wary; his teeth are sharp, as my man will no doubt attest."

Edward jumps from his seat and approaches the monkey with his hand outstretched, but the creature takes one look at the king and leaps from the fellow's shoulder to swing along the priceless wall hangings.

"Ha, ha, look at him! He is like a little devil. Can you get him down, Uncle Tom?"

It is good to be called 'Uncle Tom' again but even I cannot tempt a monkey to sit upon a king if he does not have the mind for it. We spend an hour in pursuit until I am weary, and Edward is growing disillusioned.

"Your Majesty, if we ignore the beast and pretend we do not care for him, he may grow curious and come to us, especially if we eat from your royal fruit bowl. I am told monkeys have a special love of fruit."

With one eye straying constantly toward his errant pet, Edward chatters on about his lessons, the injustices of being a king who is yet denied command. He pops half a pear in his mouth and when he falls silent, I put my fate in his hands.

"Your Majesty, I have a mind to marry."

The king swallows, coughs and wipes his fingers on his velvet sleeve.

"Do you? Who, Tom? Is it one of my sisters?"

"Nay. Mary will have none of me and Elizabeth is too young as yet."

"I can order one of them to wed you. Do you want me to do so? Which one do you want?"

"Your Majesty, I'd prefer a willing bride and there is such a lady who would, I think, be pleased to have me if she had your blessing."

He stops eating, licks pear juice from his fingers. "Who is the lady?"

Behind him I notice his new pet inching down the curtains but having no wish to distract him from the conversation, I say nothing.

"Katheryn, your stepmother. It would bring you and I even closer, Your Majesty. Instead of merely uncle, I would become a sort of father. You'd like that, wouldn't you?"

Edward's eyes narrow. It is not a sign of displeasure but rather an indication of his thought process. "You want to wed my mother? And she welcomes this?"

"Oh, I have not been so indelicate as to approach the lady, but I do have hopes that, with your blessing, she would find the idea agreeable."

193

He sits up, wipes fruit juice on his velvet doublet and claps his hands. "Then my blessing you shall have, Uncle Tom. I can think of no lady I love and respect more, and there is no fellow I prefer either, unless it is Barnaby Fitzpatrick, but my whipping boy can never be the bed mate of my mother. I shall inform her of my wishes immediately."

An hour or so later when I bow from his presence, he is feeding the monkey, whom he has named Diablo, on pieces of fig. As the door closes softly I cannot but hope that the gift of the beast will stand me in good stead with the king, and find no favour with my brother and his termagant of a wife.

By July, the news of our marriage is out. The protector and his wife are furious. Princess Mary declares her relationship with Kate is ruined, but Elizabeth, although wary at first, accepts it quite readily.

At last, six months after the death of the old king, Kate and I can relax and live openly as man and wife. But the respect my wife once took for granted as former queen is now retracted. Anne Stanhope, my brother's wife, refuses to pay the deference due to her. "She is not the queen. Why should I carry the train of the wife of my husband's younger brother? And if Master Admiral can teach his wife no better manners, I am she that will."

Anne, as wife of the protector, now demands to be the first lady in the land and although there are those who yield to her wishes, she wins herself few friends. I for one lay awake at night and dream of beating her with sticks.

I take it all in my stride until the day she physically pushes Kate aside and enters the room before her. My lovely Kate is humiliated and reduced to tears. She quits the court at once and scurries home to Chelsea, declaring she will not leave again. She declares she will remain at Chelsea where she is loved and respected by her own household.

Elizabeth and Jane Grey, who has come to live with us, try to comfort her. Jane fetches her shawl and calls for a warming drink while Elizabeth strokes her stepmother's hand with long white fingers.

Kate turns a reddened face to me and demands that I do something. This is the sort of thing I have dreaded. I have avoided marriage for just these reasons; bickering women and obsolete traditions. I think longingly of a heaving deck, the empty horizon stretching endless before me. In the end, to stem her weeping, I send the girls about their business and take Kate to bed.

Although it is not much past noon it is the only way I can think of to staunch her tears, but for the first time she is limp and unresponsive. She lies beneath me like a corpse until I am forced to acknowledge that if I want my wanton wife back I will have to stand up for her rights. I climb from her bed and prepare to journey to the palace and confront my brother.

"And I want my jewels back too," Katheryn insists as I ride away. "My wedding ring and my gold cross, and pearl pendants; they are mine, willed to me by my mother. They are not the property of the crown."

I promise to do what I can and with a heavy heart head toward court and the unfriendly company of the Somersets.

Brother Edward does not smile when he looks up from the parchment, but he puts down his pen and presses the tips of his fingers together as if he is containing his patience. "Thomas," he says by way of chilly greeting.

I am always uneasy with him. Not afraid, but wary of my contempt over-spilling. With an assumed bravado I saunter to the desk and slump in the proffered seat, take off my hat and ruffle my hair which is sweaty from the ride. "You are well?" he asks, in just the sort of voice to convince me he has no care for the answer.

"Well in health if not in spirit."

In the maddening way that is peculiarly his own, he closes his eyes slowly. I feel my jaw tighten in response. All my life he has shown me this barely concealed resentment; intolerant of the fact that I am not cast in the same mould as he. Where he is all books and cunning, I am for hunting and action. "And you?"

"I am very well," he says brightly, signalling his man to bring refreshment. "As is my wife. Thank you for asking."

Sarcasm now, as well as contempt. I balance my ankle on my knee, lean back in my chair and drain the cup. The wine is good but not the finest. For all his ostentation, he still keeps to his miserly ways. "I did not notice an enquiry after the health of my wife, either."

"Ah, yes, your *wife*." He makes the word an insult, slurring the word until it sounds like 'whore.' "How is she?"

"Not well at all, since you ask. She has been treated ill by those close to you, as well you know."

He raises his eyebrows, tries to look surprised. Once I would have punched him for such a smirk. I remember the boyhood joy of besting him in a scuffle. Recall him running to our nurse with his nose dripping scarlet juice down the front of his best doublet. I'll bet he still isn't man enough to beat his little brother in a fair fight – although the trick of getting him to play fair has ever been the greatest challenge.

196

"She wants her jewels, Edward, as is her right."

Cold grey eyes rake down my body, taking in the cut of my doublet, the fine knit of my hose and, I hope, the negligent elegance with which I carry them. I may not always behave like a gentleman, but at all times I contrive to look like one. Edward shifts in his seat a little.

"The jewels are the property of the crown, as you both know."

I lean forward, narrow my eye, unable to disguise my contempt, and growl at him. "Not all the jewels my wife held in safekeeping at the Tower belong to the crown. There are pendants and a jewelled cross that was bequeathed to Kate by her mother. It is her property and I demand that it is returned."

"Demand, Thomas? Of whom do you demand it? The king? One does not demand things from a king; one begs and waits for favours."

I leap to my feet, my chair skidding backward, the legs pointing skyward. "Unless, of course, one has usurped the ruling of the king, and stolen the position as royal advisor. I will go to Edward myself. He will not see her goods taken by the likes of you. What do you mean to do with them? Drape them round the fat neck of your own ugly wife?"

"I have had enough of this."

He is on his feet, his weight on his knuckles pressed hard on the desk. We stand eye to eye, our noses point to point, snarling like dogs ready to pounce, to fight again. I can almost smell the victory. Every inch of my body longs for it. My knuckles twitch as I glare into his bloodshot eyes daring him to make the first move.

When he backs down and looks away, my heart sinks. My dagger will not be finding a resting place in his ribs today. "Get out!" he snarls. "Get out before I have you thrown out."

The sound of our raised voices alerts the guard, and the door is thrust open. Edward raises a hand. "It is all right. My brother is just leaving."

I whirl around, storm across the room and kick his dog as it slinks in through the open door. As I hurry through the ranks of scowling yeomen and along the corridor, I can hear the mutt continuing to yelp as pathetically as its master.

I ride back to Chelsea where Kate is awaiting news. Her disappointment when I confess to having failed is great and I swear to her that, if it is the last thing I ever do, I will get those jewels back for her. God curse me if I don't.

September 1547 - Chelsea

I sit at the head and look along the table at my collection of royal women; a queen, a princess, and a cousin of a king. I should be content, but my brother and his monstrous wife continue to sprinkle flies into my ointment. From time to time Katheryn looks up from her plate to smile at me. I wink at her and as I do so I notice Elizabeth watching me from the corner of her eye. I flick a grape across the board and it lands with a plop in Elizabeth's soup.

"My Lord Admiral," she exclaims as she fishes it out. "I believe you have lost something." She flicks it back with perfect aim into my own bowl, splashing my doublet. I leap back, dabbing at the cloth with my napkin.

"You minx," I accuse her hotly, but she merely blinks and smiles a slow, maddening smile. Jane looks on, her eye darting from me to Katheryn, unsure if she should approve of our antics or be affronted. Seeing Kate's merry look she relaxes a little, and her mouth softens. Jane has not known high spirits at home; from what I gather her upbringing has been all prayer and piety. It is different here. Beside her Elizabeth is mischief, although where she learned to play such games I do not know. She leans back in her chair and looks at me sideways through her sandy lashes.

"I think, My Lord Admiral, you should not engage in a war you cannot win." Elizabeth pulls her bread apart and my eyes are transfixed by her long white fingers. She has just turned fourteen and although only a girl, her wit is as sharp as a knife. Sometimes I am at a loss as how to answer. It is not just her words but the manner in which they are spoken.

Our eyes lock for a few seconds until hers crinkle at the edges, softening the arch remark, and I am reminded of her mother and the way she could play a man on her hook.

Like a fish, I wriggle a little and turn back to my wife, who is stoically spooning broth into her mouth. Something hidden behind Elizabeth's girlish face has just silently announced that she is no longer a child. Disconcerted at what I've seen, I seek to demean her and shove her roughly back to the ranks of infancy.

"You need to spank her, Kate. Don't let the minx get above herself," I say as if in jest. My wife puts down her spoon, her gaze level and cool.

"Perhaps you would prefer to do that yourself, My Lord."

It is a sharp retort that tells me to behave. I had not realised until now that she has noticed the growing tension between the girl and I, and is injured by it. Jane dips her head low over her bowl, while Elizabeth continues to pull apart her floury bap and cast it into her soup. Conversation lags until Kate throws a pebble into the pond of our despondency and disperses our unease.

"You really must ride to see Somerset again, Thomas. He is still refusing to release my property. Despite my refusal to sell Fausterne Manor to him he has now promised the tenancy to a fellow of his; a man called Long. It is not right, Thomas. The manor is mine, I should be able to do with it as I like."

My head is weary of all this. Night and day all I hear is how wronged she is by my brother. It is as if she holds me to blame in some way. Of course, she is right; it is her property. I do not deny that, but a fellow should have some relief from business at the supper table.

These days Kate goes less and less to court. She is content to sit at home with Elizabeth and Jane, sharing her learning with them. The parlour table is littered with Latin translations, books pile up on chairs so that I am lucky if I can find a seat, and the conversation is replete with topics I cannot comprehend. I try to distract them from their seriousness with rough games and teasing, but when that palls she gathers her women about her to read and sew, and I find myself excluded again.

Sometimes the domesticity is stifling, and I long to feel the heave of a ship's deck beneath my feet, or the clash of my sword against the enemy. I am hungry for danger, for adventure, but instead we pass an insipid summer leavened only by bed-sport with my wife, and my continuing taunting of Elizabeth. In desperation I turn my mind to courtly intrigue.

It has cost me dear to secure the nine-year-old Jane Grey as my ward, but she is a worthy pawn in the game of chance I am playing. Married to the queen, and uncle to the king, I am in a prime position to usurp my brother's place in the boy's affections. As the year begins its downward journey I conceive a plan that will bring us closer.

If Edward were to marry Jane, I would be at the centre of a wheel of royalty. I would become the pivot upon which England turns, and Edward, Jane and Kate could revolve in my sphere like constellations. I begin a slow and insidious plan to bring the cousins closer and engineer a romantic royal intrigue.

At this time the trouble in Scotland breaks out again, and my brother rides north with an army. I am ordered to lead out the fleet but I feel my presence is of more worth here, close to court, so I send Vice-Admiral Clinton off in my place.

In Somerset's absence, the royal palace becomes a more amenable place. If I desire it, I have daily access to the king, and I begin to drip hints about his need for a wife, although I make sure not to mention the name of Jane Grey just yet.

I soon discover that the king has inherited more than a little of the Tudor taste for wealth and ornament. I wonder if we are to see a return to the miserly ways of his grandfather, the seventh Henry. Like him, Edward keeps a careful eye on the accounts, and when I broach the subject of marriage, he declares he will wed none but a foreign princess and she must be "well-stuffed with jewels."

"But, Your Grace, there is more to a wife than the coffers she brings with her. The greatest feminine jewel is tucked safely beneath her petticoats."

The king flushes, his ears turning as red as his cheeks. He bends his head and pretends to search the coat of his favourite dog for fleas. The beast rolls onto its back, legs akimbo, tongue lolling blissfully while the king continues his task. "You'd prefer an English wife, Your Majesty. A foreign woman can be awkward; they have strange habits and customs. It might be best to select from the ladies at court. Remember, your father only found true happiness with your mother, Jane, and she was as English as I am."

The boy releases the dog, who leaps up to anoint the royal face. With a yelp Edward pushes him down, draws his sleeve across his wet nose. "Well," he says, as his former blushes subside. "There is time yet for me to make my decision but I have a fancy for a wealthy wife, and there are few ladies of England that are rich enough to appease me."

This is a blow. I had not considered the boy's greed. Perhaps if he and Jane spent more time together an unbreakable bond would form; a love match. All I need is to discover how to get the overly pious girl to take her nose out of a book long enough to catch the royal eye.

Life at home descends peacefully into routine. While I spend much time at court, Kate prefers to stay home where she is still treated like a queen, and has a vast household to see to her every need. At the royal palace Anne Stanhope, God curse her, preens herself like a prize goose over Edward's court. Kate is not the only one who is offended by her overbearing pride and stays away. I do my best to avoid her, and pray the war in Scotland keeps my brother occupied long enough for me to plant the idea of marriage to Jane in the king's mind.

Away from court there is turmoil in the church. As my brother and Cranmer manoeuvre England away from the Catholic faith, injunctions are set against the idolatry of images, the use of rosaries, and we are forbidden to pray to saints. To Kate's delight, which she does not try to conceal, Bishop Gardiner is imprisoned for his protest at the changes.

Of course, little of this affects me. As long as I ensure the rules are followed in my own churches and chapels, my life continues much as it has ever done.

After being forced to conceal her beliefs for so long, Kate is overjoyed by this turn of events and ensures that, in our home at least, the new decrees are followed to the letter. It is the one area of government that she and my brother agree upon.

Elizabeth and Jane, who are staunchly Protestant, embrace the new ideas, but Mary, who used to write to Kate regularly until our marriage, now scarcely communicates with us at all. Her silence speaks loudly of her disapproval.

We abandon mass and now we sing our psalms in English, and moves are in place for services to be held in English too. As usual, when it is time for church, I make myself scarce; I am not a praying man. I couldn't care less about church reform, but I wonder what the peasants make of it all. Their lives have turned according to ancient laws of the church, and the innovations must be bewildering to those of low intellect. But, judging from the deprivations of their lifestyle, one would imagine they've more to worry about than how the sermons are read.

Kate, now she is more confident, resumes work on her book. She calls it *The Lamentation of a Sinner* and for a while she can talk of nothing else. At first she is nervous about publishing it but, urged on by her companions and bolstered by the glowing preface penned by her friend, William Cecil, she goes ahead.

The house fills with her admirers; the reformer, John Parkhurst becomes her chaplain, and she gives

Miles Coverdale a place as her almoner. Even the radical and argumentative Robert Cooch appears often at supper. I take no part in his arguments. Like a lecher in a house of nuns, I sit back in my chair and let my mind wander to other concerns.

Elizabeth sits opposite, putting on airs and trying to appear sophisticated in a gown I've not seen her wear before. It is crimson, clashing with the wisps of hair that peek from the edges of her cap. I guess it is a gift from Kate, who cannot resist such shades of red. Jane is likewise richly clad, but she is in yellow and it is Elizabeth who draws the eye. She makes no move to attract my attention but still, I cannot keep myself from looking.

She is arresting but not pretty. Her pointed face is prim until she turns those dark, dancing eyes upon a man. I wonder if it is only I who can see it, or if she works her spell on all men. I trace an imaginary finger along the parting in her fiery hair, down her high white brow to her fine aquiline nose, her pale plump lips. There I linger, my make-believe fingertip tracing the outline of her mouth that opens to lure me in. I imagine her hot mouth drawing my finger and become so engrossed in the scenario that I gasp aloud. Everyone turns to look at me and I laugh.

"I almost dropped off," I apologise. "Do carry on."

Cooch's voice drones on but Elizabeth is watching me now. To hide my discomfort I try to turn the tables and disconcert her instead. I pull surreptitious faces to try to make her laugh but she averts her gaze, turns coldly away, listening intently to the conversation for all the world as if she'd not rather sport with me.

Winter blows in hard. I ride home from court through a bitter wind, tiny flecks of snow stinging my face. I urge my mount onward, keeping my head low, and look forward to the welcome lights of home. When I finally slide from my horse the house is in darkness. My limbs are stiff, my clothes sodden. I stamp into the hall and throw my cloak at a retainer.

"Where is my wife?"

"She took poorly, My Lord, and retired to her chamber."

Dogs leap up from the fireside in hairy welcome, but I push them down and take the stairs two at a time.

"Kate?" I whisper as I push open the door and, without waiting for her summons, enter the room. The only light is coming from the fireplace; the only sound is the regular tic of her breathing. Before I am halfway to the bed, a figure detaches itself from the shadows and stands before me in the firelight.

"She is sleeping, My Lord. Try not to wake her."

Elizabeth, clad only in her nightgown, clutches a shawl around her shoulders. I pause, drinking in the vision of her limbs, outlined by the firelight, her red hair tumbling on her shoulders. I take a step nearer, keep my voice low, so as not to disturb my wife.

"Why aren't you in bed?"

My voice is no more than a whisper. She shrugs, her white face shadowed by the leaping flames.

"Katheryn was feeling poorly. I am her friend. She sent the others away."

Without her cap, she looks both more vulnerable and more desirable. There is a slight kink to her hair I've not noticed before. It seems like a living thing, as red and as vibrant as the fire behind her. I lift a tress, test the softness between finger and thumb. Her shawl slips to the floor as she drops her hands and when she swallows, my eyes move to her throat; her long, white, kissable throat.

My lips are dry, my blood pulsing beneath my skin, my loins tight as I acknowledge her budding breasts thrusting beneath the thin stuff of her nightgown.

"My Lord," she croaks. She knows I am looking, knows what I am thinking, and her words are both an acknowledgement and a denial. I drop the fiery strand of hair as if it has burned me, and as she flees from the room I gaze helplessly after the high tight buttocks ill-concealed beneath her shift.

January 1548

There is dancing after supper. A crush of people is squeezed into the hall, laughing at the shrill discordance of the musicians as they tune their instruments. Then, when the music begins, chaos turns to order as we begin to follow the steps of the first dance. We move in a wheel, Katheryn's hand is in mine as we promenade and turn. When I bow, she points her toe, her head balanced as pretty as a daisy upon her green-clad shoulders. We come together, her lips stretching, her eyes gleaming. She is beautiful. My mouth grazes her cheek before we part again, our fingertips touching.

For a while I am hers again, freed from the charms of the royal baggage. The evening passes in a haze of resurrected lust and that night I go to her bed. I make love to her like I did before we were wed, before my life became bowed down with domesticity and sobriety.

At first it is like tickling a kitten. I move upon her slowly, waking her dormant passion, stirring her need.

She has missed this, it is plain to see; she begins to writhe beneath me, matching my pace, issuing small mews of pleasure. I open my eyes and look down at her blood-suffused cheeks, her streaming ruddy hair. But the face I see is not hers. My mind tricks me, the dimly-lit chamber and the flickering candles turn the legitimate loving of my wife into a romp with a dangerous girl. As Elizabeth's smile is superimposed upon Kate's I throw back my head and explode with adulterous pleasure as I flood Katheryn's womb with my seed.

While my wife relaxes into a satisfied sleep, I lie awake wondering what the hell is wrong with me. *Am I bewitched?* I remember the stories that emerged about Anne Boleyn after her execution, stories of witchcraft and evil intent. Before this I rejected such wild claims, but now, with her daughter Elizabeth haunting my marriage bed, stalking at the periphery of my mind for every waking moment, I begin to wonder.

As night dissolves into a wet, chill dawn, I rise heavy-eyed and pull on my hose and slip into my shirt. One of Katheryn's dogs stretches in its bed and watches me quit the chamber, but it does not follow. Carrying my shoes I creep along the corridor, intending to plague the kitchen staff for an early breakfast, for a night of loving has made me famished.

As I near Elizabeth's apartments, her woman, Kat Ashley, emerges, still in her nightgown, her hair in two thick black braids. She cries out when she sees me and claps a hand to her bosom. "My Lord Admiral! You made me jump. Why are you up and about so early?"

"I might ask you the same, Madam. Is everything well?"

207

"My Lady has a headache." She jerks her head toward the open chamber door. "I am fetching an infusion of sage and lavender. That will set her right. I am not sure if we should summon the physician, My Lord, she has been out of sorts for a few days. Go and have a peek at her, see what you think."

I cannot refuse. As if I am being drawn forward by an invisible string, I glide toward the door, push it wide and find myself standing beside her bed. She looks up at me without surprise, her huge dark eyes more shadowed than usual. A smirk flickers on her lips. "Admiral. Are you turned doctor? Have you come to administer to my needs?"

I ignore the innuendo and she holds out a long slender arm, the sleeve of her nightgown falling back to reveal white skin, faint blue veins pulsing at the inner elbow. I push down the desire to kiss it.

"Your woman said you are sickly. You look all right to me."

"On the contrary, My Lord. I am ailing and like to die. Feel how hot I am. Do you think I have a fever?"

She takes my hand, clamps it upon her forehead, the contact bringing me closer. Too close. Her skull is hot, but not overly. Her hair is like coppery silk beneath my fingers. I can hear her breath, short and sharp. The youthful odour of her bed rises, challenging every male instinct. I try to pull away but she retains my hand. "Am I very sick, Tom?"

She speaks my name oddly. Usually she addresses me ironically as 'Admiral', or 'My Lord' but this morning she turns the single syllable 'Tom' into an invitation.

I snatch away my hand.

"What are you doing, Elizabeth? Are you mad?"

"It must be the fever. I am burning up." Restlessly she pushes back the covers with her feet, revealing long slim limbs, dainty ankles, tiny bare toes, and nails like enamelled jewels. I groan inwardly and struggle with the blankets, trying to cover her.

"Stop it. Stop it. You will have me hung."

Our faces are close, our breath conjoined, our noses almost touching.

"Hung for what?"

"You are not a child."

"No, My Lord. I am not."

We both become very still. The dream of loving her rises like a drowning tide and I struggle desperately to keep my desire from overspilling. She has my balls in a vice. I cannot move away, and I definitely cannot go forward. Anger surges.

"Perhaps you are a child. You are certainly acting like one!"

"So make me behave then." She is defiant, taunting me. Defying me to do the thing we both want and cannot have. In an instant I grab her wrist, sit down on the bed and pull her over my knee.

Her buttocks jerk firmly beneath my open palm as I bring my hand down once, twice, three times. She wriggles like an eel, her breasts, bare beneath her gown, squirm softly against my upper thigh. At each strike she emits a yelp of outraged pain, wriggling like a fish. She kicks out in vain, her long legs fighting for freedom. She is so scantily clad she might as well be naked in my arms.

"Admiral!"

Kat Ashley is standing at the door, a platter of cups in her hand. She marches toward me and slams down the tray as I release her charge. Elizabeth spins away in fury, loses her balance and falls panting onto her arse at the fireside, her nightgown above her knees.

"You'd not have done that were my father alive, or he'd have had your head!"

She glares at me through her wild red hair, her face puce with humiliation, tears wet on her cheeks. The temptress has gone and she is a child once more; an angry, rebellious child. She will not taunt me again.

I stand up stiffly, tug down my shirt to conceal my straining crotch. "Your charge needed a lesson in manners, Madam, and as her guardian, I administered it. It is a blessing you were not present to witness her words for they were unfit for female ears."

Self-righteously, I take my leave of them and, as I go, I can feel Elizabeth's eyes burning into the back of my neck.

February 1548 – Hanworth Manor

Thereafter, I spank Elizabeth regularly. The trouble with women, and princesses in particular, is that they are treated too gently. If a girl is spanked often, it helps her know her place. Elizabeth, despite being legitimate one minute and a bastard the next, has been treated with kid gloves since she was birthed. It is high time she learned some manners.

The next time I enter her chamber, she is wary. Her women squeal in horror as she backs off further into the bed and I have to fight my way through the bed hangings to find her. I roll her over onto her belly and warm her arse with my palm. She shrieks like a pig on slaughter day and I grow quite warm from the exercise. By the time I am done with her she is exhausted and quelled, lying back on her pillows with her clothes in disarray, watching me with bright eyes as I straighten my clothes and take my leave of her.

"I will see you at breakfast." I throw the remark over my shoulder as I make for the door, and feel the soft thump of a pillow in the middle of my back. I make no response but go and seek my wife who is, thankfully, still abed.

Kat Ashley harangues me for impropriety. "She deserves it," I say, deftly dismissing her protest. "A spank never did anyone any harm."

When she receives no satisfactory response from me, she takes her complaints to Katheryn. Once more I am beset with her grievances. I must be more circumspect. Elizabeth is a royal princess. She is under our protection, our guidance.

"But Katheryn, I was merely seeking to guide her. When I was a boy, my brother and I were whipped daily. It never did us any harm ... well; I turned out all right, anyway. I only used the palm of my hand on her, I didn't use a strap. She is a wayward, cheeky piece and needed to be told." Katheryn puts down her needlework and looks at me reproachfully as I continue to bluster. "Most of it was horseplay. Why not come with me and see for yourself?"

"Come with you? To her chamber?"

I shrug as if it is immaterial whether I go alone or not, as if my visits to the girl's chamber are innocent, and each time I lay hands on Elizabeth I am not wishing I were kissing her instead.

"Why not? I've nothing to hide."

I can see Katheryn is appeased, and my assumed indifference has convinced her that my actions are those of a blameless man. She fumbles for her needle again, squints in the ill light to make the next stitch.

"You should sit closer to the window; you will go blind straining to see in the dark."

She puts her work down again and smiles up at me, holds out her hand. I take it reluctantly and she draws me toward her so that I am forced to get down on my knees before her.

"Thomas, I – I do have something to tell you." Her face flushes pink, her eyes flood with tears. Instantly contrite, I think she has found me out. I reach out and capture a tear before it drops onto her gown.

"What? What is the matter, Kate? Are you ill?"

"No, no, Tom. Not at all. Not ill but, but I think ... I may be wrong but ... I think I might be with child."

Her last word is a whisper. As I absorb what she has said my mouth falls open, and I sit back on my heels, as astonished as I have ever been by anything in my life. I had thought her barren. Three husbands and not so much as a whiff of pregnancy, and yet a few months with me and.... A smile spreads across my face and I let out a whoop of delight.

"Pregnant, Kate? Are you sure?" I leap to my feet and begin to strut about the room, unable to keep still, unable to prevent myself from crowing. "All you needed was a man in your bed, my love. I bet it will be a boy. Imagine what the old king would have to say about that, hey? When is it due? How long do we have to wait?"

She laughs at my enthusiasm. "A long time yet, Tom. About six months, I should think."

"Six months? That seems like a lifetime. Still, it will give us time to plan. We must move to Sudeley, where the air is fresher and there is less chance of contagion. The girls will like it there. I will organise it, but I need to put my affairs in order here before we can go."

Although she is sickly in the mornings, Kate is as good as her word and accompanies me to Elizabeth's chamber. Somehow, in her presence, the spankings turn to tickling. Both of us join Elizabeth on her bed, tickling and pinching, making her scream with delight. For the women it is innocent enough, but during the romp I cannot help but notice the changes that are taking place beneath Elizabeth's nightgown.

She is growing, filling out, and her body scent is altering to that of a woman. Sometimes when we descend on her she is already up and fully dressed, although it is not yet full light. I am wise enough about women to know that the regularity of this denotes her monthly flux is upon her and she is reluctant for me to discover it. I treat her more gently then, for women are weaker and more inclined to weep. But the change in her also tells me she is a woman now, in all respects, and ripe for a husband.

As she matures, she puts on airs. Taking more care over the styling of her cap, the arrangement of her skirts, the cut of her gowns.

As Kate's belly begins to swell and spring begins to spread its green mantle across the gardens, Elizabeth becomes remote, detached. She is no longer a child. Her laughter is not as loud, nor as long. She watches me sullenly, not bothering to greet me when I come, or fare me well when I leave.

***

The physicians warn Kate to exercise more. She must take a walk every day in the gardens for the wellbeing that the fresh air brings. Since she can no longer hunt, I ride out alone and bring home game for her table. I want to fatten her up but at the same time I am reluctant to see the matronly swell of her once-slender frame.

I have heard it said that if a mother eats too well the child can grow too fat to emerge safely from the womb. She grows rapidly ungainly, her face and hands puffy, her eyes shadowed, and I long for the trim, alert Kate that I fell in love with.

"It is for the good of the child," I tell myself as she waddles ahead of me along the garden path. "I don't mind." I follow in her wake, full of good intentions, determined to be an honest husband. And then Elizabeth turns a corner, her figure like a wand, her face youthful and flawless. I bite my lip, close my eyes, and try very hard to love my wife.

The arbour where Kate and I are resting is not yet smothered with summer roses but it won't be long, for the air is warm. We make comment on the burgeoning leaves, the thrusting bulbs, and the way the trees are turning to a soft green. It was on a day such as this that I made love to her amid the celandine.

Life is different now.

I am holding Kate's hand; it lies like a warm fluttering bird in my palm. Her fingers are slightly swollen, her nails bitten, and it pleases me to discern, already, the rise of her belly beneath her gown. Although her pregnancy is not far advanced I know her ankles are puffy too, and that she is troubled with constant passing water. It is not often she strays so far from the close stool but today, since it was so fine, I persuaded her to come. It is still months until the birth, and I cannot allow her to be cooped up indoors for so long.

As we sit idling, a figure moves in the shadows, and another follows quickly after. We both look up, alert and squinting in the sun until the footsteps cease and we find Jane and Elizabeth have joined us.

"Good afternoon, girls." Kate holds out her hands and invites them to join us. Jane hurries obediently forward, head bowed, and gives her habitual curtsey. Elizabeth follows more slowly. She is not smiling, her mouth has a downward turn to it, and I find I miss the amused twitch that was there before.

Katherine shifts in her seat and we shuffle along so that Jane can sit down. As Elizabeth moves to join us I notice her dress for the first time. "Good God, girl. What are you wearing?"

She stops, looks down, and fans out her skirts. "What is wrong with it?"

"The colour is what is wrong. No wonder you look as sour as three-day-old milk. Tell her, Kate, that dour dismal black does her no favours. Does it, Jane?"

A scarlet-cheeked Jane makes no answer. She ducks her head and pretends to be intrigued by the book she has brought along with her. Kate frowns at me, gives a slight shake of her head.

"Don't be so rude, Tom."

"But it is a disgusting colour. Tell her to go and change. It offends me."

Elizabeth's face is reddening and her expression is akin to one I have seen her father wear many a time. Something, not just the colour of her gown, irks me. Her whole get-up is unflattering and I am dismayed to see my Elizabeth looking almost nondescript. She is vibrant; magnificent, and should be dressed to reflect that.

"Sit down, Thomas."

I ignore my wife and remain standing while Elizabeth and I glare at each other.

"Go and change it." I speak through gritted teeth. She sticks out her chin, and her lips lose their rose tint as she clenches them tight. I expect her to stamp her foot but instead she crosses her arms and looks away, over the heads of Kate and Jane to the garden beyond. I take a step forward, avoiding Kate's outstretched hand.

"Go and take it off, or I will cut it from you."

Her head jerks round, her face white, and her eyes glittering dangerously.

"You wouldn't dare."

There is a hint of uncertainty in her voice. I take another step forward and she doesn't move, just lifts her head higher and tries to stare me down.

"You have one more chance, Madam."

"I will never do as you say. You are not my father."

I grab her wrist, twist it roughly so she falls to her knees with a sharp cry. Ignoring Kate's shout of protest I fumble for my knife with my other hand and begin to hack at Elizabeth's skirts. At first she is so astounded, she does not fight back. We are both surprised as the fabric rips in two. And then, as if I am possessed, I find I cannot stop. Using the weight of my body I hold her down, but she won't keep still. Her arms and legs are flailing.

Terrified of wounding her, yet determined not to let her rule me, I trap her as tightly as I can and proceed to slice her petticoats to ribbons.

We are tangled together on the ground, surrounded by torn cloth, spilled beads, scattered jewels. Her headdress has come adrift and her hair tumbles down, enveloping both of us. She is shrieking, spittle on her lips, tears spouting from her eyes. She is wild and alive and vibrant and her vitality fuels my passion.

216

Suddenly she goes limp, lies in my arms unmoving, only the rise and fall of her breast evidence that she is not dead. I do not release her. I look upon the damage I have done, her ruined clothes, her white limbs showing through what remains of the offending garment. I dare not hold her any longer yet I dare not release her either.

In the end she turns her head, and our eyes meet. Her face is dead white, her eyes dark and deep. She moistens her lips with the tip of her tongue and swallows. She is going to speak. I move my head closer so as not to mishear. Her breath tickles my inner ear and her whispered words, when they come, croak painfully in her throat, making my balls contract.

"I love you."

I let her go, drop her in the dirt and scramble to my feet, backing away as if she has a contagion. With a pounding heart I watch her rise stiffly from the ground, and with great dignity brush the earth from her tattered skirts. Then she walks away from me, across the garden, toward the house, like a duchess, like a queen.

March 1548

I escape to court. All that I have so carefully built up, my household of royal women, my quest for power, is now in jeopardy. Perhaps I should have bided my time, should have married Elizabeth instead of Kate. Had I done so, as husband to one so close to the throne they could not deny me my share of respect

But I love Kate, I do. I do.

Things are just difficult now. She is ailing and unwieldy, leaving me lacking in the fulfilment a married man has the right to expect. There are whores, of course, and hearth wenches, but there is also Elizabeth – and beside her everything else is diminished. Like Eve, like a Siren, she is offering me the forbidden; the one forbidden thing that I long for so much. She consumes me, her face, her body, her voice....

I could take her and hang for it, but is she prepared to hang too? Does she know what she is doing? Does she know where it could lead?

My brother is lately returned from Scotland and now seems determined to get his claws even deeper into the king's flesh. He is beset by troubles as the religious wrangle continues. It is a war of contradictions, the abolishment of idols one moment, and calls for a return to traditional ways the next. I keep out of it. I am all for war if it is over something solid, something tangible like land, or power. But the manner in which a fellow chooses to pray is not something I'd bother to strap on my sword for.

There is unrest in the countryside too as landowners enclose their land, setting sheep to run where once there'd been grain. And as the coinage continues to slip, and England slides further into debt, the growing population becomes hungry. In the north, grumblings of another uprising are quelled while the London inns I frequent are seething with discontent.

I bury myself in the fug of the people's dissatisfaction, quaffing cheap ale, pretending interest in the cheapest whores. The woman on my arm will not see forty again. She cackles at my jokes, her fingers creeping up the back of my doublet as she leans in closer to whisper in my ear. A wild-eyed fellow, deep in his cups, shouts treason from his place at the hearth. I throw off the harlot's embrace and move toward him.

"What we need is another plague," I quip, thumping my tankard onto the ale-stained table. My companions are all poor fellows and, not seeing my joke, they glare at me and the atmosphere becomes thick with resentment. "There'd be less to feed, more food to go further ..." I try to explain, but it seems my joke is a poor one. I drain my cup and creep away, relocate my whore and, grabbing her by the wrist, drag her off to spend the night in a rancid-smelling stew.

Somewhat sated, in the morning I haul myself back to the palace to be met with a hostile reception from my brother, who is closeted with Dudley. My request to see the king is rejected. Dudley looks down his long nose at me, making me squirm.

"Look at you, man. You are in no state to be presented to His Majesty." I look down at my stained linen and my once pristine doublet and know they are right. "Come back when you have sorted yourself out."

Wearily, I turn away and head for my apartments. Dudley is right. I stink like a midden. A bath and a good meal will wash away the lingering stench of debauchery. I have not fallen so low as to lose sight of the upright fellow I once was. I need to put my troubles behind me and start afresh – reconsider my options and forget about Elizabeth. She is not for me.

As I soak in the tub I reflect that women were the start of all my troubles. I should be done with them, all of them, and concentrate on my wife, my political career, and my soon to be born heir.

Within an hour I am washed and my beard is trimmed and, clad in clean linen, I set about repairing the damage and making an attempt to regain my hold on my slippery fortunes. I order lavish new furnishings for

Sudeley and write to Kate, telling her of my purchases and my plan to move the household there in June.

I have been from home for weeks, and it is almost May when a letter arrives from Kate. I move to the light of the window, break open the seal, and her words pour forth with such eloquence I can almost hear her chatter. I gallop through the lines of news, dull domestic stuff about new-born kittens and dismissed servants. I have no care for such things. I am searching for a single word, 'Elizabeth', but my eye falters upon something else.

"...I gave your little knave your blessing, who like an honest man stirred apace after and before. For Mary Odell being abed with me had laid her hand upon my belly to feel it stir. It hath stirred these three days every morning and evening so that I trust when ye come it will make you some pastime."

The child has moved in her belly. My child. My son. I let the letter fall and gaze out across the garden. My son will be the future. Women are nothing compared to sons. Once I am a father, it will be easier to resist – easier to ignore Elizabeth's trap. Suddenly I am seized with the longing for home. I too want to lay my hand upon Kate's belly and feel the strength of my boy's kick. Swivelling on my heel, I holler for my man and bid him pack a bag and order my horse to be made ready.

May 1548 – Hanworth Manor

Looking up at the windows of the manor, I am filled with joy to be back. No more bawdy houses for me, no more wine-sodden evenings, no more fruitless requests to visit the king. Now I will become a paragon of domesticity. I will embrace it all; the boredom, the lack of horizon, the tedious religious conversations. The only thing I must not embrace is Elizabeth. I am determined to treat her like the child she is. I am a man, her superior, her guardian, and must behave as such.

When a groom comes running I toss the reins to him and pulling off my hat, hurry into the hall. "Kate!" I bellow up the stairs and, after a moment, she appears at the top and comes lumbering down to meet me.

I had forgotten how big she is now. Fleetingly I regret the light-footed wanton who won my heart. I kiss her cheek, stroke her belly and take note of her pallor, her shadowy eyes. For the first time Kate looks every one of her thirty-six years. I feel a pang of pity.

Keeping her hand in mine, I lead her into the parlour and make her comfortable with cushions and place a wrap about her shoulders.

"What do the doctors say?" I ask as she settles herself down. "Is it usual for you to be so breathless?"

I try to recall other women in a like condition, but apart from my brother's wife who casts offspring as liberally as a dog sheds hairs, I can think of none. But then I remember my sister, Jane, who perished so suddenly within days of giving life to the king. My heart turns sick at the thought of losing Kate that way. "Is this normal?" I ask for the thousandth time. "Should you be this tired?"

"They tell me to rest, to take short walks and to put my feet up whenever I sit." I cast around for a stool and bring it over and wait until she obediently places her feet upon it. We continue to talk for a while, catching up on the missed weeks. I hold her hand as she speaks of pointless, flimsy things; a litter of kittens found in her clothes press; a plague of mice in the kitchen; the sudden illness of one of the cooks. I listen, relishing the ennui of it all and content for it to go on forever.

When the light begins to fail, a servant comes to draw the shutters and stoke up the fire. I realise it will soon be supper time and the girls will be joining us. With a shrim of uncertainty, I gird myself against the first meeting with Elizabeth and wonder if she has changed. I hope she has. I hope she has grown ugly, put on weight, or is covered in a foul rash.

Jane arrives first, blushing puce when she sees me and dropping a deep curtsey. I greet her easily. She rouses none of the unwarranted feelings that Elizabeth does. It isn't just a weakness I have for girls or an obsession for royals. It is a weakness for just one girl: Elizabeth, the harlot's daughter.

But, when she comes, despite my mental preparation, I am not ready. There is no preparation I could have made for the impact she has upon me. At first we do not hear her tread, but then Kate raises her head and sees her hesitating at the door. "Elizabeth! There you are."

At her words my head snaps up, and our eyes meet in a clash of mutual fear. She should have the word 'Danger' emblazoned on her brow as a warning to all men. With great difficulty I battle for calm as she slowly crosses the room and curtseys, just as Jane did. Only this time I am swamped with emotion. I look down upon her bowed head, the line of her parting disappearing beneath her cap. Then she straightens up, raises her face, and I drink in her strange brand of beauty. She stands for a moment with her hands at her sides, her heart in her eyes. I notice her lips are moving and struggle to make sense of what she is saying. It is something about London, and the king.

I mumble something in what I hope is an apt reply, grateful when a page moves toward us with a tray of drinks. I grab one and toss the contents down my throat. Beside me Katheryn takes a cup and sips delicately, but Jane and Elizabeth both refuse refreshment.

The women begin to discuss the day, their words buzzing like bees about my head, the meaning of the conversation trickling away before I can grasp it.

My household. Three royal females: a child; a vessel containing my son; and a young woman holding the strings of my heart – or my loins at least. I have all that I wanted, and everything I did not. I did not look for this. I close my eyes, drowning hopelessly in the inevitable.

Supper is long in coming. I clear my throat, look about the room, click my fingers for another cup of wine and knock it back, without tasting. Soon the liquor begins to seep through my body, soothing my mind, flooding me with wellbeing.

I begin to relax.

At dinner, Kate sits at one end of the table opposite me, with Jane and Elizabeth equidistant from us both. This allows me to watch Elizabeth without seeming to. I become part of her nourishment, witness everything she places between her lips, watch the movement of her long white throat as she drinks, her long slender fingers ripping apart her bread.

Jane is a nondescript mouse in comparison to her cousin, and Kate, my once lovely wife, is like an overfed tabby cat; comfortable and unexciting. All I can see is Elizabeth. She shines like a jewel, her hair that peeks from beneath her cap matches her gown, and her tawny eyes are kept lowered, guarded; concealing what?

Allowing Katheryn and Jane to dominate the conversation, I indulge myself by trying to guess the thoughts that are running through Elizabeth's mind. Is she thinking of me? Is she hoping I will venture to her room to smack and pinch and tickle her as I have so often?

She tears off a slice of capon and pops it into her mouth, her tongue emerging to lick the grease from her lips. She glances toward me as she delicately chews but her eyes dart quickly back to her platter, a light flush mantling her cheek. Why did I not wait and wed her? Had I persisted with my suit she would have surrendered. How could she not?

After supper, although she cannot join us, Kate suggests some dancing. "It will amuse me just to watch," she says, summoning the musicians.

It is a small gathering; some of Kate's reformer friends and her household women. Usually, unless it is a court occasion, I decline the dance, but this evening I drain my cup and decide to take the floor.

I dance first with Jane, and then Kate's sister, Anne, but all the time my mind is on Elizabeth. I see her without looking, enjoying the company of the other men. She is gay, her laughter drawing my attention from my own partner. Inexorably, as the steps of the dance draw us closer, my heart begins to pound. She is but one move away; I paint on a smile, and try to deny the jagged blade of lust that darts up my arm when our fingertips touch. It is a sensation I want instinctively to shy away from but, as soon as it has passed, I cannot wait to feel it again. My eyes follow her. Elizabeth has felt it too, I can tell by the way she bites her lip and averts her eye as she winds her way through the dance.

Her cheeks are pink now, but it could be the exertion. I dismiss that idea, preferring to think it is contact with me. It is better to believe that she burns with longing for me, as I do for her.

Somehow, my former vows forgotten, I manage to get through the evening without giving myself away. The next morning I learn Elizabeth has taken to her bed for a few days with a megrim, and I begin to feel better in her absence. I am strong enough to resist her, I tell myself as life begins to run smoothly again.

I ride about the estate, putting things in order and, at the same time, continue to organise the refurbishment of Sudeley, and my plans to remove the household there as soon as they are complete.

One morning I rise early, and so as not to wake anyone, I sneak from the chamber and down the stairs without my boots. The servants are already abroad, a comforting clatter issuing from the kitchens. As I pass along the upper corridor, a grubby housemaid carrying a bucket shrinks against the wainscot. She bobs a curtsey but I do not acknowledge her as I hurry downstairs and pull on my boots at the outer door.

In the stable yard the grooms are busy; they hastily pull their forelocks as the dogs set up a welcome clamour when they see me. They drag their chains forward and leap up in greeting, muddying my clothes. "Get down," I roar and head for the stable where my favourite mare is waiting.

She has been laid up for a few weeks with a strained fetlock, and I've instructed the groom to spare no cost in her care. As I draw close she whinnies and nudges me, looking for titbits. I run a hand down her long nose, cup her muzzle that is as warm and as soft as a woman. She blows snot into my palm.

"Ah, many thanks." I pat her again and, wiping my hand on my sleeve, turn to the groom. "How is she coming along?"

"Good, My Lord," he says, tugging at his forelock. "Another week or so and she should be fit for light duty."

"Good. Good. I will ..." I pause mid-sentence as a horse clatters in through the gate. My heart leaps when I see it is Elizabeth, looking regal in green velvet. She pretends not to see me, and slides from the back of her white palfrey, looking about the yard. When she decides to notice me she stops tugging at the fingers of her gloves and her face drops a little, uncertainty stirring beneath her carefully-schooled expression. I move toward her, make my bow.

"My Lady Elizabeth, you are abroad early."

Her face is pale, her sandy eyebrows like gold in the sunshine, her tawny eyes troubled.

"I like to rise early, Sir, so as to avoid unwanted visitors."

She might as well have slapped me. I lift my chin, narrow my eyes.

"You get up at an ungodly hour to avoid me? How long have you been doing so?"

"Only this morning. Since you are back from court I thought to dissuade you from resuming your former insolent habits."

"You no longer welcome me in your chamber?"

"I am not sure I ever did welcome you, Admiral. You just never took no for an answer."

She looks at me with loathing and my heart flips. I have made her hate me, but whether that hatred is born of my former attention or my latter lack, I cannot know. With a sniff she makes to walk away but I grab her arm, her bicep small but well-formed beneath my grasp.

226

"You welcomed my attention. You welcomed it too much."

She struggles to free herself but I keep hold of her. "Come, Elizabeth," I say loudly for the benefit of the grooms. "Walk with me in the garden."

I move so rapidly she is forced to trot beside me, her ridiculous riding hat bobbing on her head like a dead chicken. When we are out of sight of the house and stable yard I pause in an arbour and thrust her unceremoniously onto the seat.

"What are you doing, Elizabeth? I know you don't hate me. I know you crave me just as I do you. But what can I do? I am a married man. You are a royal princess. If we listen to our hearts, we could both die for it."

Tears are balanced on her lashes, her chin begins to wobble. It is not like her to weep. She is usually disdainful, controlled. I have rarely seen her off her guard. Her weakness is my undoing. I can never bear to see a woman cry.

"Don't. Please, Elizabeth, don't weep." I reach for her, touch her shoulder and she rolls into my arms, huddles to my breast, her body trembling.

"Why, Tom? Why is life so unfair? You should have waited, persevered and wed me. I would have accepted you in the end. I just wanted you to be sure. I thought you would come back and try to persuade me. I didn't expect you to marry my mother."

Oh God. I could have had her. I could have wed her instead of Katheryn and let everyone else go to hell.

"I'm sorry." She is tiny, like a delicate little bird. I place my lips on her hair, close my eyes and inhale the scent of camomile and thyme. We rock to and fro for a moment and then she lifts her face. It is wet and full of grief, her trembling lips are parted.

And as I look upon her I no longer care if they hang me, they can burn me if they want to. They can tear my body limb from limb and dispatch it about the four corners of the kingdom. Elizabeth is in my arms and I will have her ... somehow.

***

It is not easy to behave as if I haven't just discovered a trove of treasure beneath my bed, but I do my best. I do not resume my visits to her chamber and treat her circumspectly whenever we are in company. The moment we find ourselves alone however, she rushes straight into my arms. Instinctively she tempts me, but I have no idea if she knows the full power of her charms. Her butterfly kisses taunt me until I crush her against the wall and all but swallow her. I long to consummate our arrangement, but it must be right; we must wait until we are sure we will not be discovered. Exposure has become our greatest fear, an all-consuming terror, but still it does not stop us.

On a wet afternoon at the end of May I come across Elizabeth alone in a music room. She puts down her lute and, after checking I am unaccompanied, she presses against me, slides her arms up around my neck.

Her lips are warm and hungry, her bosom tight against me. I kiss her back, hard, before I break away. My tongue leaves a wet trail as I slide my mouth down her neck to where her breasts pout like small doves over the top of her bodice. We fall back against the window seat, she is breathing rapidly as I kiss the taut flesh, wrenching her necklace aside, spilling pearls across the floor. With a shaking fist I struggle with her lacings, balance small

228

white breasts in my palm before placing my lips around the point of her nipple.

She gasps. At first I think it is with pleasure but then I realise she has stiffened in my arms and is pushing me away. Slowly I raise my head, my face wet with spittle and, with foreboding banging in my brain, I turn to find my wife standing like a statue at the open door.

She looks old, shattered, and I am flooded with guilt. "Kate," I croak, struggling to rise, caught up in the treachery of Elizabeth's skirts. Katheryn looks right through me, speaks with tight white lips.

"You have broken your pearls, Elizabeth," she says woodenly before she turns and leaves us, closing the door firmly.

"Don't leave me, Tom. Don't leave me." Elizabeth clings to my arms, clutches at my doublet as I struggle to lace my codpiece. I push her away.

"I have to. Can't you see what we've done to her? Oh my God, what were we thinking? We should have waited until ... oh, we should never have done this!"

"Tom!" she wails, as I throw open the door. I turn for one last look. She is sitting on the floor, her skirts pooling around her, her gaping bodice revealing the breasts I have so lately kissed. They have no power over me now. Elizabeth is shrunken, diminished against the greater pull of the woman who bears my child. I am racked with guilt and remorse. I turn away and run for the stairs.

June 1548 – Sudeley Castle

The house is quiet without Elizabeth. On the morning that she departs I shut myself away and watch from the window as she takes her leave of Katheryn. There has been no acrimony, no blame apportioned to her. She rides meekly away without looking back in search of me, but I know we share the same pain. I know how she feels and how deeply her heart is aching with the desperate need to be forgiven and be allowed to stay. When the cavalcade is no longer in sight I turn from the window and look about the bleak room, consider the interminable emptiness that lies ahead.

Kate will not discuss it. Several times I try to excuse myself, try to explain, but on each occasion she holds up a hand, closes her eyes and refuses to listen. We bumble along together until it is time to leave for the country.

I had imagined the day we set off for Sudeley would be a joyful one, but instead it is drear. A steady rain is falling, and Kate is barely speaking to me. With every mile that takes me farther from Elizabeth the strings that link us grow thinner, and tighter.

My hawk tightens its grip on my wrist as in a spurt of angry frustration I kick my horse into a canter, splashing through summer puddles, ducking beneath wet boughs. The sodden landscape races past, the wind stings my eyes and when I come to rest near a stream, I find there are tears on my cheeks. I dash them away and wait until I hear the murmur of voices and Kate's litter comes rumbling into sight.

She allows me to help her alight and together we hurry to the shelter of the overhanging oaks. Tired and pale from the journey and the constant jolting of the horses, she places two hands to her lower back and stretches with a groan.

"Ooh, I am not used to travelling in a litter. I think I would have been more comfortable on horseback."

While there has been no spoken recrimination, she is distant, there is no passion in her voice. A great wall has been erected between us and I wonder if it is too thick to breach. I pass her a flagon of wine and she drinks daintily before handing it back. While she dabs her lips with her kerchief I throw back my head and let the liquid pour down my throat. Drawing the back of my hand across my mouth, I risk a smile.

"You might do better riding with me. I can keep you safe, and the view will be better."

She hesitates and a slow flush creeps into her cheeks. "In the rain?"

I squint up at the clouds. "It is clearing now. I warrant it will be dry before it is time to ride on."

"And what about your hawk, My Lord, are you prepared to let me replace her?"

I search her words for innuendos but she looks innocent enough. I turn back to the horse and begin to tighten the girth. "Of course. You are my wedded wife and will always come before the pursuit of leisure, no matter how pleasurable."

I mount up, manoeuver my horse to a fallen log. Kate climbs gingerly upon it and I hold out my hand to haul her up before me. She clings to me for a moment before settling herself, with some difficulty. I notice how much heavier she is than before. It is yet two months until the birth. I wonder how much larger she can get.

"I will go easy," I reassure her as I signal to the horse to move on, and we leave the rest of the party to follow after.

At first she is uneasy, holding herself stiffly, trying to maintain some distance between us but, as she grows tired, she slumps against me. Her head is below my chin; my arms are wrapped around her, my hands on the reins.

231

It is a while since we have been this close. The familiar fragrance of lavender and juniper stirs the memory of my former fondness. The proximity makes me feel kinder toward her. We ride on in silence, my mind wandering, revisiting past mistakes, wrong corners.

I suppose a man cannot remain infatuated with his wife forever. Had I married Elizabeth, I might have tired of her too. It is her unattainability, the thrill of taking the forbidden that intrigues me. That is her attraction. I must learn to be content. Once the child is here, Kate will be herself again. A few months more and all will be well. I frown, unfamiliar with the feeling of guilt, but I know myself for a selfish, shallow fellow. I should recognise my good fortune and be happy with what I have. Yet, as is ever the case with me, that which I possess seems shabby and tarnished compared with that which I desire.

***

"Oh Thomas!" Katheryn exclaims when she sees the lavishness of Sudeley Castle. No sooner have we arrived than I take her to our private chambers. I have spent weeks quietly arranging to have the rooms refurbished. There is new furniture, crimson velvet curtains, gold cushions and hangings. The nursery is likewise red.

"My favourite colours." She clamps both hands to her cheeks and looks about the room with brimming eyes before breaking off to smile at me. It is the first authentic happiness I have seen on her face for weeks.

"I thought you would like it. I – Kate, all I want is to please you. From now on, I swear, there will be no more ..."

She holds up her hand, closes her eyes, stemming my words. "Don't say it, Tom," she says at last. "If you

232

make me no promises, you cannot break them. I cannot bear it again."

Leaving me speechless, she moves among the new furniture, examines the cot, rocking it gently with her foot. I stand at the window that looks across the gardens to the small chapel.

"We will be happy here, Kate. Away from the court and all the nonsense and intrigue. Here you can nurture our son and, once our little knave is born, everything between us will be as it was before."

Her smile is gentle and sad, but she makes no reply.

It takes me a few weeks to realise the vastness of the household that has followed us to Sudeley. Where I had anticipated a quieter life, I find Kate and I are still the centre of a huge train of people. It is not the intimate escape that I craved.

It seems to me that each time I seek the company of my wife, she is with Coverdale or attended by Dr Huicke. She surrounds herself with her ladies-in-waiting and sometimes it is as difficult to see her alone as it was to see the king.

I hate the conversations they hold, religious theories, learnéd stuff that I cannot hope to follow. They make me feel like a fool and, as I am forced to listen, I grow more and more alienated, more uncertain. And when I do get her on her own, she constantly harps on about her jewels, haranguing me to sort out the business with my brother. She should not be worrying about such things. Her concentration should all be centred on producing a lusty and healthy boy.

When I visit court, my brother Edward is resistant to all my attempts to see the king. We argue, as always, and he even threatens me with gaol. I accuse him of disrespecting my wife. "Disrespecting your wife?" he bellows. "She is the only thing keeping you out of gaol. You have no place in the council; I will not make you governor of the king's person. Go home and look to what you do have, you ungrateful whoreson."

It is on my tongue to taunt him. I have ever loved to raise the issue of his first wife, Catherine Filliol, who made a cuckold of him with our own father. She bore Edward two bastards before the idiot discovered he was their brother and not their sire. I cannot hide the smirk that the recollection brings and as if he can read my mind, his face shutters against me.

"Get out, Thomas. Go back to your royal brood mare and leave me alone."

My arm lashes out as if to grab him but he flinches away, raising his hand in supplication like a coward. With a mocking laugh, I tuck my thumbs in my belt and saunter from his presence.

On my return to Sudeley, I find Kate in relative solitude. As soon as she notices me at the door she looks up from her writing, puts down her pen and nods to her women to leave us. As they scuttle out I throw my hat on a chair and join her near the window, put my hand on her shoulder.

"What are you doing?" I lean over, examine the fine script.

"I am writing to Elizabeth. I had a letter from her this morning. She misses us."

A suitable reply jams in my throat. Afraid of saying the wrong thing, I hold my breath, wishing I hadn't asked, but unperturbed she picks up her pen again and signs her name with a flourish. Then she pushes the parchment toward me. "Why don't you send her word too, and let her know we are both thinking of her?"

234

I hesitate, unsure whether I should decline or not. If I refuse she might think I have something to hide, but if I oblige I may be deemed just as guilty. In the end, finding no answer, I pull up a chair and pick up the pen. I scrawl a few words and push it toward Kate for her perusal but she shakes her head.

"I do not wish to read it." She pushes the paper back to me, and before I fold and seal it, I add another line, apologising for breaking my promise. I cannot add more and I hope she will understand what is written between the lines, and hear the regret with which I write.

A few days later a reply arrives, folded in with a message to Katheryn. Assuming a casual attitude, I tear it open and absorb her words. Elizabeth writes with an artful hand, each stroke is carefully considered, each sentence conscientiously dotted.

My Lord,

You needed not to send an excuse to me, for I could not mistrust the fulfilling of your promise to proceed for want of goodwill, but only that the opportunity serveth not: wherefore I shall desire you to think that a greater matter than this could not make me impute any unkindness in you. For I am a friend not won with trifles, nor lost with the like. This I commit you and all your affairs in God's hands, who keep you from all evil. I pray you make my commendations to the queen's highness.

Your assured friend to my power,
Elizabeth

Katheryn looks up from her own letter. "She misses us."

"Yes." I clear my throat and look down at the note again. Kate won't shut up; her persistence sets my teeth on edge, and all my nerves a jangling.

"I miss her too, and I am sure Jane does."

"Yes," I say again. Like a fool I am tongue-tied, and unable to add my own feelings to the matter without bringing down Kate's wrath upon my head.

I tuck the paper within my doublet. "I, I have some business to attend to." I bend over and leave a kiss upon her cheek. Her face is a little too warm and slightly damp. "Perhaps you should get some rest before supper."

I stride through the house and into the garden and with each step Elizabeth's letter rubs against my skin, a scratchy reminder of her absence.

As the weeks pass, I grow more and more irritated by Katheryn's bevy of friends. I am worried about her and fear they tire her. I want her to myself, to lie back in the privacy of our apartments and put my feet up. She looks peaky and pale, and her eyes are dimmed with dark circles. I am losing faith in Huicke who, with his usual pomposity, declares that all will be well. He puts her megrims down to her age, tells her to exercise more, although she can scarcely place one foot in front of the other. One afternoon I lose my temper and drive him from the chamber.

"I will have no more of it, Kate. I am sick to death of his face, and his treatment is having no effect on you. Look at you, you are worn out."

Kate sighs, too cast down to argue. She reaches out her hand and I take it, join her on the bed. As we lie together and watch the scudding clouds outside the window, I feel the tension seep away.

"Things will be better soon," she promises, "just as soon as our son is born."

236

"He will be a match for his cousin. Just as I've been with my brother. I've always run rings around Edward." I laugh as I gently pass my hand across her belly. My brother's wife has just spawned yet another boy. They've named him Thomas, to appease me perhaps, but I'm damned if I will name my son Edward, after him. One of the most satisfying things about fatherhood will be ensuring that my son turns out to be twice the man of my brother's spawn. "We must make sure he has the best of everything. The best horses, the best armour ..."

Katheryn laughs suddenly.

"Tom, the little knave is not yet born, let alone ready for all that. Let the child learn the art of sitting up at least before we choose him a mount."

I grin sheepishly. "My thoughts were running away with me."

"I should say they were. A horse indeed. And of course, Tom, there is always the possibility that he might be a girl."

She looks up at me wide-eyed, afraid of my answer, but I shrug my shoulders. "No. It is a boy. I am sure of it."

A letter arrives from Mary. Kate's eyes fill with joyful tears as she takes it and opens it quickly. She reads a few lines before looking up, her face alight with joy.

"Oh, Thomas. I think I am forgiven." I notice she makes no mention of Mary's pardon being extended to me. While she ducks her head back to the letter, I stroll to the window and look out across my fine estate. Of all the property I own, Sudeley is my favourite. There is something tranquil in the rolling countryside, the soft fragrant gardens. I long for that peace to seep into my skin and dilute my raging soul.

Kate looks up again. "Mary sends her good luck for the delivery and bids me extend her commendations to you."

"Really?" I wander over and take the letter, my eye travelling over the script. "Hmm, that is good of her." I toss the parchment onto a table and return to the window.

"It is almost time for my lying in, Thomas. You …you will keep out of trouble while I am …busy?"

"Of course," I reply, but I do not turn for I am aware that my cheeks have grown very red. She is inferring that I shall not ride to be with Elizabeth, or that I should not come to blows with my brother and end up in gaol. "I am not a child, Kate. I know how to behave."

August 1548 – Sudeley Castle

Kate takes to her lying in chamber and I am kept away, only her women may enter. I lurk close by, keeping an eye on who enters and who leaves. She is a vessel carrying my most precious cargo and I must see her safely brought to harbour.

I am sitting in an alcove not far from her chamber in case I should be summoned when a footstep alerts me. When someone comes creeping toward my wife's chamber I stand up, my hand to my dagger.

"Dr Huicke."

He stops and turns toward me. "Ah, My Lord, I did not see you there."

"Where are you going?"

He smiles a slow infuriating smile, strokes his beard and issues a string of medical terminology I cannot

238

hope to follow. He is making a fool of me and anger unfurls in my belly, curling like fire through my veins.

"No. You are not going to see my wife, Sir. She has no need of you. Your constant visits tire her."

He stands open-mouthed for a while before conceding defeat and bowing his shiny bald head.

"As you wish it, sir, but I must warn you, at her age your wife is at greater ..."

"She is at more risk from bumbling quacks than from anything else. Get away from her door, man, before I have you thrown from the castle."

His face blanches and he backs off. I hope I'll not see him again.

***

I wake suddenly and lie staring into the dark, unsure what has disturbed me. The wind has risen outside, the ivy blowing and tapping against the window. Perhaps it was that. I roll over again, bury my head in the pillow, but something won't let me sleep. I turn onto my back again, stare into the darkness. And then I hear footsteps, and muffled voices. I spring from bed and throw open the chamber door to find two of Kate's servants scurrying past. They stop when they see me and, averting their eyes from my naked chest, bob a curtsey.

"What is it?" I ask, scratching my head, making my hair stand on end. "Is it your mistress?"

One of them steps forward, bobs again. "It is the babe, My Lord. He is making himself known."

I swivel on my heel and begin to struggle into my clothes, swearing at the laces that insist on tangling. In the end, still half clad, I hurry along to Kate's chamber where I am turned away at the door by her outraged nurse. I don't know why I expected anything else. It is hardly acceptable for me to be there. I point to a chair in the outer chamber.

"I will be right there. You are to summon me the moment my son is born."

She nods her agreement and I sit down, my hands to my head. My son. The thought of him makes my heart surge with gratitude. Once I have a son, things will begin to go my way. I will have someone to fight for, someone who will always be on my side. I lunge into a dream where this child is the first of many. I see myself surrounded by strong sons and pretty daughters. It is a happy thought.

Few sounds issue from the room but every so often a woman appears, takes a look at me and scurries past as if I might bite her. I sit down. I stand up. I pace the corridor. I go to the window. Return to the chair. Sit down. I stand up. I pace the corridor ... for long tortuous hours. And then the door opens. A dour-faced maid tells me I can go in.

The chamber is dark and there is a strange smell in the air, some herbal concoction I do not recognise. Women with no faces are tidying the chamber, carrying bowls covered with cloth, armfuls of linen, trays of potions and dark-hued bottles. A fire burns unnecessarily hot and in the bed, Kate is looking down at the bundle in her arms.

She looks up when she hears my soft tread and her face opens like a flower ... like a lily. "Look Tom," she says, and looks down at our sleeping son again.

The babe is tightly swaddled, its puce face crushed, its lips pouting, his eyes shut. It is the ugliest thing I have ever seen. Gently I lower myself to the edge of the bed.

240

"How are you, Kate? Are you well?"

"I have never been better," she says, as a tear drops onto her cheek.

"I was worried. It took so long."

"No," she laughs, gently. "It wasn't long. My women have been telling me it was indecently quick, and easy."

"Hmmm, let's hope next time will be quicker still."

I lean over for a closer look.

"Do you want to hold her?"

I nod and she places the child in my arms. She is no weight at all. I look down at the snub nose, the pursed lips, the bald head still coated with grease. And then the impact of Kate's words hits me.

"A girl?" I whisper, and Kate nods, her eyes nervous for the first time. With a slightly shaking finger I trace the line of my daughter's cheek. "A girl," I murmur. "Just what I wanted."

September 1548 – Sudeley Castle

I have never been happier or prouder. I receive a letter from my brother Edward, who cannot help but sneer a little at our failure to produce a son, as his wife has done. But even that does not spoil my mood. I order the wine casks to be opened and spare no cost in celebration.

We name her Mary, in honour of the princess. I cannot keep away from the nursery. For the first time I have a girl I can worship, one who will love me back, unconditionally. Long years of adulation stretch before me. I see her toddling toward me with outstretched arms; mounted on her first pony; donning her first silk gown.

I will spare no effort in finding her a high-status husband. Why, she might even make a match with King Edward. I am the brother of a queen; husband to a queen; uncle to a king; why not the father of a queen too? The future is bright. For the first time in years the smile on my face is relaxed, and I no longer have cause to be looking constantly behind me. With gusto I begin to arrange the christening, lingering long and hard over who will make the most suitable Godparents.

I am at my desk compiling a list of names when I hear a slight knock on the door and little Jane Grey sidles into the room. "Jane!" I greet her heartily, throw down my pen.

Her face flushes scarlet as it always does when I speak to her. She takes two steps closer, stops, clutches her hands before her and blurts out, "My Lord, Katheryn is sick. She has taken a fever."

Cold dread floods through my body, making my head spin and my belly turn sick. I am on my feet before I know it and thundering up the stairs. As I storm across to the bed, Kate's women part, their skirts whispering like a dying breath.

The child sleeps peacefully in her cradle. After a cursory glance at her I turn to Kate and approach the bed. Her face is red, and she is sweating, her hair tangled and damp, the veins at her temple pulsing. "Sweet Jesus," I groan. "How long has she been like this?"

"It started last night, My Lord. She was thirsty and headachy. Then, early this morning, we woke to find this."

"What did Huicke say?"

The woman blanches. "We did not dare send for him, since you forbade him the chamber."

"Get him now." I speak through tight lips. As the woman rushes from the chamber, I sink onto the mattress and take Kate's burning hand.

"Hush, sweetheart. Hush. All will be well."

She looks at me, doesn't seem to see or recognise me.

"Lady Tyrwhit, Lady Tyrwhit." Her voice is anxious, querulous. "Where are you?"

"Here, Your Majesty." The woman steps forward to the opposite side of the bed and leans over my wife. Kate grabs her arm, straining forward, her words issuing from spittle-coated lips.

"I am not well handled, for those that be about me care not for me, but stand laughing at my grief, and the more good I will to them the less good they will to me."

She is mad. Delirious. I look desperately around the chamber. "Where is that damned doctor?"

A maid bobs a curtsey and runs from the room to hurry the tardy physician. I place a hand on my wife's brow and it burns beneath my fingers.

"Hush, sweetheart. I would do you no hurt, you know that."

She wrenches away, rolls her head back and forth on the pillow. "Nay, I think so. You have given me many shrewd taunts."

As guilt sinks sharp teeth into my gut, Lady Tyrwhit casts her disdainful glare in my direction. We both know Kate is thinking of Elizabeth and all the hurt we did her. I have never been sorrier for anything in my life.

To the astonishment of all assembled, I shift onto the bed and lie down beside her, wrap her in my arms. I can feel her body heat radiating through the blankets; her hands that I refuse to release are as hot as a brazier.

243

"Hush Kate; my Kate. All will be well." To ease her I whisper little terms of endearment, words of love, but she makes no answer, nor shows signs of easement. "The doctor is coming," I say at last and she turns her burning red eyes upon me.

"I would have done better to have seen him the day after the birthing but you ... you would have none of it, and forbid him. You have finished me, Thomas. You have broken my heart, and now you have finished me ..."

Katheryn dies in a raging fever, never once looking upon me with love. At first I cannot credit it. How can God, that God that she set so much store by, do this to me? To her? To us? I rage. I storm and, with no Katheryn there to steady me, I embark upon a perilous path.

The child, Mary, now holds little joy for me. What is she without her mother? What am I? People begin to tread softly around me, afraid of my seething anger, my irrational deeds. I order a vast royal funeral; a protestant ceremony as she would have wished.

"It is to be as grand as any queen's. That is what she was, do you hear? A queen! My queen." I try and fail to swallow my tears, retreat to my room again, pour another cup of wine, tip it down my throat and hurl the vessel at the wall before I give way to another storm of weeping.

I cannot seem to function. All my life God has given with one hand and taken away with the other. Letters arrive, carefully worded, gentle letters of condolence, every one of them expressing love for Katheryn and sympathy for me. I cast them to the floor, even those from Elizabeth and Mary. I tread them into the rushes.

I don't want sympathy.

I want Katheryn.

On the day they place her in a leaded coffin and carry her into the black-draped chapel, I watch from the house with heavy eyes. The future is bleak. I have no will for it. I am lost, all at sea on a foundering ship. The Lord High Admiral – I laugh bitterly at the silent jest.

My pity is all for myself. I have little to spare for poor motherless little Mary. Someone will care for her. She will have nurses, servants, and a huge domestic staff far beyond the needs of a tiny babe. I will break up Katheryn's household. I have no care to be here, so I ride away, back to court.

***

If my brother and the council ignored me before, now that Katheryn is dead my influence upon them is even less. I am no longer husband to the queen dowager, I am just a widower. My back is uncovered, giving my enemies free access to it.

To try to keep my mind from grief, my spirit from shrivelling, I rekindle my ambition. I need to boost my power, bolster my impact upon state affairs with some influential friends. I am a popular man. There are plenty that enjoy my company, invite me to their homes, and introduce me to their daughters. But they do not offer me the benefits I need.

Soon my thoughts turn back to Jane Grey and my quest to marry her to the prince. The thing that stands in my way is my inability to get close to my nephew, the king. They keep him from me, bury him deep in the palace and, despite all my efforts, I cannot get near.

With a vague plan to form a counter party to my brother's, I begin to cultivate friends in high places. I take up residence in Holt castle, far from Edward's prying eyes, and develop tactics and stratagems.

But Kate is never far from my thoughts. I dwell upon the wasted hours, the petty squabbles, the hurt I caused her, and then I drink. Jug after jug of wine to numb the feeling of despair, the utter *desolation* of a life gone wrong.

On one such night I write to Elizabeth. A long and maudlin missive that I hope to God nobody ever sees. I ask her to marry me, but no doubt she is still torn with guilt at her past behaviour, sorry for Katheryn's loss. She will have none of me and the rejection sends me deeper into despair.

One day, I tell myself. One day I will have her and my life will run smoothly again. Wed to one of old Harry's daughters, how could my fortunes not change?

My friends warn me that my brother and his council have noticed my plotting. They do not like it. I am not the only one who desires to be rid of the protector, but I alone bear the courage to do anything about it. They are all cowards, reprobates. I will not be stopped. I will speak to the king whether Brother Edward desires it or not. I don't need his sanction.

I drain another bottle and set off after dark to the palace. Leaving my horse in a quiet alley, I climb a wall and make my way through the privy garden. I try not to remember walking here with Kate, flirting under the nose of the king, little knowing that he was plotting to steal her from me and make her his own wife.

The palace is slumbering, the moon is shadowed. I creep like a thief along the edge of the wall and into the royal apartments by an unfastened door. My brother should be hung for such laxity; any jade could break in and do harm to the king.

I know this place like the back of my hand. With great stealth I move through a room littered with the bodies of sleeping attendants, and up three steps to the inner chamber. I place my hand on the knob and turn it.

The door opens silently. I am in and the king is unattended.

The fire is low, the torches extinguished, only the night candle burns, gently illuminating the dark. From the huge canopied bed issue the high-pitched snores of the boy king. As I move forward, one of his dogs raises its head, growls low in its throat. I hold out a hand, "Shhh," I whisper. "Good dog, good dog."

He recognises me and lies back down, his muzzle on his front paws, his long ears fanning out on the floor. I am thankful the king favours only spaniels; I'd have no fancy to encounter a pack of wolfhounds. The other spaniel, of liverish hue, who does not know me, glares at me with a bloodshot eye. He doesn't see a friend, a visiting uncle, but a nocturnal stranger stalking the royal chamber.

He springs up, lowers his head and growls, far more menacingly than the first. "Good dog," I try again but it has no effect. Before I can think of escape, he is upon me with a great snarl, his teeth sinking into my thigh. I shout out in fear, fumble for my gun, as in a great snarling the other beast leaps to his feet to join him.

Doors open, footsteps come running. The king is awake, stumbling from bed in his nightgown, somehow seeming much smaller than his twelve and a half years.

Teeth, so many teeth, lacerating, relentless, sharp! I kick one beast away, it flies off, comes to a halt near the grate, but in no time is back to join the other in making tatters of my doublet.

"Edward," I cry out to quiet his fears. "It is me, your Uncle Thomas. Call off your dog." But the king stands amazed, half dreaming still. Desperate now for self-preservation, I fumble for my pistol; raise my firearm and, careless now of who should hear me, blast the beast away. The dog slumps to the floor, the other runs for shelter while I sit in a puddle of canine blood and wipe my brow. While I try to catch my breath, the chamber begins to fill with astounded servants.

The king falls to his knees, lifts the lifeless head of his favourite spaniel. I creep toward him, arms outstretched but he ignores me as he gathers the corpse closer to his heart.

"You've killed my dog," he wails, hugging the beast tighter, bloodying his nightgown. "You've killed my dog, my poor, poor dog." He buries his face in the bloodied fur and tears spill down his cheeks. As I attempt to move closer to offer comfort him, Edward draws away, glares at me and, wearing the face of his father, speaks through clenched teeth. "I will have your head for this, Uncle Thomas, God curse you."

Part Four
Elizabeth Tudor: Princess

January 1549 - Hatfield

I've been walking in the garden, but a sudden rain shower drives me indoors. I skip up the steps and pull off my cap, shake it so that freezing raindrops scatter like beads onto the rushes. I hand it to my attendant and begin to peel off my wet cloak.

It is good to be back in Hatfield. Although the Dennys did all in their power to ensure my stay at Cheshunt was comfortable, I missed the familiar walls of home. But even though I am back and my every need is catered for by Katherine Ashley, I still crave for the wisdom and gentleness of my stepmother. I thought I would die from grief and guilt when they brought me the news of her death. Poor Katheryn. She never had the chance to know happiness, not really.

I have known plenty of stepmothers, but never mourned one as I do her. And I am wracked with guilt for the horrid way I mistreated her. Katheryn offered me everything I had ever missed. She filled the gap in my soul that was carved by the loss of my real mother. I cannot forgive myself. I know I am an ungrateful, undeserving wretch.

I have to try very hard to recall my earliest days, the time before my mother stopped coming to visit. But if I close my eyes and allow my mind to drift back, I can almost reach her. I cannot see her face or remember any particular thing we did together, but I recall her presence. It is a sort of fragrance, a waft of merry laughter, a shadowy perception of warmth and love. It lightens my heart even now.

As an infant I thought about her a lot but gradually, when I realised she wasn't coming back, I stopped looking for her, and after a while I stopped thinking about her too. But after she was gone and especially now, I am always alone. Although I am surrounded by people and almost every move I make is monitored, I am solitary, separate, and I have been ever since the day they cut off my mother's head.

Katheryn soothed all that. She mothered me, mentored me, and taught me to be strong and wise. I should have held on to that wisdom when I first began to yield to the charms of her husband. I make no excuses but women are soft when it comes to love.

Kat Ashley ushers me to my chamber and I pick up my book and sit close to the hearth. "Are your skirts damp? Do you think you should change?"

I look at her over the edge of the pages. "No, Kat. I am fine."

I return to my book, hook my finger over the edge of the page, ready to turn, already anticipating that which is on the other side. A girl arrives to restock the fire and for a while the flames are dampened by additional fuel. I miss the heat on my steaming skirts and supress a shiver.

Kat scurries back in, places a cup and jug at my side, and waits with her hands clenched, reluctant to disturb my reading since she knows it annoys me. I look up with barely disguised impatience.

"What now?"

"There are some gentlemen to see you, Madam. Gentlemen from court."

I put down my book and straighten my shoulders. "What gentlemen?"

Before she can answer, the door is thrown open and Robert Tyrwhit is ushered in. He makes the customary greeting and I respond to him coolly. Something is not right. I don't yet know what it is but I am alert, my skin crawling as if there is an assassin in the room. Although I am not constrained to do so, I stand up to greet him.

"Sir Robert," I say as Kat slips reluctantly away. She will listen outside the door; I have no doubt about that. Kat has been with me since I was an infant and takes liberties I would tolerate from no other.

Tyrwhit takes a step forward, looks around my chamber. "You are alone?"

Keeping hold of my book, my finger marking the page, I spread my arms wide.

"As you can see, Sir Robert."

He looks pointedly at the girl who is sweeping ashes into a pail. I had forgotten her presence.

"Get out," I snap, and she grovels her way to the door and disappears, leaving us in peace.

His cap is in his hands; as he clears his throat he smoothes the feather and flicks away a speck of dust. "I have some news that may concern you. Your stepfather, the Lord Admiral, Thom—"

"I know who my stepfather is, Sir Robert. What has he done now?"

At the mention of Tom my heart begins to beat faster, but I pretend indifference. It is imperative that I keep my real feelings hidden. Thomas is always in some scrape or other. I wonder if he has taken to a life of piracy, or persuaded the king to realise his desire to be the royal guardian. Sir Robert hesitates, his eye intent on

251

my face, increasing my lack of ease. I lift my chin, look down my nose.

"He is under arrest, Your Royal Highness, held in custody at the Tower."

I am suddenly very cold. I do not move but I clutch my book tighter, fighting for control, determined not to let him see how deeply this news affects me.

"In the Tower?" I reply as casually as I can. "For what reason?"

"For attempting to abduct the king."

I had not expected such an answer. Tom would not harm the king.

"Abduct the king? That is ridiculous. He dotes on Edward, he is his nephew."

Tyrwhit bows his head, closes his eyes.

"Nevertheless, he stole into the king's bedchamber at the dead of night and murdered his dog."

"Murdered his dog?"

I am repeating everything he says like some brainless popinjay. My mind is darting back and forth, trying to make sense of Tyrwhit's words. Tom likes dogs, he loves the king. He would never do these things. I suspect a plot. Imperceptibly I draw in a deep breath, trying with difficulty to pull myself together. I pretend to be dismissive, as if the event is of no great matter to me. I shrug my shoulders and turn away.

"The Admiral was ever a fool. I am sure there is some mistake. The king will no doubt change his story in a day or two and all will be well again."

Running a finger along the windowsill I pick up a small pile of dust before turning my attention back to Tyrwhit.

He shakes his head, stony-faced. "Nay, that he won't. The arrest was made several days ago and in the

252

duration several other matters have come to light. That is why I have come to tell you that I am taking your woman, Katherine Ashley and your man, Thomas Parry, into custody for questioning."

My vision blurs, the world dips. I clutch the back of my chair and will away the tiny bright lights that are whirling in the blackness of my mind. I scrabble for words.

"That is ridiculous. They were not involved in any attempted abduction of the king. They were here, with me."

"That may be so but we need to talk to them about another matter concerning The Admiral ... and yourself."

How can he know? Who can have spoken of this? When she sent me away, Queen Katheryn swore she would speak of it to no one, and even Tom is not such a fool as to ...

Tyrwhit breaks into my thoughts. "In the meantime I will leave you in the care of my good wife."

At his summons Elizabeth Tyrwhit is shown in. She sinks into a low, insincere curtsey. She has never liked me and I do not want to be placed in her care, but something tells me it is pointless to protest. Princess or not, I am in no position to make demands. I never have been. Lady Tyrwhit is not a bad woman, Katheryn loved and trusted her, perhaps I can too.

I give myself a little shake and, remembering my manners, I greet her cordially and am stunned to the core when I notice the scarcely veiled hostility in her eyes. My disquiet increases; maybe, just maybe, she was the sort of friend that Katheryn confided in. Is it possible that this woman could betray my guilt to the entire world?

I imagine the shame, the ignominy. I can hear the recrimination of the people now. *She is just like her mother. It is in her blood. She is nothing but a whore, born of a whore.*

Full of shame at my imagined disgrace, I want to weep. I want to run and find Kat, hide her away somewhere so they cannot take her from me. But I remain where I am, rooted to the spot like a tree in a thunderstorm. I shrug my shoulders and turn back to Sir Robert, forcing myself to speak casually.

"Well, Sir Robert, I trust you will not detain them for long. I rely on Katherine Ashley for everything. Besides, she is not just a servant, she is my friend."

"It will take as long as it takes, Madam. But I will be back in a day or two to speak to you about the matter in more detail."

He bows over my hand and I repress a shudder of repulsion. He is dissembling. I can always tell and I can never stomach deceit. I prefer a man to speak rudely but honestly; there is no value in words that are spoken just to please.

As my attendants are escorted from the palace, I can hear Kat weeping loudly, protesting that she has done nothing to warrant the attention of the council. I watch from the window as they are bundled into a carriage to begin the journey to London. Looking through the thick green glass is like looking through tears. Kat stares wildly up at the window and, although it is doubtful she can see me, I raise my hand in farewell. As the carriage draws away, I pray to God she does not weaken and betray me. It is not just my life that is in danger, but that of The Admiral too. We are both dependent upon the testimony of those two weak and foolish people.

Inwardly I am trembling but, assuming a confidence I do not feel, I sit down and take up my book again as if nothing is amiss. Uninvited, Lady Tyrwhit takes the opposite chair, and I scowl at her. Kat would know I prefer to read alone. The woman begins to witter, trying to win my confidence.

"It is a lovely house you have here. I've not visited Hatfield before but I've heard about it, of course."

If she knew me she would know better than to try to engage with me in idle chatter. I scarcely ever waste words. I lower the book a little.

"I am trying to read."

With an outraged glare she gets to her feet, makes a sketchy curtsey and moves to the window, leaving me in peace.

Usually about now Kat would bring me a warm drink, quietly sort out my night linen and begin to ready my chamber for the night. Although the house is full of women, it is Kat I want. Hatfield seems empty without her.

The day has exhausted me and I can feel the beginnings of my monthly cramps tightening in my belly. I rub a pimple on my chin, and feel my mouth begin to tremble. I draw my breath in sharply and sniff away the silly tears, duck my head to my book again. If I have to cry I will do it later, when I am alone, tucked beneath the covers. Until then I will not give my enemies the satisfaction.

I focus my eyes on the pages of my stepmother's book, *The Lamentations of a Sinner*. There is so much of Katheryn between the pages; her aspirations, her piety, but very little of her big, warm heart. I like to read her words; they make her seem very close and it is easier to believe she is not lying cold beneath a slab of stone.

Katheryn's book begins by modestly berating her own sinfulness. My eyes mist over as I absorb her humility and match it to my own situation.

"When I consider, in the bethinking of mine evil and wretched former life, mine obstinate, stony, and intractable heart to have so much exceeded in evilness, that it hath not only neglected, yea contemned and despised God's holy precepts and commandments ..."

If Katheryn were here now, what would she think of me? Would she see me as her own failure? She tried to teach me, tried to make me good, but I am so bad ... Dark to the depths of my soul and too sinful to be taught.

Katheryn was writing, of course, of her life before she embraced the new faith, but my mind is set on more earthly matters just now. I think of her too-short life, unspotted by sin, and compare it with my own. There can be no comparison.

I am not yet sixteen years old and yet I have sinned more gravely than she ever did. I had always intended to live a spotless life, prove myself a virtuous and pious woman. But that was before I knew Tom. Now, I am so cast down by misery and guilt that I wonder if my reputation is worth fighting for. Perhaps I should be whipped through the streets for the sinner I am. Perhaps it is what I deserve.

I have no appetite. I push the food around my plate and barely eat half of it. After a restless evening when I accuse the musician of discordance, and make my woman, Meg, weep when she almost beats me at cards, I send them all away early. I am glad to retire to bed, grateful for the drawn shutters and the dark that will not show my tears.

Where are you, Kat Ashley? I wonder if they have housed her well, or thrown her into a dungeon. I hope they use her kindly for she is a weak and silly soul. She will not be hard to break. Thomas Parry is an unknown quantity but, being a man, I credit him with a courage I do not expect from Kat. I have little doubt that cruelty will swiftly crumble her resolve and loosen her tongue.

I stare into the dark until my eyeballs ache. I toss and turn, kicking off the covers and hauling them back again when the night air chills my restless limbs. By morning I am exhausted, and when Elizabeth Tyrwhit comes to wake me, I bury my head beneath the pillow and tell her to go away.

"I cannot go away, Madam. My husband will be here to speak with you within the hour."

"Tell him to go to the devil..."

"I beg pardon?"

Thankfully the pillow has muffled my words and I remember just in time that I must not make an enemy of her. I emit a huge sigh and open my eyes, see nothing until I draw the pillow away. I must think of Kat imprisoned in a dark, dank cell. Only my co-operation will free her. I must keep my head. Confess nothing and pray that my story and that of my servants is the same.

I stand shivering in the gloomy morning while they dress me. They sponge my body, comb my hair, and tie my petticoat, lace up my kirtle. I am dressed plainly as is my preference, and my reflection shows a girl, slim and taut, with a stone-white face and large blank eyes. I do not look like the object of any man's lust. My guilty conscience is tucked securely away behind a pious screen, and I present a picture of maidenly purity.

"You must eat something," Lady Tyrwhit holds out a plate but I push it away and reach for a cup instead. Wine will sustain me until the trial is over.

I have heard it whispered that my mother's trial was a farce, the charges trumped up by her enemies. I wonder how she felt on the day she had to face them accused of such heinous things. Had she had time to make up a credible story but ... the difference between my mother and I is that she was innocent of the charges. I am not.

There will be no panel of judges today, but I will be judged nonetheless. I close my eyes and silently pray for wisdom and calm. Then I pick up my prayer book and sweep from the room, moving so quickly along the corridors and down the stairs that Elizabeth Tyrwhit is forced to break into a trot to keep up with me.

When we reach the hall I am calm and collected. As they throw open the door, I cannot resist from smirking at her discomfort. She is quite out of breath, and a glimmer of sweat is beading her brow. I flash her a half-smile of contempt before I enter the room and Robert Tyrwhit and his creatures rise to greet me.

A wintry sun filters through the windows of the hall. It should be a day for hunting, or a walk in the grounds, perhaps a shooting contest in the meadow. Instead I am here, confronting my detractors.

Tyrwhit wastes no time, and as soon as he has greeted me, immediately begins to bark questions. As if I am playing a game of tennis I fend them off, send them spinning back, unanswered, dodged, dismissed, scorned.

His patience grows short. He tightens his lips, leans one hand on the table, the knuckles white against the board. I can sense he is fighting to keep his temper and for the first time I begin to believe I can best him. He raises his head, fixes me with a liverish eye.

"Have you ever contemplated or discussed marriage with the Lord Admiral?"

"No, Sir, I haven't."

"Are you sure?"

"I am very sure. I would never consider any proposal of marriage unless it was expressly desired by the king's council."

He looks at me. There is no friendship, no compassion, and no empathy in his face. Were my father still alive, this man would never dare to look at me so.

I am not lying. I have never openly discussed marriage with The Admiral but the question has always been there, unspoken between us. At first, when Katheryn was alive, it was a regret, a missed opportunity. But since her death our marriage has once more become a possibility. One day it might happen, and I know that my marriage to him is Kat Ashely's scarcely concealed dream. She is almost as much in love with Tom as I am. I remember her flushed face when she spoke of him, pressing his suit, as if I needed encouraging.

"He is a fine gentleman. So handsome, so rich, so dashing ..."

Oh yes, Tom is all those things. I sigh deeply and look toward the window. I cannot see out but I know what is there. I suppose I had lately held a dream that we would be allowed to marry, that I would achieve my desires. Now, with recent events, I realise that it will never be.

To escape the stifling confines of the hall, I picture myself strolling instead through the meadows, beneath the branches of the great oaks. The air is ripe with the smell of the slumbering earth, rotting vegetation, lately fallen rain, dank puddles. When they sense my approach, the deer in the shadow of the wood stop feeding; they raise their heads, their noses twitching, alert to my presence, deciding whether to flee or to tarry. As Tyrwhit's detested voice breaks my reverie, their tawny behinds dart for cover. I drag my face from the window.

"My Lord? I am sorry. I misheard you."

He draws breath, battling to keep his temper.

"We have been informed of The Admiral's plot to take control of the king's person. We believe that marriage to you or your sister formed part of that plan. We have it on good authority that your servants, Parry and Ashley, were intriguing to marry you to Seymour. What we need to determine, Madam, is your own involvement in that plot."

My sister Mary? I do not doubt the truth of it, although it is news to me. I can feel my face reddening as I fight to control my jealous rage. So Tom was covering all his bets and courting both of us. I take little comfort in knowing he would have preferred it to be me. Next in line to the throne or not, Mary is plain and growing old. She can hold little charm for him.

I, on the other hand, have sampled his lust, witnessed first-hand his uncontrollable desire. Had Mary been subjected to such passion, she'd spend the rest of her days praying for redemption.

Tyrwhit taps his fingers impatiently on the table. I wish I were my father that I might strike terror into this man's heart. I want to cuff him and roar out in anger as I have seen my father do, but I am not a king. I am a girl and friendless in this dangerous world.

Refusing to be cowed by him, I raise my chin, look down my nose.

"My servants; Mistress Ashley in particular, I trust you have housed her well. She is not used to the discomfort. She will not like the cold."

He casts his eyes to heaven, leans toward me, and speaks through tight white lips. "We have housed her in the deepest, coldest, darkest cell in the Tower. Now, Madam, unless you wish to join her, you'd do well to answer my questions."

Belatedly I realise that arrogance will not win with this man. I bow my head meekly, and allow a tear to trickle down my cheek before I look up again. When he sees my apparent weakness, his face relaxes and a slow smile of satisfaction spreads across his face. I make my answer, ensuring a wobble enters my voice as if I am sorely offended.

"I have never had any dealings with The Admiral other than as stepfather and stepdaughter. He is the king's uncle and has ever treated me as he treats my brother, like a dearly loved relative."

So great is his frustration that Tyrwhit all but thumps the table. He glares at me and I decide it is time to weep in earnest. Perhaps, like The Admiral, he will not be able to abide my tears and bring this interview to a swifter end.

My chin wobbles, my eyes flood with tears and I give two or three very substantial sobs, before flopping onto a nearby stool. I bury my face in my hands and my shoulders heave silently in a convincing show of despair.

There is not a sound in the room other than my weeping. A clerk, who has taken down every word spoken in the last two hours, clears his throat and shuffles his papers.

Tyrwhit sighs.

I recognise the first sign of his defeat. As I raise my head to let him see my tear-streaked face, he throws up his hands.

"All right; all right. Have done with your weeping. We will leave it for today. I will be back tomorrow, but I need answers; answers that match the confessions given by your servants."

I look up at him and dab my red eyes with the corner of my kerchief. I nod.

"Thank you, My Lord. I am sorely tired but, no matter how often you return, I will not be able to add to that which I have already told you. I know nothing of any plot or any marriage arrangements. I am barely out of mourning for my dear late father, sir."

I turn my tragic face to him and he clears his throat, looks away. I mentioned the late king to remind him just who he is dealing with. I might be a friendless pawn in this game he is playing, but I am a royal princess. He should be wary for, according to all my teachings, I am of royal blood and God and the truth should be on my side.

I pass a sleepless night in which I am beset with stomach cramps, a nauseating headache, and a bleakness of spirit. Usually I would summon Kat and she'd comfort me as only she knows how. I refuse to call for the Tyrwhit woman and, as soon as I am abed, I send all my other ladies away.

There is just one maid in attendance. She falls asleep straight away, snoring gently on her truckle bed. When I can stand no more I nudge her awake with my foot and she staggers, barely awake, from the warmth of her slumber.

While I wait for her to return from the stillroom with an infusion of ginger, I look about the shadowy chamber. Night paints the corners a deep impenetrable black. They are the sort of shadows that might conceal a monster, a spy or an assassin; the sort of malevolent corners that gave me night terrors when I was a child.

Determinedly, I turn to face the window, where the first streaks of dawn are lightening the sky. It is warm in my bed but I slide from beneath the sheets and creep, barefoot, to the window and throw back the shutter. I lean closer, my breath misting the thick green glass.

The gardens are silvered with frost, the shrubs and bushes humped menacingly. Beyond the garden wall the meadows and hills merge with a tumultuous purple-streaked sky. The world might be sleeping but the earth isn't. The wind stirs the trees, rain rattles on the casement and, in the shadows, the night creatures prowl.

On nights such as this, bad folk carry out despicable deeds. It is lonely here at Hatfield. It would be an easy task if anyone should seek to come and kill me in my sleep. Retainers are easily bribed, and the tiny village, huddled at the foot of the hill beyond the church would be no defence. Were Somerset to send an assassin against me, no one would hear my screams.

I kneel on the sill with my head drooped in my hands and feel the tears begin to well up again. When the door softly opens, my mind is still full of assassins and death and, with a cry of terror, I leap to my feet, stand defenceless in the half light.

"It's all right. It is me, Madam." The girl comes silently across the room and beams an encouraging smile. Without mentioning my terror, she helps me back into bed, draws the covers up to warm my frozen feet and offers me the cup. My pink-tipped fingers close around it, welcoming the comfort of the warm brew. I take a sip, feel the liquid slide down to my belly, thawing my blood, and soon my knotted stomach releases enough for me to breathe. I begin to relax.

"My enemies are gathering against me. Did you know that?"

She opens her eyes wide and for the first time I notice how extraordinarily freckled my companion is. Everything about her is normal and homely; I expect she has a family nearby; a litter of siblings all similarly freckled. I cannot help but smile at her over the rim of my cup and she smiles back.

"I have heard things, Madam. Things I don't rightly understand, and I've heard other talk too." She looks away, bites her lip as if regretting having spoken.

"What things?"

Her eyes grow large. "It might be better if I do not say."

"You have to say now. You cannot leave me in suspense. Come, tell me. I swear I will hold nothing against you."

"There is talk, a wicked slander, Madam, that you were seduced by the Lord High Admiral and that even now, you are waiting to bear his child."

Our eyes travel as one to my stomach that is as flat and as barren as a board. We look at each other and although there is nothing remotely funny, laughter erupts from deep within me. I sputter the decoction of ginger over the sheets and in moments, we are both rolling on the bed, gasping for breath as tears run from our eyes.

"Oh dear, oh dear." I wipe my cheeks dry. "It isn't really a laughing matter but men are so ridiculous, aren't they? Surely it is plain to see that I am not carrying anyone's child, let alone The Admiral's."

"When they realise that perhaps they will leave you alone."

I sober suddenly as fear chases mirth away again and I speak quietly into the gloom. "They won't leave me alone until I have betrayed him. He is a better man than any at court but his enemies will not stop until they have him."

She has no answer and we sit quietly until, indicating the cooling cup, she says. "Drink your medic up, Madam, it will soothe you."

"That's better," I say, handing her the empty vessel. She places it on the night stand and draws the covers up to my chin. I relax into the pillow and try not to think of tomorrow, but I do not sleep.

Every time I close my eyes, I see Tom in his prison cell; imagine my poor Kat Ashley shivering in a dungeon, her pretty fingers bloodied by the screw. My eyes snap open, staring into the dark, trying to chase away the images. What can I do? What can I say to get them out of there? If I cannot find the right words they will perish, with me alongside them. I thump my pillow, toss and turn for hours, torn between anger and despair. With fear in my heart I watch the shadows on the wall begin to lift, hear muffled sounds from the kitchens as morning creeps relentlessly closer, like a thief.

Tyrwhit, his temper well and truly lost, waves a parchment in my face. "It is all written here, Madam. Your servants have told us all."

He smacks the paper with the back of his hand to emphasise his point.

"I cannot agree or disagree with their comments unless I know what they have said."

My heart is thumping sickeningly and I try to breathe slowly and deeply so as not to let him see my fear. What have they said? He could be fooling me; leading me into a trap. They may have kept silent. I will say nothing. I will force him to read their confession aloud before I commit myself.

The silence cannot last long. I close my lips tight and listen to the scratch of the scribe's pen as he catches up with my last words. Everything I say, everything I do is being taken down to be held against me.

My heart sinks when he begins to read the transcription of Ashley and Parry's confessions. I want to scream that it is a forgery, a slanderous list of lies, but Thomas Parry and Kat's voices are apparent in every line, and when he shows me the paper with the scrawled signatures I recognise the hand, too. They have betrayed me. I bow my head, and begin to weep, real tears this time.

He makes everything they said sound sordid, shameful. How can such sweet times be made to seem so tawdry?

I remember that day in the garden, the sparring that began so innocently and ended so sharply poignant. The blade that slashed off my gown tore away my childhood too. As he held me down and ripped up my clothes I didn't want him to stop, not until I was naked in his arms. When I told him I loved him, I couldn't help myself, and it wasn't until I saw the answering lust in his own eyes that I realised the danger. I should never have spoken. It was only my innocence, my apparent girlhood that was holding him back.

It had always been a game. He came to my room, tickled and slapped me, teased me about having enormous buttocks. It was just a prank, a naughty, rough game that made us feel alive. He didn't mean to make me love him. He didn't mean to fall in love with me. We both loved Katheryn.

"Well, Madam. What say you to this?"

"I say it is back stairs gossip, My Lord. I heard a similar rumour that I am carrying The Admiral's child."

I hold out my arms, turn a circle. "Do you see evidence of that, Sir? There is as much truth in that rumour as any of that which you have just read out. If Mistress Ashley and Thomas Parry spoke of any marriage then I cannot be held accountable for that. Both they and I would never consider any union without the full consent of the council; as both Parry and Kat clearly state. The part about The Admiral so graciously allowing me the use of his house when I travel to court is true. The rest is false, gained under threat of torture, no doubt."

"You never discussed The Admiral with Mrs Ashley?"

I shrug my shoulders. "I may have, but we weren't in earnest. We discussed many, many men, as women do, My Lord. Mistress Ashley finds The Admiral charming and handsome, is it a crime that we should discuss him?"

He frowns and looks down at his notes, and after a few more questions allows me to leave. Once in my chamber I sit down, try to quell my trembling limbs, and pen a letter in my best hand to the Lord Protector explaining in detail, and with much falsehood, the events of the past year or two.

As I draw to the end of my missive, I pause, and run the quill against my cheek before adding the following.

... Master Tyrwhit and others have told me that there goeth rumours abroad which be greatly both against my Honour and Honesty (which above all other things I esteem), which be these; that I am in the Tower and with child by My Lord Admiral. My Lord, these are shameful slanders, for the which, besides the great desire I have to see the King's Majesty, I shall most heartily desire your

Lordship that I may come to the Court after your first
determination ; that I may show myself there as I am.
    Written in haste, from Hatfield this 28th of January.
    Your assured friend to my little power,
    ELIZABETH.

I will wait now and see what comes of it. If he consents to my attending court to prove my condition, it will put an end to the rumours and hopefully go some way toward winning leniency for Thomas.

But, despite my best attempts, the protector is not appeased. Although Kat and Parry's revelations are merely embarrassing and not enough to convict me of any crimes, he decides that Ashley is not a suitable governess. He suggests that Lady Tyrwhit becomes her permanent replacement.

I am not having this. If they have not found anything to convict me, why should I be punished?

After another night of stormy weeping I dry my eyes, remember my rightful status, and write again.

My Lord,
    Having received your lordship's letters, I perceive in them your good will towards me, because you declare to me plainly your mind in this thing, and again for that you would not wish that I should do anything that should not seem good unto the council, for the which thing I give you my most hearty thanks. And whereas, I do understand, that you do take in evil part the letters that I did write unto your lordship, I am very sorry that you should take them so, for my mind was to declare unto you plainly, as I thought, in that thing which I did, also the more willingly, because as I write to you you desired me to be plain with you in all things. And as concerning that point that you

268

write—-that I seem to stand in mine own wit in being so well assured of mine own self. I did assure me of myself no more than I trust the truth shall try. And to say that which I knew of myself I did not think should have displeased the Council or Your Grace. And surely the cause why that I was sorry that there should be any such governess about me was because that I thought the people will say that I deserved through my lewd demeanour to have such a one, and not that I mislike anything that your lordship or the Council shall think good (for I know that you and the Council are charged with me), or that I take upon me to rule myself, for I know that they are most deceived that trusteth most in themselves, wherefore I trust that you shall never find that fault in me, to the which thing I do not see that Your Grace has made any direct answer at this time, and seeing they make so evil reports already shall be but an increasing of these evil tongues.

He replies promptly and coldly, rebuking me for my pert obstinacy and I realise with a heavy heart that I must concede to his wishes. They do make one concession however, and allow the return of both Thomas Parry and my darling Kat.

It is then that I learn The Admiral's lands are being parcelled up and sold to the highest bidder. The undignified scramble that ensues as courtiers, who once claimed to be his friends, compete for his properties, bodes ill for the future. I take to my bed again, pleading illness; sick to the stomach that I must sit by and do nothing as they destroy the man I love.

For five days I lie abed, not knowing the outcome. I eat very little, ignoring the tasty morsels sent up from the kitchens to tempt me. I might as well be dead without

Tom, without Katheryn, without Kat Ashley. She is the closest thing to a mother I have left.

I have just finished with the close stool, and my servant is bearing it away. I am half way across the chamber, barefoot, clad only in my shift, when I hear a scratching at the door. One of my women brings a robe to drape across my shoulders before I call for whoever is outside to enter.

The door opens a little, a woman sidles in, a cloak clutched tightly about her. She raises her head cautiously, as though she expects a whipping.

"Kat!" I throw off the robe and spring across the chamber floor to drag her into my arms. She is weeping, spluttering apologies, excuses, promises to never gossip again. I do not care to hear them. I am just glad she is home. I pinch her, just for the reassurance of hearing her yelp. She is real.

"Oh Kat. I am so glad to have you back. I have been so worried. Are you well? Did they hurt you?"

She shakes her head, sniffs. I click my fingers for a kerchief and wait while she noisily blows her nose.

"I am so sorry, Madam. I swear before God that I will never speak loose words again. Can you forgive me?"

Taking her arm, I lead her to the fireside settle and we sit down, hands clasped. I am glad to see her fingers are as pretty and as unsullied as they have ever been.

"I know you meant me no ill. I am just grateful that they let you free. There are few who enter the Tower and come out alive."

She is trembling. She tries and fails to hold back tears. Her face crumples as she shakes her head. "If I'd known my words could harm you, I'd have cut out my own tongue."

"There now. We are safe, that is the main thing. We are all safe ... all except The Admiral."

I push the thought of him away and try to be grateful for what we have salvaged from this sorry plight. Kat is a foolish woman but she loves me, and had no way of knowing that her loose tongue would ever put me in such danger.

But from now on we speak only of trivial things; the burgeoning spring, the lambs in the fields, the choice of a new pup. We keep our speculation to small matters such as what we shall have for dinner. Although he is uppermost in my mind, we never mention Thomas who languishes still in the Tower, his fate all but sealed.

I know there is no saving him and I am aware they watch me still. The Protector's spies are everywhere and my toughest test still lies ahead. I turn my mind to preparing myself.

I have no clue as to how I am to bear the news of his death as if it is of no great matter. Of late I have become a marvellous dissembler but this next act of deception will prove the greatest trial of my life so far.

20th March 1549 - Hatfield

I am abed but I do not sleep. My mind is with Thomas, sharing his last night on this earth. I do not see the fine trappings of Hatfield Palace that are all around me. The walls of my chamber melt away and instead I see the grim, grey confines of his cell, a square window high up showing a patch of barred night sky.

Thomas is with me, or I am with him. I share his punishment, feel the damp cold. My bones ache, my heart breaks. Our only company are rats, our only food a bowl of watery broth.

He doesn't know I am there at first. He sits dejected in the straw with his head in hands and regrets all he has done. All his failures, all his misdemeanours are piled around him like a miser's treasure.

I reach out to touch him, take his cold and grimy fingers in mine and kneel with him in the straw, shuffle closer on my knees.

"Don't be sorry for it, Thomas," I whisper in his ear. "Remember us, and be glad for it."

He raises his head, blinks his vacant eyes, and scratches his lousy beard. He tries to grin but it is a pale shade of his former smile, a rictus grimace in the face of death. There is little left in this broken man to remind me of my shining Admiral.

That is the moment when my heart finally breaks and I realise that in losing him, I have lost everything. He turns away.

In the darkest hour of his life he has ceased to think of me. I am become nothing more than a misguided yearning, an insignificant splash of joy in the ocean of his existence. I drop his hand and turn away, walk toward the grim stone wall.

When I wake in the morning I wish my life was ending with his. I can see little to live for and I feel so alone, more than ever I have before. Without Thomas, without Katheryn, without my father, I am nothing but a dispossessed princess in an empty hall. Bolt upright on my pillow I call out for Kat Ashley and she comes running, her braided hair bouncing on her nightshift. At my bidding, she throws back the covers and climbs into my bed.

I am out of favour with the king; gossips whisper of my shame in the taverns, and my suspected lack of chastity is likely to cost me the chance of a decent husband. Without marriage I will have no future. I feel everything is over and wonder why I was born. Surely, *surely* God must have a plan for me.

In the morning when they bring me the news of Thomas' death, I am ready for them. Internally I collapse weeping to the floor, my spirit crushed, my future a great gut-churning void. But, with a great effort, I shrug my shoulders, pull a wry expression and take refuge behind clever, callous words.

"This day died a man of much wit, but very little judgement," I say, and then I walk away from them as if my world hasn't just shattered into a million pieces. For a long time I stand passively at the window while my mind screams remorse.

Sorrow, there is nothing but sorrow. It surrounds me, it fills me, and it suffocates me but I must not let them see. As the days go on, misery is all-consuming. It grows so large that it lodges within my breast and forms and moulds me into something new.

From the day they kill him I put away my gay clothes. I dress sombrely in grey and tuck every tendril of hair tightly beneath my cap. I strip myself of emotion and constrain my passions tightly in the depths of my being where they will never again see the light of day.

To the outside world I must appear flawless, pious and, although I'd like to stick up my fingers and send them all to hell, I do nothing.

I say nothing.

I feel nothing.

One day at a time; one foot before the other. I tie up my tongue and school my face not to betray me. I must

273

not speak. The world is teeming with enemies and I must always be discreet. There is no one I can depend upon and I wish, not for the first time, for someone, some unassailable friend in whom I can place my trust completely. I wish my mother was here. I try to image what would she say to me, what advice she would give.

From what I can gather, she would probably advise me to dance, to lift up my head and confound them all with my gaiety and wit, but I know that isn't the answer. It is hard enough to be the daughter of a woman who has been condemned as a whore, let alone being labelled as one myself.

I give the matter a great deal of thought and, as the future stretches before me in a depressing unlit path, my thoughts turn to my other mother; to Katheryn.

Although I injured her, while she lived she was my mentor, and my guide. How would she advise me now? I close my eyes, meditate for a while on her philosophy and, as if she is in the room, I receive the hint of an answer.

I get on my knees and begin to pray for the strength to be a better person. I close my mind to The Admiral, shut away his face and, as the darkness shifts a little and the blackest sorrow begins to recede, I begin to perceive a way forward.

The path that lies ahead may be uncertain and I know I must always tread most carefully. But, looking back at the road I have already travelled, I come to realise that my body has played tricks on me. Romantic passion has put both me and those I love in the greatest of peril.

Katheryn was a strong brave soul until she married for the last time; bonded with a man for love. She made three political marriages, one forged in the softness of her heart. It was that last marriage that caused her the most misery. Now Thomas is dead there is still time for me to turn away from all that.

I put away my jewels and my most frivolous gowns forever, and continue to play the part of a pious protestant princess. Quite consciously I mould myself into a more severe shape than Katheryn took. I become the 'dutiful' Katheryn, the woman she was before she fell for the charms of Sir Thomas Seymour.

The Admiral came close to destroying all three of us; his love for me, real or counterfeit, could have led to my own death. It was a fortunate escape and, as hard as it is, I turn my back on his memory.

I concentrate on the woman Katheryn was during the time Father was in France. It was a time when I was only learning to love and admire her but, in the absence of the king, she proved to me that women can be resilient. It is possible to be strong and stand alone in a world of men.

Even if it is a world of enemies.

I am determined to bury the part of me that is as fickle as my father, and as impetuous as my mother. If I am to survive in this uncertain world, I see it is Katheryn I must emulate, not my parents. I will strive to live my life as Katheryn lived hers.

My stepmother, Katheryn Parr, the Queen.

Author's note

In writing this novel of Katheryn Parr I have made every effort to stick to known facts but, as always with fiction, it is only an interpretation of what might have been.

We know very little of Katheryn's early life, or whether her first and second marriages were happy or otherwise.

There are no details of her personal experiences during the siege at Snape where the novel opens, but we do know that she was there with John and Margaret Neville. We cannot know if the women were subjected to any violence, but we do know that other women were badly handled during other sieges.

Sir Francis Bigod was hung with the rebels as a result of the Pilgrimage of Grace, and her marriage to his son Ralph never took place. We do not know why. The idea that she developed an infatuation for Francis Bryan is my own invention. All we know is that Margaret followed Katheryn to court after the death of her father, Lord Latimer, and died young of an unknown cause in 1545.

It is not until Katheryn catches the eye of Henry that the picture of her begins to become much clearer. She was an intelligent woman, a keen supporter of the reformation, writing and publishing her own books on the subject of religion. While not displaying any terribly original ideas, they do reveal a mind that was both fertile and keen to make a difference in the world. Marriage to the king empowered her and provided her with a real voice in the changing world of the 16th century.

We must remember that she lived in terrifying times, married to a petulant and powerful king but, from the knowledge we do have, it seems that her marriage to Henry was not a bad one. The fate of Henry's former wives must have been with her constantly, but Henry seems to have held her in high regard. He enjoyed her company and respected her intelligence.

In my opinion, there is little doubt that the king took a great deal of pleasure in confounding Wriothesely and Gardiner when they sought to arrest her and replace her with someone of the Catholic faith. Throughout the relationship she seems to have 'managed' Henry very well, understanding his moods and pacifying him where other wives failed.

Perhaps this was the real key to her survival.

Throughout most of her life Katheryn displayed great resilience of character. She wed three times, wisely and well, and proved herself to be an excellent wife and helpmeet. With the possible exception of Catherine of Aragon, she was arguably the most dedicated of all Henry VIII's wives. Her own personal downfall was her *'intractable heart,'* her love for a man who was both unstable and unworthy. It is extraordinary that so sensible a woman fell for a man like Thomas Seymour, but as Elizabeth states in her narrative, "...women are soft when it comes to love."

The love triangle that developed between Katheryn, Thomas and Elizabeth can be viewed in several ways. I do not accept that it was child abuse on Seymour's part. Elizabeth was of marriageable age. The emotions of teenage girls have not changed and their passions can be equally if not more ungovernable than those of adults. I believe the attraction was strong, possibly not the great love affair that I have portrayed but too strong for an inexperienced girl and a hot-blooded man to ignore.

Katheryn was unfortunately the injured party and met her death knowing that the two people she loved most in the world had, quite possibly, betrayed her in the worst possible way. Her daughter Mary was given into the care of Katherine Willoughby, who reluctantly took her into her household. Baby Mary was a burden, her entourage a huge drain on their expenses. We are not entirely sure what became of the child but she fades from the historical record at around the age of two years old.

By falling in love, or lust, or whatever you like to label it, with a princess of royal blood, Thomas Seymour was sailing very close to the wind. The danger increased after his marriage to Katheryn because his intentions after that date can only be seen as nefarious. Either he planned to do away with his wife and marry against the council's wishes; or he planned to deflower and ruin the reputation of a royal princess. Either way it was a risky and almost insane enterprise.

History tells us that on hearing of his death, Elizabeth expressed regret for a man 'of much wit but very little judgement.' Whether she really uttered those words or not, they seem to sum up the general consensus of opinion; Thomas was not wise.

He was brother of the protector and uncle to the king but, even so, there are boundaries. Perhaps he was fonder of Katheryn than we know; perhaps in his grief, with her no longer there to prevent him, he overstepped the limits and took liberties that the council were no longer prepared to accept.

He was accused of thirty-three counts of treason – some of them trifling. The details of his alleged crimes are as follows:

Thomas Seymour began a campaign to undermine his brother, the protector's, authority over the king, their joint nephew, Edward VI.

Seymour supplied the king with pocket money and took him treats. He also attempted to damage his brother's reputation by spreading rumours about the manner in which Somerset was running the country.

Seymour abused his position by encouraging piracy, something he was meant to control in his capacity of Admiral.

He was also accused of bribing the Vice-treasurer of the Bristol Mint, whom Seymour learned was guilty of inaccurate book keeping. To make this matter worse he used the money he gleaned from blackmail to finance a coup against the protectorship.

To cap it all, at the end of 1548, when called to appear before the Privy Council, Seymour hatched a plot to kidnap Edward VI.

On the 16th January 1549, he broke into Hampton Court Palace, entering by way of the privy garden. As he entered the royal apartments, the king's spaniel woke up and began to bark and Seymour shot the king's beloved pet.

Seymour was arrested and taken to the Tower, accused of trying to kidnap the king, of plotting to marry the king's half-sister, Elizabeth, with the intention of putting her on the throne.

The charges were perhaps trumped up to rid the protector and John Dudley of a courtier who had become too great an irritant to ignore. Other men died for much less. What remains clear is that without Katheryn's steadying influence, Thomas was a wild and ungovernable man, and a sorry end was inevitable.

Quite possibly the greatest legacy Katheryn Parr left us was Elizabeth. Although not of her blood, when she later became queen, Elizabeth illustrated many qualities learned during her time with Katheryn.

It was Katheryn who persuaded Henry to welcome his daughters back to court, and it is quite possible she had something to do with their reinstatement in the succession.

Elizabeth was at her stepmother's side while she was Regent during the war with France, and saw then the possibilities of a woman holding her own in a male dominated world.

After Henry VIII's death, Katheryn took Elizabeth into her household to continue her education, and oversee her upbringing. If Katheryn failed Elizabeth in any way, she also endowed her with a strength of mind and force of will that can only be admired.

Other works by Judith Arnopp include:

The Kiss of the Concubine: A Story of Anne Boleyn
The Winchester Goose: at the court of Henry VIII
The Song of Heledd
The Forest Dwellers
Peaceweaver

All available in paperback and on Kindle.

Please visit Judith's webpage www.juditharnopp.com to keep abreast of news and forthcoming novels.

The Tudor Roses

The Tudor Roses are a group representing the Tudor nobility in a wonderful display of authentic Tudor fashion. The group is made up of one lord and several ladies and two royal princes. During the summer months they are in residence at a number of Tudor castles and halls in England and Wales. (Details on their webpage).

Their aim is to bring alive the empty chambers and gardens of historical palaces by modelling their Tudor gowns, accessories and jewels. They will be delighted to be photographed with you to provide a long lasting memento of your visit.

The Lord of the Roses, Darren Wilkins, is also a keen photographer and I was delighted when he allowed one of his photographs to grace the cover of this novel, ***Intractable Heart: A story of Katheryn Parr.***
You can find more information about The Tudor Roses on their website:
http://www.thetudorroses.co.uk
And also find them on Facebook:
https://www.facebook.com/TheTudorRoses

Read on for an excerpt from The Kiss of the Concubine: a story of Anne Boleyn

The Kiss
of
The Concubine

28th January 1547 – Whitehall Palace

It is almost midnight and January has Whitehall Palace clenched in its wintery fist. The gardens are rimed with frost, the casements glazed with ice. Like a shadow, I wait alone by the window in the silver-blue moonlight, my eye fixed on the bed.

The room is crowded, yet nobody speaks.

I tread softly among them. The flickering torchlight illuminates a sheen of anticipation on their faces, the rank odour of their uncertainty rising in a suffocating fug. Few can remember the time that went before, and both friend and foe balance upon the cusp of change, and tremble at the terror of the unknown.

I move through the heavily perfumed air, brush aside jewelled velvet sleeves. At the high-canopied bed I sink to my knees and observe his face for a long moment. He is changed. This is not the man I used to know.

They have propped him on pillows, the vast belly mountainous beneath the counterpane, and the yellow skin of mortality's mask is drawn tightly across his cheeks. There is not much time and before death can wipe his memory clean, I speak suddenly into his ear, a whisper meant only for him. "Henry!"

The king's eyes fly open and his eyeballs swivel from side to side, his disintegrating ego peering as if through the slits in a mummer's mask.

He knows me, and understands why I have come.

He whimpers like a frightened child and Anthony Denny steps forward and leans over the bed. "Your Majesty, Archbishop Cranmer has been summoned; he cannot be long now."

Henry's fat fingers tremble as he grips the coverlet, his pale lips coated with thick spittle as he tries to speak. I move closer, my face almost touching his, and the last rancid dregs of his breath engulf me. "They think you fear death, Henry. But you fear me more, don't you, My Lord?"

"Anne?"

The sound is unintelligible, both a denial and a greeting, but it tells me what I need to know. He recognises and fears my presence. Those assembled begin to mutter that the king is raving, talking with shadows.

I sink into the mattress beside him and curl my body around his bulk. "How many times did we share this bed, Henry?" His breathing is laboured now and sweat drips from his brow, the stench of his fear exceeded only by that of his festering thigh. I tighten my grip upon him. "Did you ever love me, Henry? Oh, I know that you lusted but that isn't the same. Do you remember how you burned for me, right to the end?"

I reach out to run my fingertip along his cheek and he leaps in fright, like a great fish floundering on a line, caught in a net of his own devising. One brave attendant steps forward to mop the king's brow as I continue to tease.

"Poor Henry. Are you afraid even now of your own sins? To win me you broke from Rome, although in your heart you never wanted to. Even the destruction of a thousand years of worship was a small price to pay to have me in your bed, wasn't it?"

285

Henry sucks in air and forgets to breathe again. A physician hurries forward, pushes the attendant aside and with great daring, lifts the king's right eyelid. Henry jerks his head away and the doctor snatches back his hand as if it has been scalded.

Even now they are fearful of him. Although the king can no longer so much as raise his head from his pillow, they still cower. How long will it take for them to forget their fear?

Mumbling apologies, the physician bows and backs away to take his place with the others. As they watch and wait a little longer, the sound of mumbled prayer increases. "Not long now, Henry," I whisper like a lover. "It is almost over."

A door opens. Cold air rushes into the stifling chamber and Archbishop Cranmer enters, stamping his feet to dislodge the snow from his boots. He hands his outer clothes to a servant before pushing through the crowd to approach the bed, his Bible tucked beneath his arm.

I playfully poke the end of Henry's nose. "Time to confess your sins, my husband." Cranmer takes the king's hand, his long slim fingers contrasting with the short swollen digits of his monarch. As he begins to mutter the last rites, I put my mouth close to Henry's ear to taunt him. "Tell the truth, Hal. Own up to all the lies you told; how you murdered and how you cheated. Go on ...."

But King Henry has lost the power of speech, and cannot make a full confession. Gasping for one more breath he clings tightly to Cranmer's hand, and I know there is not long to wait before he is mine again. A single tear trickles from the corner of his eye to be lost upon his pillow.

"It's time, Henry," I whisper. "And I am here, waiting. For a few short years I showed you Paradise and now, perhaps, I can do so again. Unless, of course, I choose to show you Hell."

The Kiss of the Concubine is also available now, both in paperback and on Kindle.

Lightning Source UK Ltd.
Milton Keynes UK
UKOW03f0123190914

238785UK00004B/174/P